Spirit Trilogy

Book One
Spirit of the Mountain

Book Two
Spirit of the Lake

Book Three
Spirit of the Sky

Spirit of the Mountain

Paty Jager

Windtree Press
Beaverton,OR

SPIRIT OF THE MOUNTAIN

Contact Information: info@windtreepress.com

Windtree Press
Beaverton, Oregon

Visit us at http://windtreepress.com

Cover Art by Christina Keerins

PUBLISHING HISTORY

First Published by Wild Rose Press in 2009
Second Edition Published by Windtree Press 2014

Published in the United States of America
ISBN 9781940064840

Cover Art images:
Background photo by Paty Jager
Other images from Canstock and Dreamstime

Dedication

This book is dedicated to the people
who inhabited the Wallowa country
and held it dear to their hearts.
Special thanks to:
Jade Black Eagle and Red Wolf

Disclaimer

The daily activities and beliefs of the Nimiipu in this book are
factual—the spirits, other characters, and situations that evolve are
only factual in the imagination of this writer/storyteller. At the time of
this story there was a deep-seated distrust between the Black Feet and
the Nez Perce tribes. That is not true of their feelings for one another
today.

Glossary of Nimiipuu words

Anihm ---winter
Blackleg ---Blackfoot
El-weht--- spring
Heel-lul--- winter
Himiin (He-meen) wolf
hi•sqi--- bad luck
Imnaha --- Area along the Imnaha river in NE Oregon
Keeh-keet --- an edible root
Kehmmes --- an edible root
Kouse --- an edible root
Nimiipuu (Ne-Mee-poo) The People (Nez Perce)
o`ppah--- a smoked bread made of kouse
Pe`tuqu`swise ---Crazy One
Qe`ci`yew`yew --- Thank you
Sa-qan (Saw-kawn) bald eagle
sekh-nihm---autumn
so-yá-po (so-yaw-po) White man
Thlee-than --- an edible root
Tiw`et (Tee-wat) male medicine doctor
Txiyak---power of the spirit
Weippe --- meadow where root gathering and races were held
Wewukiye (Way-woo-keya) bull elk
Weyekin (Way-ya-kin) guardian spirit

《》《》《》

Ná-qc

(1)

Wallowa Country
1770

"YiiYaaa!" The cry of the sentry shattered the peace surrounding
Wren. Her sun-warmed skin shivered. A second cry from a sentry
posted high above the village jerked her to a sitting position. Her
vision blurred a moment from her abrupt movement and the fear
pounding her heart.

She peered through the tall pines and brush circling the boulder
where she'd come to daydream and breathe in the mountain of her
heart. Did her brother heed the signal? Tattle-Tale had passed his ninth
winter on this earth and knew to return to the village when the alarm
sounded, but her arrogant little brother was known to do things his
own way.

Wren scanned the area one last time, before sliding from the
bumpy, warm boulder and heading to the village. She refused to fall
victim due to her brother's contrary nature. Hoping Tattle-Tale
followed the warning and also returned to the village, she ran from her
forest sanctuary.

Rapidly approaching hooves vibrated the ground as she entered
the area where the village would soon stand. She glanced around at the
piles of belongings and people scurrying to gather their families to

them. The band had arrived at their summer home mid-day. Little had been done to set up camp as the people rested from the three-day journey.

Wren's father, Proud and Tall, along with several mounted warriors, entered the camp at a lope. Their horses skidded to a stop in the middle of all the chaos. Her father motioned for the others to watch the trees while he moved through the band on his favored, spotted stallion.

Wren smiled at his bearing and firm words with his people. The sentry's cry had brought fear to the villagers. Her father rode tall on his horse, his confident voice eased his people's fears.

"Our warriors will find the intruder. Do not fear. They will keep you safe."

Fringed elk-skin leggings stretched across his muscular legs. His shirt, adorned with porcupine quills and shells, showed his status. Long hair, braided with otter fur, hung to the middle of his wide back. The shorter forelock curling back from his wide forehead gathered more wisps of gray each day. She scowled. The gray had become more apparent after her last disobedience.

His wide face also hosted more lines of age. With his age came wisdom. This wisdom and his strength carried their people through hard times.

He stopped his horse next to Wren. "Daughter, did you not hear the cry of the sentry? You should find your mother and grandmother."

"I did hear the cry. I know you will keep us safe." The words slipped through her lips and her face heated. Her words were foolish. Her father would keep them safe, but her disobedience had brought pain to both her father and village in times past.

Proud and Tall slid from his horse, grimacing slightly. Wren put out her hands to help him. The last skirmish with the Blackleg had left him with a wound the tiw'et could not heal. A wound that would not have happened had she listened to her elders.

He waved his large hands, shooing her away. "I am fine. Time has been good to me, but it no longer looks upon me with favor."

"You are still the leader of our band and respected by all." The tiredness in his dark eyes disappeared for a moment and a fleeting curve of his lips showed her words warmed him. Happiness rippled in her chest. She cherished moments her actions made her father think

8

kindly of her. Lately, she found herself more in disfavor than favor. She tilted her head, which was level with his shoulder, and peered up at his impassive face, hoping to one day restore his faith in her.

The rhythmic clomp of a lone rapidly approaching horse drew their attention. The horse and rider burst into the camp. Young warriors grasped their bows and ran in the direction the rider had appeared. Women and children retreated as the older men formed a wall between their families and the intruder. Wren stood tall beside her father. He would not allow anyone to hurt her. The proof was in his limp. She cringed at the thought.

"Come listen! Come listen!" the rider shouted, sliding his horse to a stop on its haunches in front of Chief Proud and Tall. The messenger held the end of a bow over his head in a show of peace.

Wren held her breath and glanced at the men drawing knives from the waistband of their leggings. The intruder waved the bow and the men stopped, their hands resting on the handles.

The intruder wore the moccasins and paint of the Blackleg tribe. Their enemy.

Wren stared beyond the rider, to the forest he'd bolted from waiting for more to come. Before they could even walk, the Nimiipuu knew not to trust a Blackleg. The Blackleg had earned the names schemers and murderers. She stared into the trees expecting more to follow.

The agitated horse danced and frothed at the mouth. Her father pushed her behind his broad back. She peeked around him at the man, who, warily watched the warriors closing in on him.

"What is this about?" her father asked. He walked up to the intruder and placed his hand on the rider's leg. The Blackleg glanced down at the large hand keeping him on the horse. The animal snorted and sucked in air. The salty scent of sweat and tang of fear clung to the pair.

Wren's curiosity, always her failing, won. She stepped alongside her father. His large hand resting on the blackleg calmed both the man and animal.

"I have brought a request for peace from my band of Blackleg."

The elders behind her mumbled and shivers raced up Wren's arms. She studied the intruder as a hawk's shrill cry rent the air. Hair on the back of her neck tingled.

9

"Which of the Blackleg wishes to make peace?" Her father's gaze remained locked on the interloper.

The bearer of the news looked around at the people gathered. "He Who Crawls."

Murmurs of disbelieve rumbled around her. The Blackleg band he described had been their enemy since before time. What made them seek peace now? She stepped closer to hear her father's words.

The man on the horse scanned the gathering crowd. His gaze lingered on her, studying the beaded pouch hanging from her belt. When the Blackleg raised his gaze to her face, the smugness in his eyes made the air in her chest ache like a winter snow.

"There is more," her father stated, watching the man.

The Blackleg nodded.

"Dismount and join me at my fire." Her father stepped back to allow the man space to slide from his horse.

Proud and Tall motioned a young boy forward. "Take this horse and bring back one of my best runners." When the boy led the horse away, her father turned to the messenger. "You will return on one of my horses—" he nodded, "—as a sign you have brought your message to me."

Wren studied her father. Why would he ask the enemy to his fire? The Nimiipuu around her whispered and watched as the chief and the enemy walked through the village side by side.

Fear doubled her steps to follow directly behind her father and the schemer. She would never trust a Blackleg. It could be a ploy to kill the chief of the Lake Nimiipuu. The pounding of unease in her head made it hard to think. How could her father give the enemy one of his prize horses? And how could he talk to this man at his fire when the village had yet to be raised?

She watched as Proud and Tall and the Blackleg walked to the spot where the family's lodge would stand after she, her mother, and grandmother finished this day. Her father and the messenger squatted beside the rocks that would soon surround their fire.

She stood as close as she dared. This was a formal meeting, for her father requested the Blackleg join him at his camp. The other members of the Lake Nimiipuu band stood behind her, watching.

"What is it you ride into my village to say?" her father asked, studying the man sitting on his heels across from him.

"As a sign of peace, He Who Crawls asks that your daughter marry our strongest warrior, Hawk."

Wren shook her head in disbelief. She knew not of this man. But to marry him would take her far from her mountain and her people.

Her heart lurched as she scanned beyond the large pine and fir trees to the top of the carved granite peaks capped with glistening snow. You cannot send me away, not now when I have just returned. She turned her gaze on her father; surely he would not consider such a thing.

He stared at her, his eyes unfocused. His face furrowed in thought. The sorrow in his eyes twisted her heart. He would send her away. Because she found it difficult to obey rules and endangered them all. She had to make him see she could never wed a Blackleg. Her trembling hand reached out to her father to plead her love of the mountain and people. His gaze barely flickered at her hand, before he turned back to the rider, ignoring her touch.

Her heart split at his rejection. She wrapped her arms around her waist, holding herself together.

"When you have eaten, return to your people. Tell them we will not trust their word until they and this Hawk have talked with me face to face." Proud and Tall stared across the lake.

No one moved. Not even the messenger. The expression on her father's face told them all he sought answers as he focused intently on the sparkling body of water. She gulped air, forcing courage into her body to tell him she did not wish to marry the enemy. She stepped forward, and a hand rested on her arm. Her mother's eyes warned her not to interrupt. Anger and guilt warred. She had to voice her fears and emotions, but that would once again put her in disfavor.

Her father turned back to the Blackleg messenger. "Your people are to send a counsel to the River of Many Bends. We will meet when the sun has set four times. Then I will make a decision."

Wren shook her head. No. He could not give her to the Blacklegs. They had mutilated her grandmother, Proud and Tall's own mother, in a Blackleg raid. How could he even think of peace with the schemers?

She was not one for sorrow or tears, but the thought of leaving her people and the mountain caused salty drops to trickle down her cheeks and rest on her quivering lips. An arm circled her shoulders. She turned and found her friend and cousin, Silly One.

For once the young woman did not giggle. Her round face did not glow with mischief. She knew of Wren's deep love for the mountain, and how she would gradually float away like the ashes from a fire, if she could not move about the tree-lined slopes.

"Your father will seek counsel. They will not send you to the enemy. Of that I am sure."

Wren wiped at the tears tickling her cheeks and watched her father's back. His injured leg dragged along the ground as he walked over to her mother. He was at the age when men thought less of fighting and more of peace. As the chief, he would do what was best for the band. Her mother walked beside him, matching him step for step.

Morning Fawn would not allow him to send his only daughter to the Blacklegs. Wren's heart fluttered with hope. Her father held her mother's opinions in high regard. But her mother also felt her father too lenient with his daughter.

Wren glanced at the young warriors watching the Blackleg prepare to leave. Finding a mate within her own band would do nothing to improve their strength. She could find a mate in the men of the surrounding Nimiipuu bands, making their band stronger through the connection. She frowned. Why had she not taken the warrior who asked for her last summer? He belonged to a strong band of Nimiipuu only one sun away.

She scrunched her nose. He had smelled far worse than any dead animal she had ever encountered. When she told her father this was the reason she did not wish to become his wife, he had said, "You are still young."

How had she been too young one summer past to marry a Nimiipuu, but at sixteen summers considered old enough to marry the enemy? Her stomach knotted. She knew nothing good of the Blackleg.

Silly One patted her shoulder. "You will see. We need you. Your father will not send you far away."

Wren wanted her friend's words to ease the clenching of her heart, but she knew her father could see the possibilities of peace with the Blacklegs.

"When the dwellings are up, meet me by the edge of the trees," Wren said, gripping Silly One's arm so tight her friend cried out. She released her hold on Silly One and smiled apologetically.

Spirit of the Mountain

Scanning the village, she sought her mother and grandmother. The women sorted the poles for their lodge. Erecting their home usually filled her with accomplishment. This day it brought sadness. If her father agreed to the marriage, she would not work beside her elders again. She would live among people who had been the enemy of the Nimiipuu since the time coyote slay the monster, creating all the tribes.

How could the sweat and menstrual lodge stand exactly as they had in all her years? And the band go about building the village as they had for generations when the proposal brought to them by the Blackleg messenger would throw her into a life she could never understand?

She could not change what had come, but there had to be a way to stay on the mountain where her heart belonged.

Picking up two poles, Wren replayed the Blackleg messenger's announcement in her head. She wound the rawhide tightly around the smooth end of the poles. Her fingers turned white from the rage she used to pull the leather strips tight. She curled her lip back in distaste. Rage boiled in her belly. She refused to marry a man who took pride in killing and stealing.

She would not marry a Blackleg. Her stomach twisted. How could she be given to the Blacklegs without anyone caring what she wanted?

The voice and wisdom of her beloved, dead grandfather drifted in and out of her head as she worked. One phrase lingered, making her feel small for her selfishness. "He who thinks not of himself – but of others, is greatest."

The band needed her to instill peace with the Blackleg. Her stomach clenched, and her hands trembled. She knew nothing good about the Blackleg. However, her father was unable to protect the band of Nimiipuu as he had in his younger days. The destiny to save her people fell on her shoulders.

As foretold by her vision.

Lepit

(2)

When the Nimiipuu sentry's cry pierced the air, Himiin, the spirit of the mountain, remained in the form of a white wolf and moved swiftly to a rock outcropping which overlooked the Lake Nimiipuu's summer camp. To interfere in the skirmishes between enemy factions wasn't allowed by the Creator. He could witness the outcome, and with superior thinking and a little manipulation, hopefully keep such a conflict from happening again.

Why did Proud and Tall allow the Blackleg messenger to his fire? Then send the warrior off on one of his best horses? Should he eavesdrop on the village or hurry after the messenger? Himiin shook, fluffing his white fur, and headed off at a lope in the direction the Blackleg messenger disappeared.

Since the time of the trickster coyote, he and his siblings watched over the Lake Nimiipuu. Because of his father's foolishness to believe the coyote and think of only himself and not the whole tribe, he destined his children to be spirits.

Himiin rounded a budding huckleberry bush. The putrid scent of evil filled his nostrils. He tensed and scanned the surrounding area. Movement under a bush to his right proved to be a black wolf—one with glowing yellow eyes and a sinister snarl. Now he knew where the putrid scent came from. All his senses came alert. Were there more or did this evil spirit travel alone?

14

Himiin growled and circled the black wolf. Curling his lip back in a menacing snarl, he challenged the Blackleg wolf spirit. His mountain was deep in Nimiipuu territory. Blacklegs and evil spirits rarely touched this land. And for good reason. Himself.

The black wolf snarled back, baring his teeth. A glint of malice shined in his eyes.

"What are you doing on my mountain?" Himiin circled, watching for a chance to catch the other unaware, gauging the others abilities.

"It is for me to know." The wolf lunged.

Himiin leaped to the side to avoid the vicious fangs that snapped at his neck and pulled out tuffs of white fur.

They circled again.

"Answer my question, and I will allow you to live." Himiin charged the wolf. The crafty animal avoided his attack.

"You are not so impressive," the black wolf jeered. "How could one so slow be the spirit of this mountain?"

Himiin growled, no longer interested in information. How dare this lowlife Blackleg say he, Himiin, a Nimiipuu spirit, was inferior to a Blackleg? Everyone knew it took three Blackleg to equal one Nimiipuu. He leaped at the black wolf, pinning him to the ground.

"Who is superior?" he growled and scowled down on the intruder.

Why was a Blackleg here? On his mountain? Shoshone or Crow were his usual adversaries. The Blackleg only wandered this far when looting. He raised his nose and sniffed the air. Was there a raid headed this way? He'd barely caught the scent of this intruder. But he'd not miss a whole raiding party. Was that the purpose of the messenger to scout for sentries and find a vulnerable way into the Nimiipuu camp? Distracted, his hold on the intruder went lax.

The black wolf struggled and fought, clashing his teeth together as he snapped with vengeance. The trespasser squirmed loose and sprung to the attack.

Himiin dropped to the ground and rolled, avoiding the gnashing fangs of the Blackleg wolf. The interloper tested and teased, never attempting to take control of the confrontation.

"Why are you baiting me? If you wish to get rid of me, do so, rather than dance around." His heart pounded as adrenaline pumped through him.

The black wolf curled back his lip in a snarl. A spark of malicious

15

humor lit his eye. "I enjoy tormenting you. It disturbs you more than my fangs."

The insolent wretch.

Whatever the cursed spirit's motives, he would send the Blackleg away with memories of this encounter.

When they both regained their footing, Himiin pounced, sinking his teeth into the furry neck of the black wolf. The salty taste of blood trickled across his tongue. His stomach curdled. This was not his first taste of blood. His jaw sprang open, and he dropped the intruder.

As a spirit, he wasn't allowed to kill mortals. He had once and would forever hold that guilt like a rock in his heart. Dark spirits were another matter.

The wolf bit at his legs and squirmed, extracting himself from Himiin's grasp.

"You will have to kill me to stop me." The wolf lunged.

The quick assault took him by surprise, and Himiin found himself under the black wolf. The weight and ferociousness of the animal was nothing compared to the mortification. He was the spirit of the mountain. Put here by the Creator to keep the Nimiipuu from extinction. His heart raced. Fear—something he'd never felt before, and pride spurred him into action. Word could not get out he'd been bested by a Blackleg.

Using all his strength and wile, he squirmed and snapped at anything black. Twisting every direction, he pushed with paws and slashed with fangs. His muscles bunched and flexed. His head collided with the other wolf's, ringing his ears. He would not fail. Adrenaline coursed through his body. White fangs of his attacker blurred as he pushed with his legs and latched onto an ear. His teeth sliced through the tender skin. Victory warmed his chest, filling him with pride.

A yelp echoed through the trees. Himiin took advantage. He flipped the black wolf to his back, pinning the smaller animal to the ground with his paws and weight. The eyes of his attacker glowed yellow as blood streamed from his tattered ear.

"This is my mountain," Himiin growled and sucked in air, filling his aching lungs. "I watch the people and animals. If I see you here again, it is possible you will not live." To emphasize his threat, Himiin slashed the black wolf's shoulder with his fangs before allowing him up. Eyes filled with evil and hatred glittered back at him.

Himiin's heart beat with rage. He drew in air, relaxing his muscles and easing the anger pumping through him. He watched the black wolf slink away. The black wolf would return— set to kill.

《》《》《》

Dark Wolf loped until his energy drained. If he didn't need, and prefer, this form to travel about the mountain, he would leave the vessel and find another to report to He Who Crawls. But the chief would have to wait. The wolf form suited him and would soon heal if he rested.

The white wolf had proven stronger than he'd been led to believe. Dark Wolf collapsed under a rock ledge to hide and lick the blood from his fur, soothing the wounds he could reach, easing the pain of the creature whose body he'd taken.

The Blackleg band of He Who Crawls grew anxious to gain control of Chief Proud and Tall's horses. They had heard stories of how at the Weippe gathering the previous spring his horses had won every race. With fast horses, their plundering could be waged with more impact. Swooping in and out of unsuspecting tribes, they would gather the articles and food they didn't wish to waste time to make and preserve.

The Nimiipuu band by the lake was well concealed nestled at the base of the mountain. They had sentinels and boundary riders to give the alarm. He Who Crawls had been reluctant about the peace offering between the two tribes, until he realized Hawk was serious and was the obvious person to build trust in Chief Proud and Tall. For his help, Dark Wolf would become the spirit of the mountain.

Satisfaction curled in his chest thinking of the tunnel he found and how it would make the perfect spot to hide a band of marauding wolves. All dark spirits handpicked by him. Yes, this mountain would soon be his. It would give him great pleasure to do away with the white wolf who revered this mountain like a shrine.

《》《》《》

Wren worked alongside her mother and grandmother. Erecting the tulle mat dwelling wasn't hard work, but took considerable time. She laced the easy-to-handle mats to the pole frame with leather strips. The tulle mats started at the bottom and layered to the top, to allow the rain to run off.

The work before her blurred as her vision quest flashed as clear

17

today as it had the day of her ninth summer. She'd sat atop a boulder on the highest point of the mountain. Having spent three days without food and water, she'd drifted between wakefulness and dreams.

The great, white wolf had looked at her with eyes as blue as the lake and told her it was within her power to preserve the Nimiipuu of this mountain. She had taken the message as a sign and sung of this encounter before the ceremonial fire at camp every winter since. Everyone in the tribe knew it was her calling to save the people. Many felt her gift, or weyekin, the greatest to ever be placed upon a Nimiipuu maiden.

Now, as her father contemplated marrying her to the Blackleg tribe who caused them the most grief, she saw the joining as her gift.

Wren shuddered.

Far worse than marrying the enemy was the fact her father would be relieved to have her gone, and she would leave her beloved mountain. Her heart clenched.

She threw back the flap of blanket at the entrance to the family lodge and hauled their few belongings into the dwelling. Her mother and grandmother had piled buffalo hides beside their sleeping spots. It was her duty to fill the indentions with pungent scented pine boughs.

She walked into the forest, wishing her chores were through so she could enjoy the sights and sounds. However, the beds must be ready for their weary bodies this night. She carried the boughs back to the lodge. Stripping the fragrant needles from the limbs, Wren made a soft pallet to spread a buffalo hide over. When she finished with the sleeping areas, she stacked the cooking utensils in place along the wall closest to the door.

Anticipation to walk among the forest hummed through her. She'd finished the chores.

Exiting the lodge, she scanned the village for Silly One. The young woman stood near her family's dwelling, giggling and tugging on her younger sister's braid. A smile twitched at Wren's lips. Her cousin could not stay out of trouble.

"Is your family settled?" she called over to her friend.

Silly One nodded and trotted over. "I knew it would not take you long to set up your family." Her cousin glanced at the mountain. "You have been gone much longer than usual."

Wren stared at the snow-covered peaks topping the tree-lined slopes of the mountain that held her heart. The pine, fir, and alder trees, boulders, grasses, and colorful wild flowers on the mountain brought beauty into the hearts of all. She appreciated them more than most.

Her heart pattered in her chest with excitement. She was free to roam the mountain. To breathe in the sweet fragrance of the spring flowers, the dank ground still saturated from winter snow, and the clean scent of the trees.

"I have been anxious since the melting of the snow to be among my friend the mountain." She glanced around at the bustle of the people erecting the village. A small pang of guilt shot through her that some dwellings still did not stand. However, the lure of the mountain pulled.

"I can wait no longer." She grabbed Silly One's hand and together they ran into the woods following the mossy path her feet knew so well. Hearing the song of the forest—the chatter of squirrels and twitter of birds— filled her with joy. They stopped at a large, flat granite boulder where she and Silly One had spent many summers playing and dreaming.

Wren ran her hands over the rough black and white rock winking back at her as the sun danced and shimmered on the flecks of gold. This was one of the many memories she would hold in her heart.

"Do you really think your father will send you to the Blacklegs?" Silly One sat on the boulder, staring into the forest.

"I do not know." Wren glanced at her cousin. "The hope I saw in his eyes makes me believe he could."

"I cannot believe he would be so cruel as to send you from the mountain and people of your heart."

Wren cringed and wiped at the tears sliding down her cheek. Her cousin did not know of her disgrace. "If it is for the good of the people, I must go. It is my weyekin." She stared at the side of the mountain, her gaze traveled to the shimmering white peaks. "Even if I should perish."

"But what if it isn't your weyekin?"

"Did you not hear the shrill cry of the hawk when the Blackleg arrived? And did you not hear the name of the warrior asking for me?" She shook her head. It had to be her weyekin. Why else would the hawk have shrieked at that moment?

19

"I do not believe your weyekin would send you to the Blackleg. They are murderers and thieves." Silly One stood up, crossing her arms.

"Maybe through this marriage, we can stop their ways." Even as Wren uttered the words she had little faith anything could keep the blood-thirsty Blackleg from their raids on innocent tribes. Dread squeezed her chest. Would she survive among the scheming enemy?

Mita

(3)

Himiin licked his wounds from the black wolf attack. Why did this dark spirit roam his mountain? The encounter meant trouble from the Blacklegs. He sensed it in his quivering muscles. How had the intruder crossed his mountain without him knowing? He would need to be more vigilant to make sure it didn't happen again.

Thinking of all the places on the mountain the dark spirit could hide, he barely caught the cadence of happy voices mingled with the songs of the birds. Before he could duck for cover, two young Nimiipuu maidens appeared within striking distance.

The shorter one grasped the tall maiden's arm. "We should back away," she whispered.

Himiin listened and watched. His body tensed as the taller female shook off her friend's hand. The last time he'd come this close to a mortal… He didn't want to think about it. He stared at the maiden, willing her to keep her distance.

The slender young woman stopped and tilted her head this way and that. She stared at him through narrowed eyes.

"His fur is whiter than a summer cloud, and his eyes shimmer bluer than the lake. He reminds me of the spirit—" Her gaze lowered to the leg oozing blood.

"Look, he is hurt." The slender maiden walked toward him without fear. She approached, her steps slow, holding her outstretched arm offered palm up in submission. She must be either very brave or

Paty Jager

half-witted. For not many—warriors included—would approach a wolf in such a way.

Himiin remained still. His muscles bunched, ready to spring in flight. He couldn't defend himself. If he killed another... Closing his eyes, he swallowed the lump of disgust.

"Do not worry. I will not hurt you. I know you are my spirit wolf." Her gentle sweet voice eased his tension, drawing him back to the moment.

After the encounter with the Blackleg spirit, he was wary of a female walking toward him as if he caused her no threat. She could be the dark spirit in another vessel. He studied her eyes intently. The discernable essence of a spirit or person shone in their eyes. Her words registered—my spirit wolf. How did she know he was a spirit? Unless...

"Wren, you should not be so close." The plump maiden's voice shook. She stood her ground a good distance from him, while the maiden called Wren continued talking.

"There, now. Let me see to your wounds. I will not hurt you." The soft spoken words made him forget his injuries and his past encounter with a mortal. He stared into her caring eyes. Fear was not evident in her gaze, her poise, or her words. Her melodic voice beckoned his gaze to meet hers and allowed her to take his paw. He'd never connected with a mortal before. Her touch tingled his nerves.

"I do not wish you harm, only to make you better." Nimble fingers moved the fur and examined the blood soaked gashes on his leg. Her gentle touch caressed his skin like a warm summer breeze.

The last mortal to touch him... His stomach pitched. Fate could not repeat itself. He trembled and forced his mind to push the past in the far reaches of his memory.

"Wren, we must go. He could be harmful."

"I cannot let a creature of this mountain go hurt when I have the ability to help." The maiden glanced at her friend before pulling a small leather pouch from the beaded belt around her waist.

"You are a beautiful creature. Who would want to cause you harm?" She held up two fingers pinching a white substance. "This is willow bark. It will ease your pain." Her slender fingers sprinkled the powder in the wound. Her gentle hands and compassionate words puzzled him. Why would a Nimiipuu maiden care about a wolf? Even one she believed to be her spirit wolf?

He wished he could talk with her and tell her to be wary of the black wolf. The animal he'd fought would return to bring trouble for the lake Nimiipuu, he felt this as sure as he felt her soft touch. He found no other reason for the spirit to be on this mountain. He'd sensed wickedness in the wolf's eyes and what he didn't say.

In wolf form, Himiin could do nothing to convey his fears to the maiden. He whimpered as she packed moss into his wound. Her touch lightened like the flutter of an evening wind caressing his skin.

"Did I hurt you?" she asked, gazing into his eyes, giving him a glimpse of her caring and strength. Her warm fingers gently held his leg.

"Wren." The maiden standing at the far side of the trees danced with agitation.

"Silly One, I am in no danger. Besides, I would rather die on this mountain than have to marry a Blackleg."

Her words sent a knife of fear slicing through the calm her hands had wrapped around him.

Who would make her marry a schemer? And why? This new information made him even more anxious about the intruding wolf. This maiden, whose touch ignited emotions he'd never known before, brought out his protective instincts. He had questions for her and no way to ask. To change form in front of the women or speak to them as an animal was forbidden by the Creator.

He pulled his paw from her hands and backed away with a snarl. He should not treat her this way after the care and trust she'd put in him, but in this form he had no other way to show his objection to her marrying a Blackleg.

Wren watched the wolf back away, showing his teeth in disfavor. His blue eyes flashed to gold. He was upset. But at what? She glanced around. Nothing had changed since she and Silly One had come upon him.

When she looked back, he had entered the trees. "Do not get in any more fights. I may not be around to soothe your wounds," she called as his silvery white form loped into the shadows of the forest.

"Why did you help that wolf? He could have killed you," Silly One said, coming up beside her.

"But he did not. His white fur and eyes—just like the white wolf

23

that came to me in my vision." Wren stared into the trees where he had disappeared. Her heart soared. He was her weyekin. She knew it. Why did he show himself now? She scanned the trees hoping for one last glimpse. "He was magnificent! His eyes—I could almost feel him talking to me."

"And I am called Silly One. Come, your father will be holding council soon. You should listen. After all, it is your future they will speak of."

Her future. Elation soured in her stomach. Her whole life, duty to her people and father were always on her mind, even when her actions did not seem so. She must put the good of the village before her own selfishness. However, that did not mean she had to like what she was almost certain would be said tonight at the council. Her father would put the good of all over her wishes. In sending her to the Blackleg, he would not only bring peace between the tribes, but she was sure he would also be thankful to have her out of their midst.

Staring into the woods where the white wolf had vanished, she knew he was the wolf from her vision. Why else would he have sat so still and allowed her to touch him? Her fingers tingled at the memory of his soft, thick fur. His pelt was better than any her father had ever brought back for wraps.

She hoped the beautiful wolf never met that fate. It would be a shame for such a magnificent creature to be reduced to mere clothing.

Wren and Silly One did not speak of the wolf or the marriage to a Blackleg as they wandered through the trees to the village. The excitement and anticipation of seeing the mountain settled in her stomach like a heavy jagged rock. The messenger from the Blackleg had shrouded her homecoming.

Stepping out of the trees, familiarity warmed her soul. As in past summers, each family dwelling stood in the exact spot it had been every summer. No one, not even the old blind woman, would wander around lost. She peered beyond the village to the sparkling lake and rim of land so like the creator's hands which held the body of water for her people.

This was where she came into the world and where she wished to be put to the earth. To leave would not only break her heart, but leave her circle unfinished. These were not thoughts she should harbor. Her circle would be made by the greatness she could bring her people by the marriage.

Wren scanned the village for her father. The ceremonial lodge remained a pile of sticks and hides ready to be erected. She spotted elders and warriors gathering around the fire in front of her father's lodge.

A shiver of apprehension slithered down her back. Not only did she not want to leave the mountain—she did not want to be the possession of a Blackleg. They were cruel. She had witnessed this many times during raids on her people.

She crossed the village, stepped up to the circle of men, and nodded to the oldest members, but avoided eye contact with any other than her father.

"Since this meeting concerns my future, may I listen?" She did not expect her father to consent. However, under the circumstances, she was prepared to argue her need to listen.

Proud and Tall stared at her through narrowed troubled eyes. Tradition was to say "no". Instead, he glanced at the men seated around the fire and nodded his head.

"But you must not say a word." His tone held the authority she had come to love when he oversaw a council. Gone was the softness and joking.

She took a seat where she could watch him and bowed her head. To make eye contact with the elders would be wrong. It would be an injustice to try and sway them with sentiment. Tilting her head allowed Wren to watch her father out of the corner of her eye and catch telltale movements from the others seated around the fire.

One of the elders stood. He raised his hands to the Creator and chanted a song of wisdom to help Chief Proud and Tall and those seated around the fire make a decision for the good of the people.

His voice carried into the darkening sky. Wren shivered. His song would be heard, and the decisions made tonight would be watched over by the Creator.

The old man slowly sat, giving a nod to her father. Proud and Tall stood, illuminated by the firelight. Crevices of age carved a path of wisdom across his face. His eyes shone black and sharp.

"We all know why this council has been called. The Blackleg band led by He Who Crawls has asked for peace." His deep voice floated above the fire and mingled with the wisp of smoke.

The younger warriors fidgeted. Wren presumed one opened his mouth to speak, for her father raised a large hand for silence and continued.

"I know we have been at war with this tribe since before the time of our fathers and grandfathers. The Blackleg are cruel people." His eyes glistened. Did he think of his mother, her grandmother, who had died at the hands of a Blackleg? "This is a time to change things. Make the lives of our people more peaceful. If we feel the Blackleg can be trusted." He looked at the warriors and elders seated around the fire.

"I would like those who have spent as many and more suns upon this earth as I to speak their hearts and minds." Proud and Tall sat cross-legged and listened as the oldest members of the band stood and told of the Blackleg raids.

The last man who stood raised a gnarled hand and pointed at Wren. He bestowed upon her a heartfelt toothless smile. "This maiden has a weyekin stronger than any ever given to one so young and innocent." He twirled his knobby hand before him. "I believe this offering will bring about changes for our future and the future of our children. I have seen the coming of many who are not like us. We need to join with the Blackleg to be strong against the intruders." He sat down, keeping his eyes focused on Wren.

His attention to her and his words twisted her stomach with dread. How could she save the whole people? Worse, did she want them all to believe she could? Her hands clenched in her lap.

Her father stood. "If the Blackleg truly want peace, this is good. We have wasted lives and horses to them for far too long." He glanced at each man. Many heads nodded in agreement. When his gaze rested on the younger men gathered, his eyes took on a gleam, almost daring them to confront him.

Pride swelled in her chest. Her father may find his body failing him, but his presence and courage would forever hold the respect of his people.

"To make this peace they have asked us to give them Wren to marry and bring the tribes together as a family."

She looked up. His words shook with emotion. This had never happened before. Everyone stared at him, especially the young men.

"It is true she has been given a great gift." He sighed heavily. "And my daughter has at times caused me grief."

Wren flinched and her gaze strayed to his bad leg.

"I do not wish to hand her over to schemers." He looked around the circle. "But to have peace for all the village," he paused and took a deep breath, "we need to meet with the Blackleg to see if they speak with truth of this union."

He glanced down at her, his eyes filled with sorrow. "We know you love the mountain and the Nimiipuu of the lake." He again took a deep breath. "But we also know you will do what is best for the family."

Wren cautiously nodded her head as her chest ached. Her heart had torn in two. It was her duty and weyekin to do what was best for the people and forget her own happiness.

"I have chosen the six to ride with me at first light. We will meet the Blacklegs at the River Of Many Bends. We will speak with their council and the warrior Hawk to see if they are trustworthy."

The elder who had spoken of her great gift tipped his face to the sky and chanted a song for the Creator to give them the wisdom to tell if the Blackleg merely schemed or wished for peace. The others joined in, raising their voices to the star-filled sky.

Wren stood. She wished to flee, yet her feet dragged across the ground like boulders. With each step, her world dimmed. Panic squeezed her chest, making even small breaths painful.

She had eight setting suns to roam the mountain and seek out those she held dear. If the group, meeting the Blacklegs, decided she would marry the Blackleg warrior, she would live out the rest of her seasons with the enemy.

Her stomach knotted.

She swallowed the lump of sorrow in her throat and stared at the side of the mountain. Her heart ached. If she fulfilled her weyekin, the gift which every Nimiipuu lived for, watching the mountain sleep under a silver moon would only be a memory.

《》《》《》

Silver moonlight danced across the surface of the lake. Himiin stood at the bank. Small ripples appeared where fish emerged to capture the insects hovering above the water. The snow had moved up the mountain only a few weeks earlier, yet, the rhythm of the warm season sung in the animals, plants, and people who lived within and along the lake.

As the night air blew down off the snow-covered peaks, he welcomed his thick fur.

A splash warned him his brother, the spirit of the lake, approached. Through the ages, Nimiipuu passed down stories of the great beast with antlers who lived in the lake. The tale of the great beast, who came out of the water and took the disobedient children, always made him smile. For his brother was far from being a monster.

He stared at the shimmering lake. An elk emerged from the depths. Water flowed from his thick, dark coat as he shook his head and antlers.

"You look distraught brother," Wewukiye said, stepping next to the log Himiin sat beside.

"I battled with a Blackleg spirit on my mountain."

"Here? That cannot be." His brother glanced about as if the creature were in the shadows.

"I have the wounds to prove it." Himiin raised his paw to show the marks.

Wewukiye sniffed. "They cannot have this territory. It belongs to the Nimiipuu."

"I do not know what the schemers have planned, but I heard a maiden say she would rather die than marry a Blackleg." He looked at his brother. "What have you heard?"

"It is true. When the women came to the lake to wash, I heard them talking. The Blackleg asked for the hand of Chief Proud and Tall's daughter. With the match, they will bring peace between the tribes."

Himiin growled. "I do not believe this. The Blackleg are plunderers and would rather die than befriend the Nimiipuu." Fear for the maiden sliced through him like a bolt of lightning. The fierceness of the emotion confused him. In all his days as a spirit he'd carried out his responsibility to protect all the people on his mountain. The maiden had captured his very essence, and his need to single out and protect one, surprised him.

"The chief and men he has chosen leave in the morning to see if the messenger speaks the truth." Wewukiye preened, licking the water from the hair on his shoulder.

The flapping of wings drew their attention skyward. Sa-qan approached. Her wingspan stretched wide, blocking the moon behind her and highlighting her white head.

She landed gracefully on the log and smiled. "My brothers, it is good to find you both."

Himiin could not help but smile. It had been a joke of the Creator to make their younger sister the strongest, fastest, and wisest of the three. She was the spirit of the sky, watching the people and animals of a larger area than he and Wewukiye.

"What brought you to us tonight?" Wewukiye asked, moving closer to her.

"I saw a black wolf running from the mountain. I followed. He ran in the direction of a band of Blackleg warriors camped two suns away by land."

Himiin growled low in his throat. He knew the wolf was trouble.

"I believe that wolf is the one to give our brother wounds," Wewukiye said.

Sa-qan turned her sharp eyes and pointed beak at Himiin. "Why was a Blackleg spirit on this mountain?"

"He would not say. When I challenged him, he fought fiercely and went away with hatred in his eyes." Himiin did not like the wolf meeting with a band of Blackleg so close to the mountain. Nothing good ever happened where Blacklegs were concerned.

"How did you tend your wounds?" Sa-qan asked. Her eagle-eyes missed nothing.

"A maiden came upon me in the woods. She had no fear of me. And her voice so soothed, I sat like stone as she applied herbs." Since their meeting, Himiin couldn't shake the maiden Wren from his thoughts. There had to be a reason he felt compelled to help her other than her warm gentle touch and caring eyes. If she were the chief's daughter, she was in peril. Was it the Creator's wish that he protect her?

Sa-qan watched him intently. "You were not fearful to have a mortal so close?"

His sister worried about his encounters with humans.

"And she showed no fear?" Wewukiye twisted his neck and peered at him. "How can that be? You are a large fierce wolf."

Himiin ignored his sister's concerns and answered Wewukiye. "She told her friend it would be better to die on the mountain than marry a Blackleg."

29

"She is the chief's daughter." Wewukiye nodded his head, flinging his heavy antlers like weightless dried weeds.

"What of the chief's daughter?" Sa-qan asked.

As his brother explained to his sister the message brought to the Lake Nimiipuu that day, Himiin visualized the maiden Wren. Heard her sweet voice and experienced the same calm she'd wrapped him in when healing his wound.

She was too young and innocent to be sent to the Blackleg. The schemers couldn't be trusted. They had proved it over and over again through time.

"If this maiden is indeed to marry the Blackleg, there will be peace." Sa-qan leaned back and puffed out her feathery chest.

"How do we know the schemers are not using the marriage to get into the Lake Nimiipuu village?" With the Blackleg there could never be any good. They had been vile for far too long to become believable now.

"If that was their goal, the schemers would have stormed the village and taken what they wanted." Sa-qan tipped her head, studying him. "Why are you untrusting of what could be a good thing for both tribes?"

"I have a feeling there is more to this than the Blackleg wanting to make peace. Why would they send a dark spirit to prowl the mountain if they wanted peace?"

"Now we know what bothers you." Wewukiye smiled. "He is mad the black wolf got the best of him." He bumped Himiin with his shoulder. "Did he get you down? Was the powerful Himiin feeling vulnerable?"

Himiin snapped at his brother. "I will never be bested by a schemer spirit or any spirit."

Wewukiye laughed. "When one talks big, he falls hard."

"Brothers, this is not a time to bicker among ourselves. If the Blackleg are up to something, we need to know before trouble starts. Have you forgotten our purpose?"

Sa-qan's yellow eyes drilled into him. Himiin had a hard time standing still under her scrutiny.

"I have not forgotten how our father's selfishness made us the eternal sentinels of the Lake Nimiipuu."

"Then stop arguing and find out what is happening. I will watch over the band of Blackleg off the mountain, you keep an eye out for the dark spirit." Sa-qan spread her wings, preparing to fly. "And the two of you get along." She leaped in the air and disappeared.

Himiin looked at his brother and smiled. Wewukiye grinned back. They got along, they just enjoyed the bantering.

"Brother, watch yourself and let the maiden and her people decide her fate." Wewukiye walked into the lake. Himiin watched the water rise, covering the great brown body as it submerged in a ripple.

If only the problems with the Blackleg and his infatuation with the maiden would disappear so smoothly.

Pi-lep

(4)

Wren cursed the pine boughs and dry grass she used for her bed. For the first time in her life, they poked like rocks rather than the spongy grass. She stared through the smoke hole in the top of the lodge watching the night sky lightened to a new day. She had thrashed about all night which left her body tired and aching.

She did not want to become the wife of a Blackleg. One had to ride for many suns to arrive in Blackleg territory. Who knew where Hawk's village resided? Her stomach squeezed as panic gripped her. She belonged with her people and mountain. They were more important to her than eating and breathing.

The flap on the entrance to the lodge flopped open. Her father had returned from his morning bath in the lake. A cold breeze swirled through the interior, matching the chill of dread inside her. The rustle of leather and crackle of flames from a stick tossed on the fire announced his movements as he prepared for his journey to meet the Blackleg.

She would miss the intimacy she shared with her family in their lodge. As the daughter of the chief, she did not have to live in the dwelling with the other young maidens.

Her face heated. She would live with a man she did not know should Proud and Tall go through with this strange notion peace could come of her marrying a schemer. Could she live among people with different customs and behaviors—people who thrived on plundering and killing?

The rumble in her stomach had nothing to do with hunger. Fear unsettled her belly and her mind. If the Blackleg proved to be sincere, her father would jump at the chance to instill peace between the tribes.

Tears trickled down her cheeks. This time she must not allow her stubbornness to influence her thoughts. As the daughter of the chief, it was her duty, just as it was his, to think of the whole village when making a decision. If taking a Blackleg for a mate would save her people from sorrow and fighting, she had to make the sacrifice. Her heart cracked and bled, weeping at loss that already sat heavy in her middle like a large boulder squeezing out her last breath.

Before leaving the dwelling, her father stood over her. He whispered to the Creator and bent to touch her hair. Wren could not ignore him.

"I know you will do what is best," she murmured, swallowing a lump of fear.

Proud and Tall crouched next to her and whispered, "You have tried the patience of many, daughter. Yet, I promise I will not send you to the Blackleg if this Hawk is not worthy of you."

"I know you would never make a decision you felt would harm me. If you say this Blackleg is a good man, and it will bring peace to our people, I will go to him. But know my heart will be forever with the mountain and my people."

He cleared his throat and patted her cheek. Straightening, he walked to the opening and paused with his hand gripping the flap. His dark gaze lingered on each person as they slept. The longing and unease on his face before he pivoted and left startled Wren.

A shiver of apprehension snaked up her back. She hadn't thought about the meeting being an ambush until this moment. Her father's lingering glance at his family brought the notion to her like a blow from a club.

She worried about leaving the mountain and her family while her father could walk into a trap, or worse the Blacklegs could swarm down upon the village while Proud and Tall was away. Her selfishness caught in her throat as a lump of shame.

Now she understood his strange choice of one elder and five young warriors for a counsel with the Blacklegs. His selection made sense. Her father wanted to be prepared if the meeting turned into trouble.

The thud of hooves faded in the distance. The council had left the village. She closed her eyes and sent a prayer to the Creator. Great One watch over my father and those who ride with him. I fear the Blackleg are not what they seem. If it is your wish for me to marry the schemers I will, but know my heart will forever be with my people and mountain.

If the Creator wished peace between the tribes, he would take care of those members of the Lake Nimiipuu who worked toward that goal.

Unable to remain in her bed any longer, Wren sat up. She tied a belt of woven tulle around her waist. She raked her fingers through her hair, and then braided the long black tresses with soft furry strips of otter skin. When the ends of her braids were secured by short lacings, she attached her herb pouch to her belt and left the dwelling.

She breathed in the crisp morning air and slid her toes through the icy dew-dotted grass. Shivers raced up her spine. The sensation chased away the dread, making room for the anticipation of a new day. She wrapped herself in the beauty of the day which crept over the rise. The golden halo of sun, peeking over the hill across the lake, lightened her sad heart.

If she left tomorrow, she would have this memory of her beloved mountain to take with her.

Wren snagged her woven gathering pouch from beside the lodge and ran into the forest. She would gather moss for soup and return in time to help with the required chores.

The birds in the trees twittered as she ambled higher and higher up the mountain slope. Now and then, she stopped to appreciate the bright color of a new spring blossom, inhale the crisp morning air, or watch a small creature move about its morning business. She had no destination in mind, just a need to cover as much of the mountain as she could. If the meeting between her father and the Blackleg went well, before long she would no longer have the beauty of the mountain to see, hear, and walk upon.

She stepped into a clearing and stopped.

Sunning himself in the middle of the small meadow was the white wolf. His thick shiny coat sparkled in the early morning sunlight. Elation and hope raced within her heart. Wren knew not why, but this creature filled her with pleasure and acceptance for what was to come.

The even rhythm of his rising sides proved he slept. Did she dare approach? If she startled him, he might not be as friendly as the day before.

Hoping he would not run, she backed into the trees and sang a song about the creatures of the mountain. She raised her voice and willed her feet to walk unhurried into the clearing. Her racing heart fluttered with anticipation. Would he remain or flee? Please do not be angry and run away.

The wolf did not run. His head rose slowly, watching her approach with unblinking eyes.

"White Wolf, what a surprise to see you." She continued to walk toward him. He made no attempt to run. Rolling from his side to his belly, his grey eyes held her gaze. She stared into their depths. "You may come closer" whispered in her head. The invitation encouraged Wren to walk right up to the reclining, white body.

"May I sit next to you?" She indicated a spot beside the wolf.

His muzzle dipped slightly as though agreeing. Wren sat next to the animal, curling her legs underneath her.

"You are beautiful. May I stroke your fur?" Again his eyes appeared to answer. She put a hand on his back. Her fingers sank into the warm thick fur. The beating of her heart lessened as she sat next to the animal running her hand over and through the soft pelt.

The contentment of the moment wrapped around her like hot steam from the sweat lodge.

"I believe we have met before." The wolf leaned closer as though to listen. "In my ninth summer, I set out on a vision quest. In my dream you came to me." The wolf peered into her eyes. "I am almost certain you were the one. The eyes are different, not as blue, but I will never forget." The wolf tilted his head. Deep in the grey depths she could see herself as a young girl and the wolf of her vision quest. He had to be the one.

Her daring soared. She stroked the shorter, sleeker hair on his wide, strong head. His ears lay back as her hand moved downward.

"In my dreams, you told me I would be the one to save my people." She looked away— No longer able to talk for fear her own selfishness would upset the one who bestowed her prophecy. Her hands picked at the rough cloth of her dress. Had the wolf known then her weyekin would make her leave everything she loved? He nudged her hand with his warm wet nose.

Wren stared into his grey eyes, which searched hers. She sensed he saw things in her even she did not know.

"You bestowed upon me a great weyekin. A gift all the elders say is more special than any other given to a maiden." She gulped, not sure whether to be pleased or upset to have been given such an honor and hardship.

"Ever since the day on the mountain when you told me of my gift, I have felt unworthy of such greatness." She ducked her head with shame.

Taking a deep breath, she returned her gaze to the wolf's eyes. "A Blackleg wishes to marry me." Each time Wren spoke of the Blackleg marriage her chest clenched with deeper pain. "To become his wife will secure no more battles with the Blacklegs." She swallowed the panic bubbling in her throat at the remembered tragedy of the past. "I lost my grandmother and cousin to a raiding party. And my father... I fear I have caused trouble too many times. If I go to the Blackleg, it will lift burdens from my father and my family." She gulped and blurted, "But I fear there will be some Blackleg who do not wish me in their village."

To tell the one who bestowed her weyekin upon her she feared its outcome was foolish. Yet, she had to confide in someone, and the creature leaning against her, giving her support could not speak her fears.

She swiped at the warm drops sliding down her cheeks. Anger seethed inside at her show of weakness. Tears had never come so easily to her before the Blackleg messenger entered their village. She was unfaithful if she could not accept her weyekin with an unburdened heart. But just as her headstrong thoughts had brought her trouble before, they now nagged her to stand up for herself.

"I love this mountain and all who live here. Animal and people." Looking into the wolf's eyes, she found sympathy.

Himiin had never, in all his time as a spirit, found another who loved the mountain with the same passion. This woman of the real world, held the mountain in her heart as firmly as she did her family.

He yearned to answer all her questions but was helpless to console her.

Spirit of the Mountain

Frustration seethed in him. He wished to talk with her, yet, was forbidden. He could only sit and listen to her heartfelt declaration to the mountain and her people.

When she'd first approached him, his instincts had been to flee, to save the maiden from him. But as she spoke, he realized she could be the one to turn his misdeed around. If he helped her through this, and the Blackleg stopped raiding the Lake Nimiipuu, he would save not only The People, but his honor.

He bumped her hand with his nose and studied her sad face. The fear and anger she felt toward leaving all she loved and venturing into the violent world of the Blackleg was understandable. That she dealt with it so serenely and with confidence showed valor and her belief in her weyekin.

Wren's beauty encompassed her whole being. Her flawless skin appeared as smooth as the rocks which tumbled down the mountain streams. The long thick midnight-colored braids touched the curve of her hips. Long slender fingers gently plucked at his fur. Her trim firm body came from traveling the paths of his mountain.

He growled softly. He'd never thought about a mortal or non-mortal like this before. Having such thoughts—now—for this woman was inexcusable. She belonged of the real world, and he in the spirit world. He should keep his distance—for both their sakes.

"Did I hurt you?" she asked, softening her touch even more. "Or say something to upset you?"

The wonder of it all—she held no fear of him. Not even when he growled. Was she so sure he would not harm her because she believed him the wolf of her vision? Or was she this daring with all animals of the mountain?

"I must pick moss for soup, would you like to join me?" she asked, slowly standing.

Himiin raised to a sitting position, then stood and stretched. He had nothing better to do this day. For all he knew the Blackleg wolf would come back. The Creator had put him on this mountain to watch over and protect all the creatures. Wren might be in danger from the dark spirit.

For her protection, he would stay with her whenever she came to the mountain. The idea brought him happiness. To watch the maiden walking in front of him would be no hardship. She crossed the clearing with the grace of a doe.

Himiin followed, enjoying the sway of her hips and the cheerful hum of her song.

"I did not mean to be disrespectful telling you I did not wish for my weyekin. I am honored. The idea I would have to leave the mountain and people of my heart to give them my gift never came to me." She blushed. "I have dreamed of living my life here with these people and bringing up children who love the mountain." Sighing, she rested a hand on his head. "Now I will bring children to this earth and try to teach them not to kill innocents."

Fear for her and what she could walk into caused his tail to quiver. How could such a gentle soul be asked to live among the schemers? She gathered moss while he followed and tried to think of a way to stop the marriage without causing a war or bringing the wrath of the Creator upon him.

Her pouch overflowed with moss, and she headed down the mountain humming. Himiin enjoyed listening to Wren's sweet voice. He was a loner other than his siblings. Yet, the beauty of her voice and her presence soothed a wound deep inside his chest he'd not realized existed until she came upon him. Even in her distress of leaving her people, she brought goodness and warmth into his world.

He was a spirit who lived on the mountain. She was a woman of the Lake Nimiipuu. How and why they came together, he didn't know. The joy her presence brought surprised him. Fear had always gnawed at his gut when he had to be near a mortal. Ever since…

Bringing his thoughts back to the present, he realized they stood only a few feet from the edge of the trees near the camp. Wren scanned the village, patted the pouch of moss, and straightened her back. She glanced down at him and smiled sadly.

"We must part now. For you to walk into the village with me, would put you around someone's shoulders for the winter." She reached down stroking his back. "Your fur is the softest and thickest I have ever felt. I do not wish you to lose it because of me."

Himiin flinched. She spoke the truth. The men of the village would take great satisfaction in placing his skin around their women's shoulders. If it should happen, he would float into another form.

"I will be walking upon the mountain every day until I must leave. I wish to keep the mountain and my people in my heart. If we meet again, I would be pleased." She knelt next to his head. "Thank you for listening to my selfish thoughts. I know if I said these things aloud to my people, they would become fearful. I do not say these things in disrespect to anyone. Only to say what is in my heart. I am happy you allow me to speak and not make judgments. You are a true friend." A tear glistened at the corner of her eye. "May I give you a hug?"

Himiin stiffened. The human he'd harmed before had been a threat to the Nimiipuu. Wren was neither a threat to him nor her people. Wanting to feel her closeness, he nodded slightly as his head pounded.

Her arms wrapped around his neck, and her sweet breath trailed across his face. His heart fluttered with the sudden heat of his body. Confusion swamped him. He enjoyed her touch more than anything he'd experienced over the ages. The fact that a mortal could bring these emotions out in him was troubling.

She placed her head upon his and whispered, "Thank you. I need a friend like you very much right now."

A warm wet drop seeped through the hair on his head. She stood abruptly, swiped the tears from her eyes, and walked into the clearing, calling out to the people along the edge.

Himiin stood in the shadows and watched the villagers greet her. Many called back, their faces a glow and smiling. Several small children ran up and threw their arms around her legs. She was well-liked. How could they think of sending her to the enemy?

He studied each dwelling, watched who went in and out. Proud and Tall's lodge sat near the water and in a favorable spot for early morning sun to warm the interior. To know where she slept could come in handy if he should need to seek her out. To keep her safe.

How could the young warriors find peace with the Blackleg acceptable? Over the years too many raids and too many Nimiipuu had been slaughtered by the schemers. And if there were those who resented peace with the Blacklegs, he would have to keep Wren safe from her own people as well as the Blackleg spirit.

Sa-qan had offered to follow the father and his council to the meeting. She would not be able to stop an attack, but would help the Nimiipuu take the right counter actions. The outcome of the meeting was important to the spirits. The marriage to the Blackleg would affect Wren as well as the whole Lake People village and their tribe.

Knowing the doubts of the Nimiipuu maiden and the past

aggressions of the Blackleg made his part in the coming peace offer difficult to undertake. He did not feel the Blackleg would be found honest in their offer of peace. And how would he prepare Wren for what could be a trip to her worst nightmare if he could not talk to her?

Himiin glanced up at the sun. The outcome of the meeting between Proud and Tall and the Blackleg would alter life on the mountain for all. This knowledge sat like a boulder in his stomach.

After hearing the maiden's devotion to the mountain, how could he sit back and wait to see the outcome? He didn't have the patience of his brother and sister. His major flaw. And one that had put him in disfavor with the Creator many times.

He should have ripped the answers out of the black wolf. He had small reserves of tolerance, but he didn't have a stomach for killing. His head pounded with a memory of long ago. Yet, he had killed another.

Himiin hung his head as shame rolled up his throat choking him with the foul taste. Since that incident he'd held himself in check. He'd kept his distance from mortals and managed peace on the mountain with minimal force.

Before meeting the maiden, he'd been willing to kill the Blackleg spirit for answers and because his intuition told him the spirit was there to harm the Nimiipuu. He had to control his emotions.

Himiin looked at the far side of the lake. He wished to talk with Wewukiye, but knew to sit beside the lake in daylight would bring trouble for both him and his brother.

He walked back and forth up the mountain, moving farther and farther away from the dwellings. The sun shone bright on an outcropping of rock. Standing on the warm stone, he peered down. The villagers went about their daily chores. He spotted Proud and Tall's lodge and watched a group of men erecting the council lodge by the edge of the lake.

He lowered his body to the warm rock and watched the people. Scanning the village, he found Wren beside the plump maiden who'd been with her when they met. Their heads were bowed together as they ate their meal. Would Wren tell her friend she had walked through the forest with him? What would others think if they knew she spent time alone with a wolf and had no fear?

It mattered little to him what they thought as long as he kept her safe. His duty was to protect her from all harm. Not because of her caring touch and caressing voice, though the memories of her holding his paw and soothing his wounds warmed him.

Her voice and caring eyes seeped into him, offering his lonely heart hope. Until she left his mountain, he would not let anyone or anything harm her.

Including him.

Pá-xat

(5)

Wren moved through the village, sidestepping fires. Tendrils of pungent smoke fluttered toward the sky as the women placed strips of venison to dry on racks over the fire. Others stirred mouthwatering baskets of soup made from the *keeh-keet*.

At Proud and Tall's fire, her mother stabbed willow branches through trout and jabbed the other end of the branch into the earth around the edge of the fire pit. The supple willow bent toward the flames from the weight on the end. Wren's stomach rumbled from the sweet aroma of roasting fish. The early morning trek up the mountain had given her a healthy appetite. Her thoughts drifted to the white wolf, and she smiled.

Their encounter had revived her spirits.

She Who is Wise, Wren's grandmother, placed glowing, hot rocks in the basket of water to boil the keeh-keet. The small onion-like bulb was one of the first bounties Mother Earth provided in the spring. They'd run out of supplies from the summer before. On the trip from the winter camp the women searched the meadows for the young edible bulbs and roots. Soon they would travel to Weippe and gather *kouse* roots.

She enjoyed the gathering, but the nutty scent of the root baking in the ground until it was black, soft, and chewy made her mouth water thinking about it. Kouse was a main food. She helped her mother grind the dried root into a powder with a two rocks. Mixed with dried salmon, the powder provided nourishment for the men when hunting. The men wrapped this mixture in leaves and tucked it in the bottom of their quivers.

The outing to Weippe was one of Wren's favorite trips. She took great pleasure in greeting old friends at the digging and bringing back stores to keep the band fed through the coming year.

All the scattered Nimiipuu bands came together at the Weippe. Along with the harvest, they held dances, horse and foot races, and other games. She smiled, remembering her father's pleasure over the outcome of the races during their last trip to Weippe. The horses from their herd had won every race.

The Nimiipuu from other bands, and even the other friendly tribes, camped in the meadow, had traded for mares from their herd. Would this year prove as profitable for their band? Even the young warriors had gloated over the victories to others. The horse races were one of her favorite things to watch.

As the women and children dug the roots, they took care to refill each hole with earth. During the harvesting, the women sang songs to Mother Earth thanking her for her gifts. When their voices were not raised in song, the older women told stories. Wren treasured the stories which told how the Nimiipuu were created and of the spirits who kept them safe. She especially enjoyed stories of the trickster coyote.

The evening dances around the campfires brought great joy. The beat of the drums seeped into her body, filling her with Nimiipuu tales of courage and honor. The rhythm and voices raised in thanks to the Creator compelled her to dance, showing her thankfulness and respect of those who came before.

With her marriage to the Blackleg, she would have little to be thankful for, except the peace it would bring her people.

Her chest throbbed. If her father agreed to the Blackleg marriage, she could very well leave the Nimiipuu before they traveled to Weippe. Wren ground her teeth and bit back her resentment.

Why had the warrior Hawk chosen her? He could have asked for any number of Nimiipuu maidens from other bands and secured a peace offering.

A furry, white face with blue eyes emerged in her thoughts. She was the only one with the gift to save her people. The task had fallen to her, thus making her the only maiden able to secure peace. She sighed heavily, pushed her hands against her pitching stomach, and wished she had not been chosen for such a vital task.

"I am hungry," Tattle-Tale said, pushing past her to stand before their grandmother with a bowl carved from mountain sheep horn in his hands.

"Little brother, I am sure Grandmother has made enough for everyone." Wren smiled fondly at her brother. His name, Tattletale—and for good reason—made it hard to take him seriously. He was to go on his vision quest in seven moons. She shook her head. She found it hard to believe the tattletale in front of her could—if deemed strong enough and wise enough—one day lead the band. He would have a lot of growing to do to fill their father's place and the hearts of the Lake Nimiipuu band, as well as the other bands in the tribe.

"I need to eat plenty to prepare for my vision quest." He smiled. "I will have a vision of wisdom in which the weyekin will bestow upon me a gift greater than yours."

She shook her head at his foolishness. To boast of such things could keep the weyekin from even visiting him on his first quest. "You should not boast so, little brother. You have yet to spend more than two moons out alone. It takes nerve and faith to wait for your vision alone on the mountain."

He puffed out his chest. "Red Sparrow has prepared me. He even said as the son of the chief my vision will be of great importance."

"Only if you have one. Sometimes it can take several quests before you see your vision." With his boastfulness and disregard for sacredness, he would be lucky to receive a visit from a weyekin.

Tattle-Tale frowned and took his place next to the fire. Once seated, he turned mischievous eyes on her.

"I saw father talk to you before he left." He slurped the soup from the bowl and smacked his lips. "And you left right after him. Where did you go as the sun topped the hill?"

Wren stared at her brother. She would reveal nothing to him. Everyone in the village knew better than to tell the tattletale anything.

She held out a bowl to her grandmother. The twinkle in the woman's eyes told Wren to pay no mind to her bothersome brother.

She Who Is Wise cleared her throat. "The boy reminds me of old man coyote. He, too, could not keep his nose out of trouble. Always

44

sniffing for information that did not concern him." She turned her bleary-eyed gaze on Tattle-Tale. "Do you know what happened to Coyote?"

Her brother's eyes were round with interest as he shook his head.

"He found his nose snipped by the crawdad."

Wren giggled as Tattle-Tale touched the tip of his nose. Their grandmother chuckled and spooned the flavorful broth into Wren's bowl. The old woman winked. Conspiring with her grandmother would be one more thing she would miss if the marriage to the Blackleg took place.

Feeling the need to separate herself from her family, she wandered over to Silly One's dwelling and fire.

"You were up before the Sun Herald rode his horse through the village," Silly One said, as they took seats on a log away from her mother, sister, and grandmother.

Wren looked at her friend. "How do you know?"

"Tattle-Tale."

Wren wrinkled her nose and glanced at her brother crouched by the fire talking with their grandmother. "He sees too much." She turned back to her cousin. "And says too much."

"He is called Tattletale." Silly One giggled. "Are you anxious about your father's return?"

Wren shivered. She feared for him and the news with which he would return. He was old and wished the village to remain at peace. They had lost several warriors the previous summer to warring Blacklegs. She grimaced, that was when he received his wound. When she had disobeyed. Guilt swirled in her stomach. She swallowed the bitter taste creeping up her throat.

Unless the Blackleg attacked the council meeting them at the River of Many Bends, she would leave her home. Not only would they have peace between the tribes, her father would no longer have to worry about her endangering the band.

"I am afraid his return will mean I will soon marry." Her stomach, which had rumbled from hunger, now felt too full. She gazed at the slopes of the mountain. Her home. Where she'd been born and yearned to remain.

Silly One patted her arm. "I'm sorry to have asked."

"This is not your fault, or, your problem." Wren wished to relieve her friend, but failed. Tears burned behind her eyes and her lips refused to curve into a smile. Anger caused her breathing to quicken. She was a Nimiipuu who wandered from area to area throughout the year to find food and shelter from the seasons. How had her heart become rooted to one spot?

"This is also my problem if it takes you away." Silly One frowned. "Why did this Blackleg ask for you? It makes no sense."

"I do not know. Maybe he only wanted the daughter of the chief, not necessarily me." Did he know her name and specifically want her?

Silly One got a gleam in her eye. One that told Wren her cousin was up to something.

"We could have someone else pretend to be you when this Blackleg comes."

"Father would not do something so dishonorable. I cannot try to fool the weyekin or the Blackleg. It could bring disfavor to us with the Creator and the Blackleg."

"You are right. But I will continue to think on how to keep you here." Her cousin's bottom lip quivered. "I cannot see my future without you here to listen and give advice."

Wren felt the same. They had grown up together and talked of the many things they would experience as wives and mothers.

She walked back to her family's fire with a heavy heart. There were many chores to get done this day. With so much work to do, her hope was to keep busy and forget whatever her father would say upon his return.

As the morning wore on, she worked hard to fill her mind with thoughts of the white wolf. The friendship she shared with the wolf while strolling through the trees, fascinated her. She wished to wander the mountainside aimlessly with him for all time. Her heart quickened. If only it could be so.

A sigh slipped between her lips.

"You are quiet, my daughter," Morning Fawn said, as she scraped the hair from an elk hide stretched on a willow frame.

"After you work the brain into that hide it will make a fine set of leggings for father."

"Yes, it will but that is not what you are contemplating so hard." Her mother raised an eyebrow.

Wren stared at the deer hide she scraped to make a shirt for Tattle-

Tale. He would wear this shirt when he came back from his vision quest. She hoped he had a strong vision. Then they could have a naming ceremony and give him a more grownup name. She frowned. Why must he take his name seriously? No one liked a tattletale.

"Daughter?"

Wren glanced at her mother. The woman's creased forehead and searching gaze did little to gather her wayward thoughts. "Yes?"

"Your thoughts have not been on your work all morning." She pointed to the small spot where Wren had nearly scrapped clear through the hide.

A lump formed in her throat. She had come close to ruining the hide as her mind wandered to the mountain.

"What is troubling you?" her mother asked, moving her whole body forward and back as the sharp stone scraped the hair from the hide. The rhythmic swish sparked a memory of younger years playing near her mother as she worked. The sound had been a reminder her mother was always near. It was a feeling she would cherish in the days and years to come.

"I am only thinking good thoughts for Tattle-Tale when he goes on his vision quest." Her mind had not been entirely on her brother, but she refused to tell her mother the emotions in her heart. She carried enough guilt over the negative thoughts about her future with the Blackleg. Her duty was to the Nimiipuu. If her marriage prevented more deaths then her gift would be bestowed on her people. She knew this to be true. For why else would her weyekin have come to her at this time?

"I fear you are not telling me everything. Life is not always simple. Many things come into our lives which make us stronger. Are you feeling weak?" Her mother set aside the scraping stone, and turned to her. Her dark eyes were misty.

"I do not wish to say. It would put me in ill favor." She could not meet her mother's eyes.

"The news came as a shock to many." Morning Fawn scraped at the hide once more. "You have a right to feel. But you must not show how you feel." Her mother looked around, surveying the village. "You are the daughter of Proud and Tall. It is your duty to do what is best for all, just as your father and your grandfather before him." She turned her searching gaze back to Wren. "If the song you sang at the winter

47

campfires about your weyekin is true…it is your gift to bestow upon your people. You cannot ignore your weyekin. Nothing good will come of it."

"That is why I must marry the Blackleg." Wren squeezed the stone in her hand so hard her fingers ached. "I would never dishonor my weyekin, family, or people, no matter how sad my heart."

Her mother placed a hand over her clenched fingers. "You must hold your head up and smile. If others believe you are unsure, they will lose hope and faith in you and your weyekin."

"I know, Mother. I am counseling myself. But it is hard. I so love this mountain and my people. And do not look forward to the day I will leave it all behind to go to people who live an angry life."

Tears glittered in Morning Fawn's eyes. "We all have heavy hearts over you marrying a Blackleg. You must always remember The People love you and wish you the best."

Wren set to scrapping the hide with added determination. Her mother was right. She would not let anyone see how the upcoming match tore her up inside. One creature would listen as she voiced her concerns. She thought of the white wolf and dreamed of the time when she could walk the mountain with him once more.

《》《》《》

Himiin woke from a nap on his rock above the village. Laughter from a group of women and girls echoed up the mountainside as they walked to the lake. Wren's voice lifted in gladness. The sound sent his body humming.

Scanning the group, he found her in the middle next to her friend. Even from a distance, he could easily find her among the others. Her shape and gait were etched in his mind. When a grove of cottonwood trees hid them from view, he became agitated.

He'd made up his mind to watch over the maiden. It was his duty as spirit of the mountain to make sure all was right with everything and everyone in his territory. Thoughts of the Blackleg wolf and Wren's marriage tightened his muscles and rage seethed in his gut. Something wasn't right, and his gut told him it had to do with the innocent Nimiipuu maiden.

His temper abated as he remembered Wren's love for the mountain and her people. He'd never before witnessed this deep devotion from a mortal. Her dedication intrigued him, made him want

48

to keep her close and safe.

He stretched, his muscles warmed and relaxed, he yawned and squinted at the sun glaring overhead. When he felt limber and ready to proceed, he jumped down from his perch.

Surveying the area, he listened and sniffed the air. Birds trilled sweet songs in the trees. Their melodies floating through the forest meant all was well. The slight afternoon breeze brought the forest scents of plants, living and decayed, a foul smelling skunk in the underbrush to his left, and his own anticipation.

He loped down the mountainside toward the lake. The sun overhead heated openings with bright light while thickly wooded areas remained dark, cool, and musty. He heard the high-pitched laughter of women and caught their female scent before he neared the edge of the woods.

His pace slowed. He lowered his body and crept under a bush to watch the female mortals. Crawling on his belly, he moved forward to look. His breath caught when Wren walked out of the lake.

She tossed her long wet hair over her shoulders, revealing a naked body gleaming with droplets of water. The muscles in her legs were taut and well-defined. The joy on her face as she pranced along the water's edge chasing and splashing her friend lightened his heart. The woman was so innocent and child-like. How could Proud and Tall think of sending one so young off to the enemy? Her purity and beauty would be lost on the Blackleg.

His anger at the chief for even thinking of sending a maiden into the den of the Blackleg turned to a different kind of fire as he watched Wren move about. Her small breasts moved slowly up and down with each step she took. The movement caught and held his attention. The gentle curve of her hips proved she was no longer a child though her joyous enthusiasm for life said otherwise.

He'd never witnessed a woman's body unclothed. Never even cared to see one.

But this.

His mouth felt dry.

Her dark skin glowed with good health as she moved about. Snippets of her conversation floated to him on the wind.

"Do you think Tattle-Tale will actually have a vision?" she asked the plump maiden next to her. The maiden replied, and Wren's lilting laughter soothed his ears.

"He is too full of himself." She dragged her fingers through her hair.

The memory of those hands running through his fur and caring for his injuries accelerated his heart.

He swallowed the lump in his throat. What was it about this woman that made him quiver with emotion he'd never before experienced? As a spirit, he knew only duty, commitment, and devotion to the mountain. This woman stirred thoughts he'd smothered long ago.

She braided her hair. Though she stood among other women doing the same thing, he had eyes for only Wren. The sight of her slender fingers deftly twisting the strands as she smiled and conversed with the woman next to her hit him with longing to have her all to himself.

He shook his head to rid his mind of the ridiculous thoughts.

Wren bent to pick up her dress.

Swallowing, he closed his eyes. His pulse pounded and his body ached. He slowed his breathing and gathered himself back into control.

Opening his eyes, he found Wren pulling the woven garment over her head. She pulled tufts of otter fur out of the pouch on her belt and stuffed them into her long black braids.

He wanted to feel her hair, her skin. His heart thrummed in his chest.

He must touch her.

When her hair was decorated, Wren turned to an older woman. "I am going for a walk. Do not worry. I will be back in time to finish the hide." She walked into the woods. Bushes rustled and her sweet voice sang a song of praise to the Creator for making the forest beside the lake for the Nimiipuu.

His heart thundered as indecision plagued him. Should he show himself? Would she know he had watched her bathe? It would mean nothing to her; she saw him as a wolf. But could he ever again see her as anything other than the lovely creature who walked out of the lake? And could he willingly let her go to the enemy Blackleg?

He debated with himself as she moved farther and farther into the woods. He had to watch over her. The dark spirit could be out there waiting for her to walk right to him. Spurred on by his need to protect her, he raced through the forest. He leaped over a log and nearly ran into the back of the maiden.

"Oh! Are you chasing your dinner or me?" she asked, holding her hand to her chest.

Embarrassed by his arrival and his need to watch over her, he backed away, growling.

"Do not treat me like a stranger. I know you are the wolf I have been talking to, so do not try and act any different." She put her hand out to him in submission and smiled. "Were you looking for me?" She sat down on the log and patted her lap.

Her acceptance, sent vibrations of elation skittering through him. She was so small and vulnerable, yet, she hadn't once acted as though he would harm her. He sat on the ground in front of her. Staring into her dark eyes, he saw fear, guilt, and pleading swirling in the depths. How he wished he could talk to her.

"I cannot show my unworthiness to the others. My mother says I am to show them I do not fear the marriage." She placed a hand on his head and moved her palm back and forth, smoothing the hair, then ruffling the fur the other way. The contentment that settled in his chest from her touch unnerved him and made it hard for him to concentrate on her words.

"It is not that I fear the marriage," she continued. "I am angry I must leave." Her dark eyes searched his. "You will not stop joining me on my walks if I tell you how I truly feel, will you?"

Himiin shook his head and held his breath. Would he be able to make her see she should be cautious of this match between her and the Blackleg?

"I wish to fulfill my weyekin. My people are my heart, and I wish to do what is best for them." She sighed and glanced at the forest around her. "I came to this earth on this mountain and wish to be put to rest here. How will that happen if I am to never see the land of my heart after I marry the Blackleg?

"Everyone watches me closely." She swallowed and looked away. "My past has been filled with disobedience. I fear they are all waiting for me to object and cause a war."

The sorrow in her words and the pain in her eyes crept through him like a cold wind. He laid his head in her lap, covering her legs with its width. As a wolf he had no other way to comfort her. Her tiny hand stroked his head as she hummed softly.

The shadows grew long and the light dimmed. He should patrol the mountain and watch for the dark spirit. Her hand stopped and she sighed.

"I must go. My mother will be worried if I remain gone any longer." Putting both hands under his muzzle, she tipped it up to gaze into his eyes. "You are a dear friend to listen to my fears, doubts, and selfishness." She placed a kiss on the top of his head. "Thank you."

He stood and stepped back to allow her to stand. Following behind her as she walked back to the village, he vowed, before she left the mountain, he would hold her as a man held a woman. Not only to comfort her, but to appease the growing need in himself.

`Oylá-qc

(6)

Himiin hid within the forest waiting for the village to quiet for the night. When the last person disappeared into a lodge and the moon hovered directly overhead, he would meet his brother by the lake. He planned to ask Wewuikye if he had ever experienced and craved the same fire this mortal woman brought to his body.

The panic and excitement the Nimiipuu maiden brought out in him intensified with each encounter. He feared the yearning he had to be near the woman; yet, felt the friendship between them an omen. She could be his chance to right the wrongs of his past.

A movement to his left drew his attention from the shimmering lake and his thoughts.

Someone crept from the village.

Himiin made his way through the underbrush, following the whisper of rustling leaves and muffled crackle of dried pine needles. Catching the familiar scent of his prey on the wind, he picked up speed. His heart thrummed in his chest as he hurried up the mountainside to the meadow where he'd napped.

Himiin stopped in the darkness of the forest and looked out into the clearing. The images in the half moon became shrouded in grays and blacks with a shimmer of silver on the edges. In the middle of the meadow with her hands raised to the sky, twirling and singing—a vision captured his gaze and his heart.

Wren's hair hung loose, floating and shimmering as she swayed and chanted. The slim moonlight caught her features, giving her an ethereal glow. Himiin stood entranced, listening and watching. His body swayed and matched her movements to the rhythm only she heard as she sung of her love for the mountain and the people of the lake.

The melodic words echoed his beliefs for those he watched over. Knowing she held the mountain they stood upon with such reverence intensified his need to protect the maiden.

Her rapturous chant ceased. All was calm. Not a bird twittered nor an owl called as if the whole mountain had been enthralled by her song.

Himiin peered at her silhouette while the moon became shrouded by clouds. She stood motionless, her head bent and silent. The hush of the meadow roared in his ears. Should he approach? Did she wish to be alone?

Wren hugged her sides, let out a mournful sob, and collapsed to the ground. Her sudden change from joy to despair rippled his skin and choked Himiin's throat with fear.

He rushed toward her. The tall grass slapped against his body. His panting echoed in his ears as he approached the maiden sitting on the ground, clutching her knees to her chest.

He stopped next to her.

The sight of tears trickling down her cheeks when moments before she had danced with joy, tightened the knot in his throat. He yearned to hold her in his arms and take away her grief. Before entering the meadow, he should have turned into man form. His ears twitched with irritation. It was wrong to want to hold her. However, his body shook with need to comfort her.

As a wolf he could do little to console her. He licked the salty tears on her cheek. She shifted, wrapping her arms around his neck and burying her head against his shoulder. Her ragged breath ruffled his fur and warmed his skin.

Frustration again caused him to growl. But she clung to him as if a great wind would pick her up and carry her away. Breathing in her scent of herbs and camp fire, his anger abated.

"White Wolf, it seems you always see me at my worst." She sat back, wiping at the tears. Her small hands scrubbed the wetness from her face. She managed a smile. "You are my friend. I feel sad I am forever using you and not returning any favors. What could I do for you?"

He wanted to know why she snuck out of the village and chose this clearing to dance. The question could not be asked as a wolf. Annoyed once again at his inability to communicate, he was left feeling inadequate. All his years in this world, he'd never been at a loss of how to handle a situation.

"Come sit here." She patted the ground within her crossed legs. He glanced at the spot she indicated. The idea of his large body sitting within her slender legs was ridiculous. The idea of being that close didn't frighten him as it would have before meeting her.

He moved closer and sat beside the maiden, instead. She put an arm around his shoulders, resting her head against his.

"To be as free as you, my white wolf, and not have to follow the ways of our people, that is my wish tonight." She twirled his hair with her fingers. "But my disobedience in the past has brought nothing but trouble to my people. This once I must do as I am told." She sighed.

Her body slumped. "I will marry the Blackleg to bring peace, but my heart will slowly die every day I am away from this mountain and my people. I know it as well as I breathe this sweet cool air." She peered at him. "You are the only one I can tell this to. For I know you will tell no one." She kissed his jaw and hugged him, staring into the sky.

Himiin looked up. His gaze followed the wisp of clouds that veiled the cheerful twinkle of the scattered stars and the slender curve of white moon. Her plight tugged at his conscience and his heart. The more time spent with the maiden, the less frightened he became of harming her. Her innocence made him protective, not angry.

Pointing his nose to the moon, he let loose a long and mournful howl. The sound echoed through the meadow and rose to the murky sky.

Wren did not know why the magnificent beast howled, but the woeful sound matched the heaviness in her heart. She released her hold on his neck and tipped her face up to the sliver of moon. Pulling from deep within, she voiced a howl full of the despair she felt.

55

She sensed the wolf watching her. Turning to him, she stared into his eyes. As they gazed at one another, the color darkened to the deep dark blue of a summer sky at night.

Her thoughts and fears became lost in the color and clarity. A shiver of anticipation and excitement swirled inside, warming her. His presence wrapped her in a blanket of security and belonging.

Was this creature truly her weyekin? If so, why did her body warm and tingle when she stared at him? Should she not be fearful of such a strong virile animal?

"I have so many questions for you. If only you could talk and answer them."

A gust of wind tossed her hair around them, whipping her face, and tangling around his muzzle. She pulled the strands from the wolf and brushed the dancing hair from her face.

The wolf stood and walked toward the trees.

"Do not leave, I will not ask questions." A shiver ran through her at the absence of his warm body. He stopped, waited a moment, and then came back. Grasping her hand in his mouth, he gently tugged. His teeth and tongue were warm. The blunt ends of his teeth bit down only enough to pull her from the clearing.

She had not upset him. He wanted her to leave with him.

"I'll come. But I must get my pouch. I dropped it while dancing." The veiled moon left the ground in darkness. Crawling around on her hands and knees, the tall grass tickled her arms and face surrounding her with its sweet scent as she groped along the cool ground for her pouch. Her fingers touched the soft leather. Elated to find her beaded pouch full of trinkets and herbs, she chuckled and wrapped her hand around the object.

With the bag in her hands, she glanced around to see if the wolf still waited. His white fur glowed in the darkening night, giving him the appearance as she had seen him in her vision. Warmth tingled through her to know he remained and watched over her.

His head tipped toward the trees, telling her to follow.

The wind whipped her hair about her, making it hard to see. Collecting the long strands into one hand, she looked up into the sky and realized the dark clouds gathering would bring more wind and possibly rain. The frosty bite of the wind reminded her the cold time was not long gone, and the warmth of the growing season had yet to mature.

The white wolf stopped at the edge of the trees, beckoning her once more. She hurried in his direction. When she stood abreast of him, she grasped the fur on the back of his neck. Together they moved down the mountain. The darkness and her unruly hair made it hard for her to see.

Stumbling, she fell forward. Thrusting her hands out to stop the fall, she landed on the thick fur and stout body of the wolf. His warmth and softness was welcome after the battering, cold wind. She lay upon him longer than was necessary enjoying the respite from the weather. Slowly, she stood, and they continued down the mountain.

The wolf stopped at the edge of the trees before the village. The world around them and beyond resembled a dark black hole. Even the wolf's white coat barely sparkled in the gloomy night. The pressure of his body against her legs and his eyes glowing like distant fires, reassured her he remained by her side.

Dropping to her knees, she wrapped her arms around the animal's warm furry neck. Her heart pounded, snuggling against the wolf. Fear didn't enter her mind as she clung to him. He would never do anything to hurt her.

"I don't know why you have come to me at this time, but I know there is a reason." She wanted to cling to his neck forever and never have to face her family and the fast approaching marriage to a man she did not know. With her wishes and what she must do at odds, she bit back tears and hugged the wolf one more time, breathing in his scent of animal and forest.

She released his neck and stood. Drawing a breath to steady her voice, she cheerfully said, "Thank you for getting me back to the village. We will meet again I am sure. Until then, stay safe my friend."

She walked out of the trees with steps more confident than she felt. Trepidation squeezed her chest as she snuck back into the village. With her father gone, she knew of no one who would care. However, with her being crucial to the peace with the Blackleg, it would not surprise her if her father had instructed someone to watch her while he was away.

Wren cautiously made her way through the village, careful to not trip into a fire or knock over drying racks. The dwellings loomed like small mountains amidst the acrid wisps of smoke and the faint glow of dying embers in the fires along the way to Proud and Tall's lodge.

Wren dropped to her hands and knees, parted the blanket flap at the narrow entrance, and crawled inside her family's dwelling. The small yellow flames dancing skyward from the fire pit in the middle of the lodge helped guide her to her sleeping mat.

"Why are you sneaking into the lodge?" Tattle-Tale rose up onto his arm and leaned toward her.

Her heart stuttered. Did he never sleep? "I am merely trying to not awaken anyone."

He snorted. "You woke me."

"To have heard me enter, you must not have been sleeping, so I could not wake you." She turned her back on her nosy brother.

"What were you doing at this time of the night?"

Could he be her father's eyes while he is gone? No, her father would have left the job to someone older and wiser. One who would merely watch and not ask questions.

"Seeing to my needs. Go to sleep."

"You should have done that before the storm began."

How did he know about the storm coming if he stayed in the lodge all night? Perhaps he *was* the eyes of her father. She would have to be more careful when she walked the mountain and talked to the wolf.

Sighing, she closed her eyes to dream of a white wolf and spring days on the mountain.

《》《》《》

Himiin stood at the edge of the trees until Wren made it safely back to her lodge. He shook his head. The spirit in the woman was commendable, but he didn't think the Blackleg asking for her hand knew what he would have to battle. Her longing for the mountain would be hard for her to hide. Every day her husband would see her shrink little by little and not know what brought on her grief. In that state, she may not produce the offspring the Blackleg and Nimiipuu coveted.

His chest ached, and his head throbbed at the thought of a Blackleg holding her and making children. What he wouldn't give to be the one to make babies with her. To touch her in the way a man and woman consummated their joining.

He knew they should never become so close, even as his body throbbed for the chance. From two different worlds, one of them would be hurt. With his past, it would be her. He wouldn't be able to live with himself should his acquaintance with Wren bring her harm.

Even this knowledge did not lessen his emotions for her, nor curb his desire to bring children into the world with her.

Himiin thrust his muzzle in the air and breathed in deep. He was a spirit. He had to clear his thoughts of this mortal.

Since meeting Wren, he'd thought little of the mountain and only of her and his need to be with her. His obsession with her endangered his ability to conduct his responsibilities.

He must forget the maiden.

His chest squeezed, and his heart ached to think of not seeing her. To carry on his duty, he must remain alone.

He stopped at the edge of the lake. The wind fluttered his fur as he stared into the darkness. He spoke his brother's name and waited. Icy rain sliced through the black sky, pelting his coat, slipping through, cooling his thoughts and skin.

The lake came alive with swells and small white caps as the wind whipped down through the valley and stirred the water. Out of the frothy breaks stepped his brother. First his antlers, his long regal neck, and then his massive body. Wewukiye stepped ashore and shook, shedding more water than the deluge of rain.

"Your call sounded strange. Did you battle another black wolf?" Wewukiye asked.

Himiin snapped at him and leaped onto the log closer to his brother's height.

"I am battling something far worse than the black wolf." He stared into his brother's dark eyes.

"I see." Wewukiye stepped closer. "Is it the maiden?"

"Yes."

"She knows you are not what you seem?"

"No. Not yet."

"What do you mean, not yet?" He pushed his square nose in Himiin's face. "You cannot go before her as a man. We have been given the gift of man form only to help when there is no other way."

His brother's reaction did nothing to dampen his desire to go before Wren as a man.

"I am thinking of talking to her in man form." He slowly shook his head. "She is feeling as though she will die should she leave the mountain. She needs someone to tell her the mountain will always be with her in her heart and her memories." He lifted a paw. "She is too sad to see this herself."

"Why must it be you who talks to her? I would think an elder could give her this wisdom." Wewukiye shook his head and slashed his antlers through the rain. "And what about before."

Himiin flinched. He knew Wewukiye only brought it up out of concern, but his previous blunder had hurt them all.

"I feel no anger toward her. And I have learned to control my emotions."

"Are you sure? You aren't controlling your emotions if you wish to go before her as a man." Wewukiye stomped a hoof.

"I am doing this for the good of the Lake Nimiipuu." How could this half-truth slip so easily off his tongue? And worse, Wewukiye saw right through it.

"You are doing this for the maiden and yourself." His brother glared at him. "Do not become our father. I would hate to see what fate awaits us if you choose the wrong path."

Himiin stiffened and growled, "I am nothing like our father. I do this for the sake of the people and the maiden."

"Then prove it. Stay as a wolf when with her. Do not use excuses."

The last words shook Himiin as much as Wewukiye likening him to their father. He hated excuses. His father had been full of them when the Creator snatched his children and made them spirits.

"I do not like excuses. I was merely pointing out if the villagers knew Wren's thoughts they would feel she is letting them down. When in fact she is willing to make the sacrifice, knowing she could very well die at the hands of the Blackleg.

"She tells only me of this. The maiden keeps everything to herself while with her people. She feels she is being strong for them." Deep down he knew no one would listen. It was a learned attitude of the Nimiipuu. They hid their emotions and did what was expected of them. It was how they stayed strong and united—all thinking as one.

No doubt her curious nature in the past had brought nothing but heartache. He shook his head. There were times when emotions needed to be considered. And this was one of those times. A young maiden could walk into a life of torture and no one would listen because her leaving was for the good of the village.

"To show yourself, will make things more complicated. Not only will she know you are a spirit, but you will be tempted." Wewukiye shook, sending the rain gathered on his back flying onto Himiin.

"She already thinks I am her weyekin."

Wewukiye stared at him. "How is that?"

"It was a white wolf who came to her in her vision. That is why at our first encounter she did not fear me. She believes I am the white wolf who bestowed her gift. To have found me now means her marriage to the Blackleg will fulfill her duty." Himiin scoffed. "Our meeting has nothing to do with her gift. I can feel it. But I do wonder at the emotions this maiden has stirred in me. And how to ignore them."

Himiin thought of the stroke of her gentle hands across his fur, and her sweet voice in song for her love of all the things he held dear.

He stared at his brother. "I need to talk to her, to touch her."

"Ahh, now we have the truth, brother. It is not just to console the woman, but to abate your own desires you wish to take the form of man." He shook his head. "This is not good."

"Have you ever felt this way? I have been on this earth as a spirit many, many seasons. Never has a mortal or any spirit touched me as this maiden."

Wewukiye stepped closer. "Brother, it is unusual for a spirit to feel what I see in your eyes." He thought a minute. "How is it you care this strongly for a mortal, when your essence should be focused on the mountain?"

"I do not know. I too have wondered this same thing. My body, my head—" heat flashed through him as he thought of Wren walking from the lake after her bath. "When I look upon this maiden, it is as if I need her to continue to exist."

"This is strange." Wewukiye took a couple steps back as though Himiin had caught a contagious disease. "You should only care this strongly for the mountain." He stretched his neck and whispered. "Do you think the Creator is playing a trick on you? Seeing if you are like our father."

Himiin shook his head. "It is a cruel trick. I do not think the Creator would torture me so. But something must come of my encounter with this maiden, that I am certain." He swallowed the lump of despair in his throat. "Even if it means I am to help her go to the Blackleg to instill peace."

Wewukiye shook his head. "You are stronger than I, my brother. If my body yearned for another as you show, I would not be able to hand her over to the enemy. Even if it is her gift."

"It is not going to be easy. That is why I wish to be able to talk to her. To know that helping her go to the Blackleg is truly what she must do for the better of the people." He couldn't look at his brother. Her sacrifice would not keep the schemers from future raids on the Nimiipuu. This he believed. But he would help her fulfill her weyekin even if it brought him to his knees with despair. "She needs someone strong to help her through this."

"Do not show yourself unless it is necessary. Sometimes just having someone to listen to your words is as good as someone to hold you." Wewukiye turned. "Remember my words and stay as you are around the woman. To get any closer to her could ruin not only her, and her duty, but you as well. Heed my words."

Himiin watched his brother walk back into the lake. The conversation left him more upset and unsure. His emotions for Wren raged stronger than anything he'd experienced through all the ages. He sensed her sorrow and wanted to ease her pain. Yet, he knew not how without holding her and talking her through her decisions.

He stared across the lake, wishing for a sign from the Creator to guide him in his encounters with the maiden. The wind picked up and the rain slowed to a drizzle. He walked away from the lake and back up the mountain to the ledge above the village.

Lowering his body at the edge of the outcropping, he placed his head on his paws and watched the village below. She would take to the mountain again tomorrow. How he would show himself he did not know, but one thing was certain, he would be with her.

`Uyné-pt

(7)

Wren stretched, rubbing the sore muscles near the base of her back. Bending over to stretch hides on willow frames was a job for the young and the reason Morning Fawn left this chore for her daughter. Wren had stretched four elk hides and three deer since the morning meal. The sun hovering directly overhead washed over her with warmth that rivaled the cooking fire. She wiped at the sweat beading her forehead and glanced around.

Commotion at the far end of the village captured her attention. Her heart lodged in her throat as her father, and the warriors who traveled with him, rode into the middle of the village. She'd secretly wished this day would never come. Walking the mountain with the white wolf the last five suns, she had let the return of her father and the news he would bring, slip from her thoughts.

Morning Fawn ran up to Proud and Tall's horse. Half the village lay between where Wren stood and her parents, making it impossible for her to hear what they said or see their expressions.

Fear of her future made her feet shuffle back and forth. She could not decide whether she wanted the news now, or wanted to run and never hear what her father had to say. The indecision lodged in her throat like an un-chewed piece of meat.

"Father is back," Tattle-Tale said, running to her with a mischievous grin.

"I have eyes." Wren bent over the deer hide. She grabbed the hide and yanked, battling with the skin to force her anger to the job of stretching the hide on the willow frame.

"Do you not want to know what he decided?" Her brother tugged on her arm.

She shook his hand off and glared at him. "Father will seek me out if he wishes to tell me."

Tattle-Tale smiled and nodded beyond her. "I think he wishes."

She turned in the direction he indicated and froze at the sight of her father moving toward them. She felt small for making him walk across the village. After all the riding, his bad leg dragged along the ground, giving her father an undignified gait. His injured leg, having to walk to her—these were her fault. She swallowed the guilt burning her throat.

Worse than his seeking her—the whole village followed behind him. Her mother kept a slow pace alongside her father, clasping her work-roughened hands together so tightly the knuckles turned white.

The news was not good, Wren could feel it. Her knees shook as her family and friends approached. Fear squeezed her chest and stalled her heart.

"Daughter, we have returned with our decision." Her father stopped far enough away he would need to speak loudly for her to hear. He wished his voice to carry to the whole band gathered around. The thought made her shiver. Once the words were out for all to hear it would be done.

Her arms hung listless at her side when she wished to reach out to him and tell him how she felt before he made his decree. Panic strangled her throat, allowing no words to come forth. Obedience had always carried challenges. In all the times past, she would have voiced her thoughts and taken the disapproval. But no more. She nodded her head for him to continue even though her heart screamed for him to say nothing.

"I have spoken with the Blackleg warrior, Hawk. He believes peace can be held between our two tribes by taking you in marriage." Proud and Tall stepped forward, placing his large hand on her shoulder. "Daughter, he is a good man. He is strong and will treat you well. He has given his word."

Proud and Tall faced the crowd gathered behind him. "After

64

talking with the Blackleg, I have decided they speak with truth. Our
Wren will leave the village at the full moon. Hawk, a Blackleg warrior
seeking a wife and peace between our tribe and the Blackleg tribe of
He Who Crawls, will come with two escorts. We will let them pass in
peace."

Wren heard the announcement made as though she were a horse to
be traded. How could she have no say in her life? Even as the thought
flashed through her head, guilt washed over her. Her wants could not
come before the greater good of the village. If there would be peace
with the marauding Blacklegs, it would benefit all. Her father was in
no shape to battle with young warriors whose only thoughts were to
plunder and squash those around them.

Silly One put an arm around her shoulders. Wren peered into her
cousin's face, garnering comfort from the sympathy her friend's eyes.
After the full moon, Wren would never know if Silly One found a
good husband and had the children of her dreams.

"I know this is for the village you must leave, but that does not
lighten the sadness in my heart." Silly One squeezed her shoulders.

"I can barely breathe. I feel as though I am being crushed under
the large boulder by the path leading to the huckleberries." She could
not look into her friend's face. If she saw the reflection of sorrow she
felt, the tears would come. To cry with the village watching would
show weakness. She had to stay strong and show the marriage would
bring peace for all. To dishonor her father and family and show
anything less than her acceptance of the situation would be wrong.

She smiled stiffly and swept a steady gaze around the village.
Soon the gathered crowd returned to their chores with an occasional
glance cast back. Were they expecting her to once again do something
unfavorable? She squared her shoulders and held her head high. They
would not see her lose control in front of them.

The smile on her face wavered when only Silly One and Tattle-
Tale remained. She turned from her brother's observant eyes. He
would not have the satisfaction of saying she had behaved anything
other than proper.

Her parents walked back to their lodge. It was a long journey to
meet with the Blacklegs. Her father had to be tired and hungry. Her
parents would not notice if she slipped from the village. When Tattle-
Tale ventured off to speak with a cousin, Wren took hold of Silly

One's hands and squeezed.

"I need to go to the mountain." She glanced at the outcropping of rocks above the village. The silhouette of a wolf standing upon the ledge filled her heart with hope. He remained. As he had since the day they met.

"Now?" Silly One peered over her shoulders.

"Now. I must talk with the white wolf."

"You and the wolf have formed a strange bond." Silly One stared at her intently.

"I can talk about what is to come and not feel guilty. His eyes and acceptance helps me take on the burdens put before me." She scanned the area for her brother. He still talked with another boy. "Please, keep Tattle-Tale busy so he cannot follow me." She turned toward the line of trees.

"How?" Silly One secretly glanced at Tattle-Tale.

Wren shrugged. "However you have to. I do not want him ruining my time on the mountain. Or telling my father what I do." She waved and ran into the trees.

In the forest, the coolness of the shade sent shivers through her body. She moved in a direct path up the mountain toward the meadow where she had met the wolf on several occasions. Wren pushed through brush and navigated around trees. Her heart pounded with anticipation. She had to see him, talk to him. Her father's news filled her with dread and grief. The full moon was not far off. There would be little time to continue her treks on the mountain and spend time with the white wolf.

She stepped through the last barrier and into the clearing. Her stomach lurched.

A tall flaxen-haired warrior stood in the center of the meadow. Her gaze slid from his beautiful hair, down long muscled dark arms, and buckskin clad legs, back up a flat stomach and broad chest. The sight of such a man made her stomach flutter like she had swallowed butterflies. The warriors in the village were fine looking men, but this man— took her breath away. Raising her gaze to his face, she stared into familiar eyes— the exact color of the white wolf.

The warrior raised an arm and motioned for her to come forward.

She knew not of this man. He was not from any of the Nimiipuu tribes. He would not have gone unnoticed. She had heard stories of a band with flaxen hair who lived before the coming of the horse in the area far beyond the River of Many Bends. Could he be of that band? If so, why was he here, on this mountain?

"Come, Wren," he bid in a deep soothing voice.

She started forward at his command then stopped. How did he know her name?

Wren moved a foot backwards to step into the trees and run if necessary. "How do you know me?"

"Your friend called you that." His gaze never left her face. Looking into his eyes, a flash of recognition warmed her to her toes.

His presence didn't threaten her. It puzzled her. How did a man she had never met know her name? And why did he stand in the clearing where she met the wolf? She took a step forward.

"You are called?"

"Himiin," he said with a slight tip of his head.

Wolf.

She stared in disbelief. Was he *the* wolf? She gazed into his eyes. The recognition she saw within the depths set her heart racing. How could he be? It was not possible.

"You have received bad news?" His light blue eyes turned a deep blue, showing her he was the wolf she sought. But how could this be?

She took a step back unsure of this man and the turmoil within. Her mind grasped at all the tales told by the elders around the winter campfires. Many stories told of shape shifters and how they showed themselves to only a few. Could her wolf be a shape shifter? If so, could this be a sign about her future? Her heart thudded in her chest. If he truly was the wolf, he knew everything about her, and she knew nothing of him.

"How do you come to be both man and wolf?" Her father always told her she asked too many questions, but this seemed a very good time to ask many.

"I am the spirit of the mountain." He shrugged. "I can take many forms."

"How is it you have come to me?" She took a step forward. The warmth of his voice and unguarded stance drew her.

"You came to me. I was merely tending my wounds, when you came upon me."

She gulped in air and choked.

He was truly the wolf.

Only Silly One knew of their encounter in the woods with a white wolf. Her thoughts spun, making her dizzy. The knowledge she spoke with a man/wolf and held strong affection for him sent her fragile emotions spinning, unsettling her shaky hold on her future.

"Why have you come to me, as this—" she moved her hand up and down indicating his body, "—now?"

"When I saw your father's return and the sympathy of your friend, I knew you would need someone to consult. Not just listen." His words flashed memories of her walks on the mountain with the wolf. His thick coat as she hugged him and told him all her fears, and his sympathetic eyes giving her the courage she needed to fulfill her weyekin.

He opened his arms.

She hesitated. The accepting gaze and strong arms overrode her caution. She ran into his embrace, wrapping her arms around his middle. He was solid, warm, and smelled of the mountain.

She no longer held back the tears.

No one but this man could see her weakness. And the man holding her knew everything in her heart. When the tears ceased, she drew her head back far enough to look up into his well-formed face.

"How?" She tentatively touched his solid shoulder.

"Come sit with me under the tree, and I will explain the best I can." He moved her to his side, and they walked to a large pine with a patch of soft spring grass underneath.

Once settled, Wren leaned against his side where she could see his face. There could not be a more perfect man. She traced his angled cheek bones and square chin, resting her fingertips against his full soft lips.

"Please tell me how you can be a man and a wolf." She whispered, for her breath had caught in her chest, and her heart battered against her ribs.

"I am Himiin, the spirit who lives on this mountain."

She squeezed his muscled arm. "But you feel real. My hands do not go through you like mist."

"I can take different forms. I prefer being a wolf." He stared into her eyes. "Until now."

His gaze was so intense it started a fire smoldering deep inside her. She squirmed, wondering what mysteries this spirit could teach her.

"W-why now?" she asked, licking her dry lips.

"Because I felt your need to discuss your future. What news did your father bring?"

Leaning against his hard body with his strong arms around her, she had pushed the news out of her mind. His insistence to know what was to be, brought back the words of her father. And her doubts.

"I am to marry Hawk of the Blackleg tribe of He Who Crawls at the next full moon." Her heart twisted at the thought of not only leaving behind the village and her family, but this man as well.

Himiin worked hard to tamp out the anger and fear which gripped him upon hearing she was to marry a schemer. He refused to trust the Blacklegs. Not a single one of them. He couldn't send her away having doubts about what she felt she must do.

"The full moon is not far off." He placed a finger under her chin and lifted her face. Gazing into her dark eyes that revealed her emotions had become one of his favorite things about their talks. "You will have only a short time to visit the mountain." The thought of not seeing her every day sat like a poison berry in his stomach.

"I will find a way to see you and walk the mountain." She leaned against him, her breasts molded to his chest as her hands wound around his neck. Her actions reflected that of a drowning person.

The feel of her body set off needs he'd repressed since becoming a spirit. His head told him to set her away, instead, his arms wrapped around her, pulling her close. He savored the feel of her young curves and the fresh scent of her clean hair. Nuzzling her long neck, his lips registered the vibrations in her throat as she sighed.

He gathered Wren onto his lap, running his hands up and down her body, learning her shape. Her hands twined in his hair before drifting down his back. This caressing would only make the separation harder on them both, but he could not let her go without knowing how she felt in his arms.

She snuggled her head against his neck and sighed again. Himiin looked down. Her eyes were closed. An innocent smile curved her mouth.

He traced a fingertip across her smooth lips.

Her tongue darted out, touching his finger. The soft pink tip sent a bolt of lightning straight to his groin. If this caressing continued, he would take her right here under the tree. The thought brought him to his senses. He could not harm another mortal.

Even though his intentions were to please her, to touch her in this way would dishonor her and possibly damage the peace offering.

"We should walk." He helped her to her feet and stood.

Her eyes questioned, but he couldn't tell her the emotions raging inside. She could never know how her leaving would rip him apart. Her decision was hard enough without him complicating matters.

He would cherish for all eternity the bond they'd created while walking through the woods. He took her slender hand in his and started at a slow pace up the mountain. For once Wren didn't talk of her fears. She pointed out the small yellow flowers, citing their dainty beauty and sweet scent.

"Do you think this bush grows in Blackleg country?" Her question brought an awkward silence as they both stared at the dogwood bush.

He wasn't sure she wanted an answer so much as an assurance everything around her would not be entirely different. He couldn't do that. For in his heart, he believed she would not survive in the Blackleg world. Either her longing for the mountain and her people or the violence of the schemers would be her undoing.

Her time on the mountain should be filled with pleasant memories and not filled with his fears. Thinking of this, he showed her his favorite spot. A large granite boulder surrounded by giant pine trees. The sun beat down on the trees, releasing their tangy scent and heating the rock.

Himiin helped her up onto the boulder. They lay side-by-side, holding hands, soaking in the warmth and watching the clouds.

"Look!" Wren pointed to a large cloud drifting by. "That looks like you when you were sleeping in the meadow."

He stared at a white formless blob, not a noble wolf. "I look much better than that as a wolf."

Wren giggled. "I did not mean to upset your dignity. But it did look like you as a wolf all sprawled out sleeping." She glanced sideways at him. "I should be able to determine what you look like better than you. When have you seen yourself as a wolf?"

"When I look into the lake."

"Oh." She looked at him, her eyes searching, for what he didn't

70

know. "And as a man, have you seen yourself?"

The question took him by surprise. He rarely shifted into man form and had no idea how he looked. From the fire in her eyes, he knew he was not repulsive. Or did she see only the wolf who listened?

"No, I do not know what I look like as a man."

She sat up, reaching out a hand, touching his hair. "You have hair the color of the sun." She sifted it through her fingers. "It is soft and smells of the forest." Her gaze moved to his face and her fingers trailed along his cheek. "You have eyes which see more than most. Your nose is long, straight, and male." Her fingertips fluttered across his lips. "Your mouth is full, soft, and knows all the right things to say." Her gaze flickered from his lips to his eyes then down to his chin. "And your chin tells me you have a stubborn streak and are strong willed."

He captured her hand before her fingers skimmed down his neck.

"I do not need you to tell me more." His husky reply did little to hide the effect she had on him. Her soft touch and lingering gaze could not go any lower. His need for her throbbed, and she mustn't find it.

She watched him intently. Did she see the connection between the wolf and the man? He wanted her to see him only as a man. From her description and trailing hand, he knew she appreciated this form. His hands itched to roam across her body as she had his face. To do that would surely push him over the brink of control. They could never come together.

"Come, you must go back." He slid off the boulder and held his hand out to her. She placed her small hand in his. Her eyes glistened with trust.

Such great faith humbled and scared him. As the spirit of the mountain he'd held the trust of many creatures and not given it a second thought. But to have this woman, a mortal, look at him as though he could make everything right, frightened him. His gut told him her life with the Blackleg would be a nightmare. He wanted to beg her not to follow her weyekin. Duty to the mountain and the people, held his tongue.

Helping her off the rock was impossible without grasping her waist to lift her down. When her feet touched the earth, he leaned into her, pushing her against the rock.

Her eyes widened in surprise before a spark of desire grew in their russet depths.

He wanted her.

Using every ounce of control, his hands resting on her waist remained loose while all the other muscles in his body flexed. The desire raging in him was new.

And terrifying.

Controlling the vessel his spirit resided in had never been this hard.

She ran her hands up his chest, wrapping her arms around his neck. Her innocent unhurried movements were the exact opposite of his lustful inner turmoil. But then, she was mortal and had experienced these emotions before.

He shook his head. She was mortal and already spoken for. His life was to maintain harmony on the mountain. Her marriage to the Blackleg would do this.

Himiin gently untangled her arms from his neck and pushed away from the rock and the woman his body yearned. He could not have her.

Ever.

He grasped her hand and headed down the mountain. The need to have some form of contact with her was greater than his conviction to the mountain and the Creator. The contentment washing through him as he walked his beloved mountain holding her hand took him by surprise. Until this moment, he'd not realized loneliness had started to blur the beauty of the mountain.

Shadows grew longer as the sun slipped behind the snow-capped mountain top. They stood not far from the ledge above the village. In the grove of aspen trees they could not see what was below, nor could anyone below see them.

"You must go back. They will wonder where you have been so long." Even as he squeezed her hand and released her slender fingers, he wished to never let her out of his sight. The emptiness which flooded him as he stepped away from her hurt far worse than the knowledge he had stepped beyond his duty.

He looked into her eyes and saw the same emotion dancing in her dark eyes. Their being together was wrong and would bring them both nothing but grief. Yet, he knew he would watch her from his ledge and meet her in the clearing again when she slipped from the village. He couldn't help himself. She had become his reason to exist.

"You will be in the meadow tomorrow?" she asked as hope shone in her eyes.

"Yes," he answered in a voice harsher than he'd meant. She studied him a moment before her lips curved into the heart-stopping smile he would never forget. Yet, he would send her off with the enemy because his honor would not allow him to get between her and her weyekin. No matter how shredded his heart became knowing she walked into trouble.

`Oymátat

(8)

Wren slipped into the village from a different direction than she had left. No one could find out about Himiin. He was the one person she could tell her thoughts and not feel she dishonored herself or her people. No one could know how it troubled her to marry a schemer. Her father believed in the peace it would bring. She would not fail him again.

She peered around the village to see if anyone noticed her arrival—especially, her tattletale brother. Few heads turned her way and those that did glanced past her uninterested. No one seemed to care she had left after Proud and Tall's news, nor that she returned a long time later.

Wren looked for Silly One. Her friend hunched over deer hides alongside other young women her age at the far edge of the village. Wren made her way through the dwellings toward the maidens. The older women bent over fires drying fish and pounding the dried meat into powder. The children gathered firewood and attended the babies. Men gathered in groups telling stories of past hunts and preparing their bows for a hunting trip into the mountains.

Tattle-Tale did not appear to be in the village, relief washed through her. He must be out watching the horse herd. She did not want him following her, asking more questions than she cared to answer. Stealth would be needed to make sure he never saw her leave the village when she met Himiin.

"Daughter, you have been gone since your father's return." Her mother looked up from the evening cook fire as Wren approached. "You are well?"

"Yes, Mother. I needed time to set things in my mind." She thought of Himiin, standing in the clearing his arms open to embrace her. Wren flashed her mother a smile brighter than she could have managed had she not spent the afternoon and evening with him.

"You are settled in what must be?" Morning Fawn watched her intently.

"Yes, I will make the most of the days I have left with the mountain and my family." She smiled. Yes, she would spend much time on the mountain with Himiin, gathering memories of their time together to carry her through the coming years as a wife of a Blackleg.

Her smile faded. How could she leave him behind? In a short time, he had become a part of her just as the mountain and her people.

Tattle-Tale ran over to the fire. "Where have you been, sister? Why did you leave right after Father's return and announcement?"

Her brother's appearance and words jostled Wren from her sorrowing thoughts. She pasted a smile on her face. He would not find out about Himiin. This was one secret the tattletale would never learn.

"I walked among the beauties of the mountain, filling my heart. Father's words, though I thought I was prepared for them, came as a shock. I needed time to let his words and my future settle without someone badgering me." She stared pointedly at her brother. "As you heard, at the full moon I will no longer be among the mountain and my people and wish to make them strong in my heart. And, you will no longer be able to taunt me." She patted her brother's head and set a stick of wood on the fire.

"You left before Father made another announcement." He puffed out his chest. "I leave for my vision quest tomorrow. Father has expressed his wish that I have this experience before you leave."

She laughed at the excitement in his voice and seriousness of his face. It was good he went on his vision quest. She just did not believe he would have a vision. A large part of the quest was meditation, something Tattle-Tale did not sit still long enough to accomplish.

"You laugh at my vision quest?" he asked, glaring at her.

"No. I find it hard to believe you can stay in one place long enough for your weyekin to find you."

"Daughter, your words do not do justice to your brother." Morning Fawn frowned at her.

"Sorry, Mother, but there is so little these days I can speak how I feel about. This is something which does not put me in ill favor with the band, only my brother." She smiled at Tattle-Tale. He rewarded her with one of his big goofy grins.

"I forgive her Mother, for I am going to have a far greater vision than she."

Morning Fawn turned her scowl on her youngest. "To boast of such a thing will make the spirits angry."

Wren felt sorry for her brother. His belief he needed a gift bestowed upon him greater than hers was foolish. She would gladly give him hers if she could. Leaving the mountain and Himiin was a greater sacrifice than she had ever dreamed her weyekin would ask of her.

"Wren, you left before I could talk with you." Her father's deep voice startled her as his head and shoulders ducked through the entrance of their lodge.

"I wished to think about what you said." She walked over to her father. "I will do what is best for the people." *Even if it breaks my heart to leave.* It would be hard to leave Himiin, but thoughts of spending time with him until then put a song in her heart. She smiled at her father. If she kept Himiin in her thoughts, she could face anything.

"You are stronger than your mother and I. We carry heavy thoughts to have you leave our village and our sight. For you to live among a tribe who has been our enemy for so long, disturbs our hearts." He placed a hand on her head. It had been some time since he'd touched her so.

Tonight, his hand rested heavy on her head. Her father seemed to need the comfort more than she. The wrinkles on his face had deepened since he left. His heart should have lightened with the new knowledge the village would no longer fear the Blackleg tribe.

"You have met this Hawk? You said he is a good warrior?" Who was this man who would become her husband?

His sorrow lifted and his eyes shone bright. "Yes, he spoke well and cared that we make peace. He will make you a strong husband.

Together you will bear children who will belong to both tribes, uniting us." He shook his head. "It is hard to believe we could have peace after warring with the Blacklegs my lifetime, the lifetime of my father, and the lifetime of his father."

Wren nodded her head. "We have lost many to the Blackleg." She barely remembered her father's mother. But the night her grandmother was killed still haunted Wren's dreams. The woman had died while hiding Wren. She shook off the memories, finding it ironic her grandmother died to save her from the Blacklegs, and she would soon marry and live with the Blacklegs to save the band.

"And Hawk?" Wren felt a shiver of apprehension. Was he man enough to keep her safe when she set foot on Blackleg territory? There had to be some of his band who didn't want the peace or a Nimiipuu living among them just as there were those among the Nimiipuu who believed the Blackleg would not stay true to their word.

"He is a match with us in wisdom and honor. He does not carry hatred in his heart. Nor the blood of Nimiipuu on his hands, of this he was clear." Her father squeezed her shoulder. "He will keep you well."

Proud and Tall walked over to the fire and picked up a bowl. Morning Fawn filled it with the fish soup she stirred.

Hunger did not stir in her belly even though she had covered much of the mountain that afternoon. To put food in a stomach which twisted and clenched with trepidation and sorrow seemed foolish.

"Daughter, you must eat. You cannot go before your man as skin and bones. He will think we are giving him a sickly wife." Morning Fawn handed her a bowl of soup.

"How would he know what I should look like? We have never met." The disrespectful words were uttered before she could stop them. Her mother stared at her with disbelief. The Nimiipuu had married to build relations between bands and tribes since their creation. Feelings on either person's part were not thought of, but to be given to the enemy was more than she could handle. Especially since meeting Himiin and learning there could be harmony between a man and a woman which filled one with great joy.

"You need not meet before a marriage to make children and prosper." Her mother aimed a shy smile at her father.

Morning Fawn and Proud and Tall married to merge two Nimiipuu bands and make them stronger. Over the years the two had grown close and cared for one another. But they belonged of the same tribe. They did not have to learn new customs. Morning Fawn knew her husband would not plunder and raid innocent people.

Wren shook with revulsion. How did one welcome back a husband who brought you bounty from a raid on weaker tribes?

"I do not see this as the same. You and father were of the same tribe. I know only the Blackleg enjoy killing." She glanced from her mother to her father. "Am I to be faithful to a man who would think nothing of killing me should he find me unappealing?"

"I have talked with Hawk. He is not such a man. He does not believe in killing the innocent. This he spoke clearly." Her father stared into her eyes. "This man I give you to will only honor you. Do not dishonor your family by disobeying." His face darkened and formed the hardened mask he wore before his enemies.

Shame burned her cheeks. She stood. Her parents' stares held disapproval. She had witnessed these expressions before. This was not the first time her stubbornness to go against them had surfaced.

She wanted to do as they asked and help her people, but deep down, what they asked of her did not feel right. Her unsettled stomach and worried mind were proof. Unless her weyekin or the Creator showed a sign, her father would not go against the offering of peace with the Blackleg.

Clutching the bowl of soup, she hurried over to Silly One's fire. She wished to eat without the weight of her father's disapproval and her mother watching her every move. Or her brother's impish smile.

Silly One motioned to sit beside her on a log. "What is wrong? You do not look well."

Wren sat beside her cousin. The lump of shame lodged in her throat made her unable to speak. Tears burned the back of her eyes. She'd spent the afternoon with a man other than her betrothed and could think of nothing else. She had to forget him and look to her future with the Blackleg Hawk. But thoughts of the Blackleg only increased her agitation.

"Wren, did your walk not go well?" Her cousin placed a hand on her arm.

The comforting gesture nearly brought Wren's tears to the surface. It would do no good to show her fear of the match between she and Hawk. Her father had set his mind to the marriage. She gulped back

78

the tears and scrubbed her eyes with her hands.

"My walk was good. I saw much of the mountain and have placed it in my heart to take with me on my journey." She kept her head bent. Remembering the walk brought back the magical moments with Himiin. Her family had not seen the excitement in her eyes over her discovery of the flaxen-haired man, but her friend would not miss it.

"That is good. You know my father was with your father when they talked to Hawk."

She nodded, lifting her head to see the expression on her friend's face. Silly One could hide nothing.

"He said this warrior, Hawk, is much like a Nimiipuu. He talks of peace and has much wisdom." She giggled. "He also said he is not as ugly as most Blackleg."

Hiding behind the bowl she held in front of her mouth, Wren giggled. Everyone knew the Blacklegs were the ugliest. They thrived on yelling and killing. How could anyone bent on attacking peaceful tribes be pleasant to look at? She cringed. How could she live among a tribe constantly at war?

"I'm sorry. You will have to look at him for the rest of your life. For your sake, I hope what father said is true." Silly One patted her hand.

"Do you think if someone is pleasant to look at they are also pleasant in disposition?" Wren had often pondered this. Could the reason the Blackleg carried a mean streak have anything to do with their unpleasant appearance?

Her cousin thought on this. "Little Bear is pleasing to the eye." She blushed. Wren knew Silly One wished Little Bear would ask for her hand. "And is pleasant."

Wren bumped her cousin with her shoulder. "Look beyond those which you have eyes for."

Silly One giggled and scrunched her face. "I think it is true. All warriors I find hard to look at are also unpleasant." Worry crossed her pretty round face. "That does not promise good things for you at the Blackleg village."

The smell of the soup suddenly made Wren's stomach churn. She set the bowl down and hurried to the edge of the trees.

Breathing deeply of the scent of pine, she longed to run until her legs no longer moved. She did not want to leave this mountain, leave

Himiin, and live with a tribe who killed and took slaves for pleasure. If something happened to Hawk, what then? Would she be forced to live with a warrior who liked to kill? Would he treat her as a slave? Her chest squeezed at the memory of tales told around the campfires by those who were once Blackleg slaves. She shuddered.

The sun had set and the chill of the night slid across her skin and seeped to her bones. She stared up at the moon. It grew each night. Before long, she would leave with a Blackleg warrior. Sorrow filled her heart as she hugged her sides and wished she were on the mountain with her arms wrapped around Himiin.

《》《》《》

Himiin stood on the ledge overlooking the village. Wren ran toward the forest. If she had continued, he would have hurried down to her, but she stopped, dropping to her knees and hanging her head.

It made his insides ache to see her hurt. He knew of no way to ease her pain. She would leave at the full moon to marry a Blackleg warrior. The pact had been made, and they could not go back on it without causing a war. He shook with rage at the thought of her in another man's arms, especially a Blackleg.

Her innocence and love of the mountain would be lost on a Blackleg warrior. Her gentleness and caring would be scorned in a village of murderers and thieves.

He sat down, pointed his nose to the sky, and let loose a mournful howl filled with sorrow and frustration.

The creak of a branch above interrupted his song. He opened his eyes and found yellow eyes peering down at him.

"You are full of sorrow, brother." Sa-qan settled herself on a thick branch above him.

"The Nimiipuu maiden who helped me is being given to the Blackleg warrior at the full moon." He couldn't hide the wrath and anguish in his words.

"You cannot keep her. She is of the real world. You are a spirit. One who was set upon this mountain to help the creatures who live *here*."

"Is she not a creature of the mountain?" He looked up into his sister's glowing eyes. "How do I let her go, knowing she will lose her gentleness and love for beauty after being among the Blackleg?"

"She must do what is right for her people. Not you. Or her." Sa-qan dropped down to the ledge and stood beak to nose with him. He didn't back away even though his sister at times could prove fiercer than any dark spirit he'd ever faced.

"You cannot respond to a creature of the real world the way you are this woman. It is not good." She walked away, spun sharply, and returned. "Brother, do not follow her off this mountain. You have to let her go. If you leave this mountain you would become nothing more than a wisp of smoke with no meaning. No longer able to watch over the people and creatures." She tilted her head. "Do not follow in our father's footsteps."

Her words sent a shiver of dread down his spine. He would prefer to be a wisp of smoke if he could not be with the mountain.

Or Wren.

Life without the mountain or the maiden was unthinkable. He gulped. Wren held the mountain in her heart. But what of him?

"I know what will happen should I leave. I will not. But to see the sorrow it brings her to leave—I feel she will perish should she remain from this mountain too long."

Sa-qan touched his chest with her wing. "You cannot think with your heart on this matter. It will only bring you both more sorrow." She frowned. "It is distressing to me that you show more than duty for something other than your mountain. It has never happened before, to you, or Wewukiye, or myself."

"I have wondered the same. Why do I crave this mortal? Why does her plight capture my heart and rip at me?" Himiin asked his sister, the wisest of the three.

"I do not know, but it has been on my mind. You must fight the desires for this woman. Her gift is to save her people. This marriage will fulfill her weyekin, you cannot stand in the way or she will suffer greater than leaving you behind."

"What if her death comes before she fulfills her weyekin?" His gut twisted at the thought of the enchanting maiden taken before she could give her gift to her people. It would make her walk on the other side more harrowing than living with the Blackleg.

"We have no guarantee. We can only watch over her until she gets to her new village."

"That is my plan, to stay close to her until she is off the mountain." But how will they know she made it to the village and was well? He watched his sister as she straightened a feather on her wing. She could travel greater distances than either he or Wewukiye.

"When she is off the mountain will you watch her?" his voice pleaded. "And see that she arrives at the Blackleg village safely." He wished no harm come to Wren and would do whatever it took to keep her safe. Even if it meant stirring the anger of the Creator.

"I will watch over her when they leave the mountain. Until then we both must return to our duties."

Loud voices in the village below caused them to both walk to the edge of the rock ledge and look down.

Two groups of the younger warriors pointed fingers and waved their arms in agitation. Wren stepped among the young warriors sending the hair on Himiin's back to prickle and rise, his ragged breath nearly caused him to choke.

He was too far away to protect her. Anxious about her safety, he scoured the growing crowd for her father. Surely, he would step forward. But the man stood back, his arms crossed, watching.

"You must let her stand on your own. She is the only one to make her decisions." Sa-qan opened her wings.

"The decision to leave was made for her. She is only doing what she feels is her duty."

"Then you must see it the same." Sa-qan leaped in the air, flapped her wings, and was airborne, leaving him to suffer alone as he lost sight of Wren in the bodies moving around her.

Kúyc

(9)

Wren heard the young warriors arguing and knew she had to say something before the peacefulness of the village became threatened. She pushed between the warriors crowded around two of the young men who would one day be on the council due to their daring and wisdom. She stepped in the middle of the argument and used the courage she had not known she possessed until her betrothal to a Blackleg.

"No bickering." She moved between Little Bear and Eyes of Snake.

"We should not make peace with the Blacklegs. They will not honor it." Eyes of Snake glared at Little Bear over her shoulder.

"Do you think my father, Proud and Tall, would do this if he did not feel it to be right?" She stared at Eyes of Snake, who was several summers older. At one time she'd thought he would ask her to be his wife, but he had turned to another.

Eyes of Snake glared at her. "Your father is getting old and is not as strong as he once was. I believe he has made a bad decision." The defiance in his black eyes made Wren take a step back.

How many others thought the same? Was she to live with the Blacklegs and no one truly believed it would help? Swallowing the fear burning her throat, she thought of his disrespectful words for Proud and Tall. She would not let this warrior talk of her father in such a way. Proud and Tall was the chief, and a wise man, whose judgment they must all follow.

"I agree with his decision." She stepped forward, forcing the warrior to retreat into his friends. "If this Hawk, who has spoken for me, has wisdom and the strength to try for peace between our people, we should embrace it with open arms. I do not wish to lose any more of the Nimiipuu to the Blacklegs." She turned to Little Bear. "What is it you believe?"

"If Proud and Tall feels this is good and you are willing to live with the schemers to make it so, it is right for the Nimiipuu."

Wren smiled at Little Bear. He was well-liked and many more would listen to him than Eyes of Snake. "You speak with wisdom. That is more powerful than strength."

The flash of indignation on Eyes of Snake's face said he understood her cutting remark. He glared at her, then Little Bear before turning to the few who stood behind him.

"You will see the wisdom of an old man who wishes for peace because he can no longer fight will be the undoing of us all. This I believe." He nodded to the small group gathered before him and stalked off.

Wren turned to Little Bear. "Thank you for believing in my father."

"It is easy. He has carried us through many hard times. Your father only wants what is best for the village." Little Bear took her by the arm, directing her away from the others. Dropping his voice, he added, "But, I too fear it may not be the best for you." He quickly moved on, for to be alone with a woman betrothed to another was not welcome.

Panic squeezed her chest and froze her limbs. She wished to call him back, but he had disappeared among the lodges. Why did everyone voice their worries to her, but not her father? Because no one had yet to meet an honorable Blackleg. And no one wished to go against the man who had thus far led them well.

She glanced at the ledge where Himiin watched the village. His lonesome cry earlier wrenched her heart. It took all her control to not run to him and soothe away the pain.

A hand rested on her shoulder. She turned to the weary wrinkled face of her father

"Well done, daughter." Proud and Tall pulled her next to him.

"You will be missed when you go with your man." He embraced her. "Your words were well spoken. Use them with the Blackleg and our tribes will one day be united."

"Did you hear the words of Eyes of Snake?" She watched her father closely. When there was discontent among the band, he counseled the naysayer. She wondered if Eyes of Snake would even come to a counsel with her father. The warrior's anger had burned in his eyes like a raging grass fire.

"Yes, I heard the words of an angry young warrior. His heart is full of hatred for the Blackleg. He does not see beyond the deaths of his family and what could happen if we do not become friendly with the Schemers. He will see this is the best for all when Hawk comes to our village to get you." His eyes softened. "Hawk seeks wisdom. He is a warrior who uses his head and thinks things through. Be wise with your choice of words, and he will listen."

Wren laid her head on her father's chest. "I will try."

"I know you will my daughter. You have wisdom given to you from your weyekin and beautiful words float off your tongue for which you were named." He stepped away, clearing his throat. "Go to your bed now, daughter. You will begin your readiness for your man soon."

The uncertainty in his eyes troubled her. Although he spoke with clear words about her journey, he was not of clear mind all would be well. This knowledge made her already strained hold on doing the right thing even harder.

Wren walked to the family lodge with weight as heavy as a tall pine on her shoulders. She dare not glance at the ledge. If she saw Himiin, she would not be able to keep her feet from carrying her to him. There was so much she needed to say to make sure her decision was truly right for her people. He was the only one who would listen and not make judgments.

"You are moving slow, sister," Tattle-Tale said, dancing up beside her.

"Someone of your age should be asleep at this time of night." She ignored his irritating habit of walking backwards in front of her.

"It is not so late." He tipped his head, peering into her face. "If you did not get up before the sun herald and slip out to be on the mountain, you would not be so tired."

She stopped. "How I make my heart feel about the coming journey is my business and no one else's." She stepped closer. "I'm glad you are going on your vision quest tomorrow. I will not have to worry about you shadowing me."

"Ah, but I will be on the mountain. And if I do see you, I would not mind knowing what it is you do." Crossing his arms, he stared at her. "It is hard to believe you only walk the mountain the long times you are gone."

"Brother, you do not want to look for me. I do not like to have my private moments with the mountain disturbed. If you should do so—I would not want to be on the other side of my anger." She ground the sentence out between clenched teeth. It was one thing to hold her resentment with her elders and peers, but she would not be kind to a younger brother who would ruin everything should he discover Himiin.

Tattle-Tale stopped. His mouth dropped open, and he let her pass.

Wren stomped into the lodge. In her haze of anger, she did not greet her grandmother nor did she acknowledge her mother sitting by the fire weaving a basket.

"Daughter, what has upset you this night?" Her mother rose, crossing the lodge to Wren's sleeping mat.

"Why must my brother always make comment of my actions? It is of no business to him if I want to visit the mountain before I do my chores." She grabbed her mother's hands. "Make him see, it is only a short time I am able to be upon the mountain that fills my heart with joy."

Tears trickled down her cheeks. "When I leave with the Blackleg, it is unlikely I will set foot upon the mountain again, or see you, my family." She wiped at the droplets sliding down her face and looked into her mother's caring eyes. "I need the time to let all the goodness of this place I love seep into my heart so I may use it to carry me the rest of my summers."

Morning Fawn placed a hand on her cheek. "You show true courage. There is not a warrior among this band who would do what you are doing." She wiped at a tear. "Be strong. You may walk your mountain, but seven moons before your man comes, you will be in the old woman's lodge preparing for him. You will not be able to roam the mountain for that time."

Her heart stopped. She had forgotten about the purification. Panic clenched her throat and twisted her insides. How would she go so long without seeing Himiin? Without their conversations?

"If I am to wed a Blackleg, should I not do their rituals?"

"The wedding will be Blackleg, the purification will be Nimiipuu." The finality of her mother's words, told her there would be no getting around the seven moon seclusion in the old women's lodge.

《》《》《》

The next morning, Himiin watched from the ledge above. Before the golden rays of the sun barely skimmed the top of the hills, a shadow crossed the village and headed toward the base of the mountain.

He leaped off the ledge, his heart humming, and headed to the area he'd come to think of as their meeting place. In the trees at the edge of the clearing, he raised his muzzle to the sunny blue sky. Closing his eyes, his spirit floated out of the wolf body and swirled into the form of a man.

Stepping into the meadow, the sun swathed the clearing in an early morning glow. The sight astounded and awed. In wolf form, he sensed things and moved about with little concept of the beauty around him.

The glittering dew-covered grass fluttered around his legs as he crossed the meadow. He stood in the center, warming under the sun's rays, and breathed in the sweet scent of clover and wild flowers. His awareness of the mountain had grown deeper.

"Why are you grinning like a child with a favored token?" Wren asked, appearing through the trees.

Himiin hurried across the meadow. He had to see her with this new appreciation.

"The more I am in man form—the more I see the beauty around me." Her eyes widened, and her mouth formed a shape much like the bud of a wild rose. "You included." The rosy color darkening her cheeks brought a smile to his lips.

"Your pretty words will not bring you any favors from me," she said, though her eyes sparkled with interest.

"Come, we have little time, let's not waste it." He took her hand, pulling her into the trees and down a path he hadn't shown her the day before. Her steps lagged.

"Do you not wish to walk upon the mountain today?" He stopped and faced Wren.

"I want to never leave the mountain." The sorrow in her words coiled his stomach.

"You can stand up to your father. You can tell him of your fears." He wanted her to stay. How her father could think sending his daughter to the schemers would make peace made no sense to him.

"But I must do this for my people." Her words were not as strong as the day before.

"Do you really think by marrying a Blackleg you will save the Nimiipuu?" He shook his head and walked a few steps away. "It takes more than one person to change the years of thieving and plundering." These words should not be spoken. To influence her against her weyekin was wrong. Yet, his instincts told him to send her to the Blackleg would be her death and would not fulfill her gift.

"There will be my husband. He feels the same." She glared at him.

"Are you sure? You only know what he has told your father. How can we believe a Blackleg? When have they ever stopped long enough from killing and stealing to say something a Nimiipuu could trust?"

Her eyes glistened with unshed tears. "My gift is to save The People. The weyekin who came to me in my vision quest said this." She wrapped her arms around herself as if staving off a cold breeze.

Himiin hated they argued when they should relish their time together. He moved to her, drawing her against his chest, embracing her. The shape of her body molded to his. Her curves pressed against him. Holding her this way flamed the need he'd tried to suppress.

He placed a hand under her chin, raising her face to his. The sorrow in her eyes tugged at his conscience. To make her leaving any harder was wrong. But having experienced her in his arms, he was grieved to let her go. Even for the sake of their people.

Her eyelids fluttered closed. Her pulse quickened under his fingers. Shrugging off the consequences, he lowered his lips to hers. They were softer than he imagined. Her breath hitched as he touched her intimately. Parting his lips, he touched her with his tongue, wanting to see if she tasted as sweet as she smelled.

Honey.

She tasted of sweet honey straight from the bosom of a bee tree. One taste was not enough. He pulled her closer, moving his lips across hers, tasting, and savoring the feel of them. Her mouth opened and she sighed. His body came to life.

The sensations transcended anything he'd experienced before. How could one woman make him feel powerful and vulnerable at the same time? Why did he wish to crush her to him and never let go, and yet, was compelled to treat her with the tenderness one would give the tiniest of creatures. He couldn't continue this way. To hold her, to touch her soft skin. He would never be able to let her go.

He must.

He released Wren and stepped back, avoiding her eyes. How could he show her the sensations she brought to him then turn around and tell her they couldn't see one another anymore?

"Himiin? Did I do something wrong?" The pain in her voice drew his gaze to her face.

The anguish and fear in her eyes cut through him like a knife.

"You did nothing wrong. It is I. I should not touch you so. It is wrong." He took one step forward, before remembering he could not touch her and remain sane. "You are spoken for. We should not be together."

She moved quickly, grasping his hand before he could pull away. "I could not bear to not have you to speak with these last days." She stroked his hand. "Or to touch." She placed his hand on her cheek. "I may never feel this touch from the Blackleg." She kissed his palm. "I wish to have this to remember."

He growled and pulled her into his arms. "I wish I were the one to touch you so, but I cannot. It is wrong."

"Why?" She leaned back, studying his face. "I should be the one to say if it is wrong or not. It is my heart, my body. My life."

"You belong to another. He has spoken." Himiin released her and took a step back. He should not have shown himself to her as a man. Wewukiye was right. It complicated things.

The desire and possessiveness that surged within him, he'd never dealt with before and didn't know how to control. He had no right to her. His job was to watch over the mountain and help keep everything living and plentiful for all.

Wren marrying a Blackleg would keep peace on the mountain. This he should welcome as it would benefit the Nimiipuu. But at what cost to her?

Foreboding snaked up his spine causing him to shake. Was her marrying a Blackleg really the best for the mountain and her people?

"How can elders say what is right for all? Why must we be obedient even though deep down we do not believe it is right?" She turned her back to him, but not before he saw tears shining in her eyes.

"It is the way it has always been. It has worked. Age brings wisdom."

She turned back to him. "But is it not good to voice opinions? Maybe there are others who do not believe that which the elders decree."

"The elders have been of this earth longer and have heard the stories of those before." He preferred arguing to the other thoughts which ignited his desire.

"They do not know everything." She wiped at the tears and looked so lost; it took all his strength to not pull her back in his arms.

He decided to change the subject before she told him spirits also ranked high in her disgust with the elders.

"When do you leave?"

"Hawk comes at the full moon." She straightened her shoulders. Fulfilling her gift was her goal. One she would take on no matter the consequences. This devotion to her people and her weyekin made him proud.

She twisted her hands in front of her. "After today maybe it is best."

"Because we became closer?" He hoped she didn't regret the kiss. It would be all he had to remember the strong maiden once she was far from the mountain.

"No. I will cherish your touch until I am placed within Mother Earth's arms." She gently touched her lips and smiled.

"What happens after today?"

"I will be kept in the old women's lodge for seven moons before Hawk's arrival. That is three suns from now." The look in her eyes bordered on hysteria. "I will not be able to see you or the mountain while I am secluded."

"You will be fine." He took the wolf fang hanging on a piece of leather from around his neck. Draping it over her head, he kissed her shiny black hair, and settled the talisman upon her chest. "Look at this and think of the mountain. You will not be alone."

He glanced at the sun. "You must get back to the village or they will come looking for you." A part of him wanted to make things better for her, but he didn't know how. It was one of the few times he could not fix the situation.

She clasped the fang in her hand and looked at him from under dark, wet lashes. "Thank you."

Turning, she ran out of the clearing. He watched her disappear through the trees. Would she return to the mountain before she left? Would he be able to go on as if nothing had happened after having touched her? He staggered backwards at the realization he would do anything for her, a mortal.

《》《》《》

Wren touched her fingertips to her lips. He had kissed her. The tenderness of the touch and his gentle exploration of her mouth, sent shivers of excitement dancing across her skin. Her feet barely touched the ground as she walked down the mountain.

Himiin's touch and compassion meant more than a thousand sunny days. She kissed the wolf fang he hung around her neck and dropped it inside her dress. It nestled between her breasts, next to her heart. He would forever hold her heart.

Leaving the mountain and Himiin was surely a test. One her weyekin made harder with each visit she had with the spirit. Himiin, in a short time, had become as special to her as the tree-lined mountain slopes and sparkling streams.

Perhaps even more.

She stopped inside the trees and studied the village. These people would only be memories after she married the Blackleg. It was inconceivable she would ever visit the village again. The two tribes never came together except to fight.

Tears trickled down her cheeks as her mother and grandmother bent over the racks of drying fish. Who would she work beside at the Blackleg village? Would anyone care if she became homesick? Or that her true love lived on this mountain?

Glancing back the way she came, she wanted to feel Himiin's lips on hers and run her hands over his strong back. But to do so, would only bring them both more sorrow. It was best to stay off the mountain—even if it broke her heart.

Her brother stepped out of their lodge followed by their father.

Today he would leave for his vision quest. The Sun Herald rode through the village calling all to gather around to help send her tattletale brother off with best wishes and chants for greatness.

Tattle-Tale stood in the middle of the village with every man, woman, and child watching only him. He grinned at being the center of attention. Preparing for his vision quest he had dreamed of this moment when all would wish him well and those younger than he would wish to be him, heading off to learn his gift to The People.

He smiled at Wren when she walked into the village. His gift would be grander than hers. The people talked non-stop of the great gift bestowed upon her—a mere girl. He would have a more powerful one. This he was sure. After all, he was the son of a chief and should, therefore, receive a very grand gift.

"Son, keep your mind and heart open as you journey forth. And your weyekin will come to you." Proud and Tall placed a large hand on his shoulder. The weight and strength of his father brought comfort and confidence.

"I will, Father. I have looked forward to this day for many summers. I will make you proud."

His father smiled and waved his hands to make the crowd part. "Answer the call of your weyekin."

The Ti-wet chanted and danced around Tattle-Tale twirling a ceremonial stick.

Tattle-Tale smiled at Wren and his mother before he walked through the opening allowed him by the villagers. The day was warm with a slight breeze. Perfect for climbing to the highest point of the mountain. The closer he was to the Creator, the faster his weyekin would find him.

《》《》《》

When the sun hovered high in the sky, his stomach rumbled, but Tattle-Tale ignored it. He was not to think of food or water on this quest. His heart and mind must be open to the weyekin.

The moon and stars lit his way when he found refuge under a great tangy-scented pine tree. Stretching out under the large limbs of the tree, the hair on his arms tingled as the screech of a cougar pierced the air higher above him on the mountainside. As was the way, he had no weapons, only his wit to keep him safe. Judging from the echo, the cougar would not be a threat to him this night. Before exhaustion overtook him, he stared up the side of the mountain. There was still a lot of hiking to do to get to the high point he determined would be the perfect place to wait for his weyekin.

The next day as he moved steadily up the side of the mountain, the air grew crisp and fresh, blowing down off the snow-filled crevices and valleys. A herd of mountain sheep watched him climb past them. His arms hung heavy as if he carried boulders, and his legs wobbled under him, but he trudged on. Determined he would reach the ledge he had spotted from the base of the mountain.

When the ledge he sought was under his feet, he collapsed on the outcropping and stared below at the small glimmering lake. The lodges appeared as tiny lumps in the ground from this distance. He sighed and surveyed the hills on the far side of the lake. From the lake they made a person feel small, but from his vantage point, he thought he could step right over them like a downed tree.

He glanced up. The yellow rays of sunlight radiating from the shimmering ball blinded him. Blinking and rubbing his eyes, the warmth of the sun seeped into his tired limbs, and he fell asleep.

Tattle-Tale awoke when a shrill cry of a hawk pierced the quiet around him. His first thought was of his sister being taken away by the Blackleg, Hawk. He knew it was his sister's gift, but it weighed heavy on his heart. He did not wish her to leave. She was strong and good for the band. Her smile and warmth pulled them together. He enjoyed teasing her, and only did so, because he cared for her.

Her threat had surprised him. As he tried to make sense of her actions, his eyelids slid closed, and his teeth chattered from the frosty night air. He had brought no blanket as was the way with the vision quest. You came to the mountain pure of thought, cleansed of worries, only as you came into the world.

He dropped into a fitful sleep, tossing and turning. In his dream, a cougar with glowing eyes came to him.

"Boy, you are to keep your sister from marrying the Blackleg. It will bring death to her."

"How can that be? Her weyekin is to save the people by this marriage?" Tattle-Tale sat up, trying to focus on the floating image of the cougar.

"She has misinterpreted her gift. You must stop her."

Tattle-Tale stared at the apparition as it slowly faded into the darkness. He shivered. How was he to stop the marriage when Wren and the whole village believed in it? He rubbed a hand across his face and stared into the darkness. Well, maybe not the whole village. He thought of Eyes of Snake's argument with both Little Bear and Wren.

The cry of a cougar pierced the air not far above him.

He jerked into a sitting position. Sweat stung as it trickled into his eyes. His heart beat faster.

Stars twinkled overhead. The glimmer of the moon dancing across the lake far below drew him back to the present.

Did his weyekin visit him or was it a bad dream? When did one weyekin try to stop another? He had not heard of such a thing in all his years. Should he ask an elder? A vision quest was not to be spoken of until the ceremonial winter dance. Then he could sing of this vision, and his weyekin with glowing eyes and the head of a cougar.

He shook his head. Until then, he would do his best to stop the marriage between Wren and the Blackleg warrior, and hope he did not dishonor himself with his father and the others.

Pú-tim

(10)

Wren remained in the village for three suns. She kept busy grinding roots for storage and twisting dried grass and dogbane bark to make pouches to carry her belongings to her new home. Tending to her chores, she visited with the people she would miss when the Blackleg, Hawk, took her away to his village.

"You have not been to the mountain?" Silly One questioned as they beaded a belt Wren would wear on the day of the marriage ceremony. The design depicted her journey of life at the Nimiipuu village. Silly One punched a hole in the leather with the bone awl as Wren strung white dried bone beads on elk sinew.

"I have much to do these days."

"One would think you would spend the last of your free days roaming the mountain." Silly One pointed to the beginning of a wolf design in the beadwork. "I have heard a wolf's lonely call every night. Is it him?"

Wren had forced herself to shut her ears to the mournful sound and not think about Himiin's strong arms and magical mouth. Thinking of him, made her decision to marry a Blackleg harder to swallow.

"It is he."

"Why are you not with him while you can?" Silly One stopped beading and took her hand.

"He is not what he seems." She had not planned to tell anyone of Himiin's truth.

"He has turned on you?" Silly One's eyes widened with shock. "He is your weyekin. He would not do such a thing." She shook her head. "Unless he does not approve of the marriage." Her eyes grew large and her mouth dropped open.

"He does not like the marriage. But—"

"You have spoken with him?" Silly One's voice raised and people nearby glanced their way.

"Shh. He is not my weyekin." She was at a loss how to get off the subject of Himiin. Her cousin could be as tenacious as a badger when she wanted something. Talk of Himiin made her wish to see him and the mountain she had avoided the past days.

Silly One leaned closer. "If he is not your weyekin, how do you speak with him?"

Sighing, she leaned over and whispered in her cousin's ear. "He is the spirit of the mountain. He has shown himself to me as a man."

Her friend sat up straight, her mouth opening and closing like a fish out of water. She sputtered with no coherent words forming.

"What have you done to my daughter?" Silly One's mother stepped around the fire and stared at her daughter.

"Nothing, she poked her finger." Wren grabbed her cousin's hand, shoving Silly One's finger in her mouth.

Her aunt moved away, and Wren yanked on her cousin's arm as she hissed. "You cannot tell anyone what I have said. No one can know of this."

Silly One nodded her head and whispered, "What does he look like? I mean, when as a man?"

Wren smiled and thought of the moment she stepped into the clearing and found him. "Tall, broad of chest, hair the color of the sun." She sighed. "His eyes are the same as when he is a wolf. Light blue almost gray most of the time, but they become as blue and deep as the lake when—" Her face heated, and her heart thrummed, remembering the desire which blazed in his eyes before the knee-weakening kisses.

"When what? When what?" Silly One tugged on her dress sleeve.

"When he looks at me." She had to see Himiin one last time before she left the mountain. To leave and never touch or speak to him again would break her heart more surely than leaving the mountain and her people.

"You are right. I must see him and the mountain." She set her work down and stood. "Do not tell anyone what I have told you. It is a secret that must remain so."

Silly One nodded. "You are going now? What of the things you must prepare for your marriage?"

"They can wait. I must see him. It may be my last chance."

Wren scanned the area. She did not have to worry about Tattle-Tale following. He was on his vision quest and should be high up the mountain waiting for his weyekin.

She walked into the trees as though on a normal task. Once out of sight of the village, she broke into a run, heading to the meadow. The need to see Himiin one more time before they confined her to the old women's lodge raged in her equal to a hot fast-burning pitch fire.

Out of breath, she stood in the middle of the clearing. Anticipation fluttered her breath and hummed in her heart. He would come. She knew this as strongly as she knew she had to see him one more time. Eyes closed, she clutched the wolf fang around her neck, tipped her head back, and sent forth a song of forgiveness.

Creator, who put my people on this earth, bring them peace and forgive my selfish thoughts.
I am weak and unworthy of their lives.
Give me the wisdom to prevail.
And the strength to love a mountain, and yet, let it go to serve my people.

Himiin walked into the meadow. He would never be able to let this maiden go. She belonged to him. Her song was clear, breathtaking, and painful. It spoke of the torment she faced in leaving all she loved. Her marriage to the Blackleg would not solve the long-standing bitterness between the tribes. It would take more than one young maiden to stem the evil in the schemers.

He walked up behind her, settled his arms about her waist, and held her against his chest. Her song took on a deeper, huskier tone as she sung of warmth, contentment, and the mountain. He would give her all she sang about—if she stayed.

Her body melted against his as the last note echoed into the blue sky. He leaned down and kissed the back of her neck between her braids. Her herbal and womanly scents along with her soft curves brought out animal instincts.

He wanted her.

Forever.

She turned, slid her arms around his middle, and gazed up into his face. Sucking in her breath, she stared at him with wide, worried eyes.

"Your eyes. They glow red." She cupped his cheek in her hand and moved her thumb back and forth across his jaw bone.

"I am sorry to scare you. My emotions change the color." He leaned down, taking possession of her lips. He tried to keep the kiss light. Her breasts pressed against his chest. The sweetness of her mouth did nothing to lessen the anger he suffered at her leaving. He deepened the kiss, allowing all his torment and need to ravage her mouth.

Wren pulled back when he became rough.

"Forgive me." He stepped away, dropping his arms to his sides.

"No, I will forgive nothing. You have done nothing wrong." She moved toward him.

"We—I cannot go on seeing you and know you will not remain on the mountain." Himiin turned away. The anxiety on her face hurt him as deeply as knowing she would soon be in a Blackleg's arms. The futility and fury which overtook him lanced sharper than any he'd encountered over the ages of watching the feuds between the tribes and being unable to do anything to help.

"Please, do not deny me these last few hours of being with you and the mountain. My heart would break should I leave here knowing we were kept apart because of pettiness." Wren wrapped her arms around him, pressing her breasts and face against his back. Her warmth and pleading proved hard to ignore.

He wished to hold her and talk of pleasant things, but his mind would not let go of the notion he would never see her again. That he must let her go.

"Over the ages, I have experienced many things watching this mountain and its creatures. Your leaving is the hardest thing I have yet to face." He turned to her. "You, my sweet Wren, have embraced me with your love for this mountain, your caring ways, and your strength."

He tipped her chin and gazed into eyes bathed in the glistening tears of sorrow. Catching a tear with his finger, he touched it to his chest. "I will hold you in here for as long as the sun rises and the moon glows."

She flung her arms around him, clinging to him like a great wind would pluck her out of the meadow. The treasonous moon grew overhead as he held Wren in his arms and savored his time with her.

A change in the wind brought the scent of another. Himiin scooped her into his arms and hurried toward the trees.

"What are—?"

He placed a hand over her mouth and whispered in her ear. "Someone is coming."

Well hidden behind a wall of bushes, he set her feet on the ground. He rested his head next to her ear and whispered, "I must not be seen with you, it will bring you dishonor. But do not worry. I will not be far." She turned to him, trust shimmered in her eyes.

He kissed her soft lips and regretted the necessity to hide. If not for her betrothal and the dishonor his presence would bring, he would have stood by her side and claimed her as his. He could not bring her shame. Instead, he deepened the kiss, leaving her dreamy-eyed, and stepped behind a tree.

Pushing aside the contentment his kiss wrapped around her, Wren turned in the direction Himiin had watched before they entered the trees.

Tattle-Tale stumbled into the clearing. Had his weyekin come to him? How did he come to stagger about the forest? She rushed forward to keep him away from Himiin's hiding place. When he caught sight of Wren, he hurried her direction.

"I have seen my weyekin," he said, grasping her arm. His eyes glowed with a wariness she had not witnessed in him before. His gaze jerked, and a frown etched his brow as he studied the trees.

"You are not alone." He started to step around her.

"Your eyes are playing tricks on you. I have been singing to the mountain and thinking of my future." She took his arm to lead him away from the trees he seemed anxious to explore. The same trees which hid Himiin.

"You are trying hard to keep me from something." Tattle-Tale's mouth curved in a smirk. He pulled from her grasp and darted into the trees.

Wren fidgeted. Should she call to him or follow? Bushes shook, a low growl rumbled, then a sharp gasp rent the still air. Her brother burst through a clump of dogwood, running straight at her. He snatched her hand at a run and pulled her across the meadow.

She glanced over her shoulder and smiled. A large white wolf stepped out of the trees. She waved and let her brother lead her off the mountain.

Away from the man who held her heart.

Inside the village, people followed them to their lodge. Their parents and grandmother sat around the fire in front of the family dwelling. Seeing the crowd headed their way, the adults hurried forward.

"Wren you have brought Tattle-Tale back." Her father turned to the boy. "Was your gift bestowed upon you?"

"Yes, Father. I have seen my weyekin." Tattle-Tale's gaze flickered across her before leveling on their father.

Proud and Tall placed an arm around his son's shoulders. "That is good. Yes. Very good."

The warmth of her father's smile and his relaxed posture was something she rarely saw. It was good to know her brother's vision could bring pleasure to him.

He turned to her.

"Where have you been daughter that you would bring Tattle-Tale home?" His eyes shone hard and dark in the firelight. Did he know she was with another, not her betrothed? He could not. Unless the happiness Himiin brought to her heart showed on her face.

"My need to visit the mountain became stronger than my desire to stay in the village. I had remained in the village far too long. I wished to walk in the forest, listen to the birds, and sing my farewell."

He turned to Tattle-Tale. "Is this true? Did you find her alone?"

She stared at her father. Had she so shamed him before that even now, as she prepared to live with the Blackleg, he still did not trust her? It hurt deeply to think he had lost all faith in her. Her heart lodged in her throat as her brother straightened his body and looked at her.

"She was not alone." The conviction in his voice made her stomach lurch. He did not see Himiin as a man, she was sure of it.

Why did he sound so convincing?

Morning Fawn gasped. Her father turned his dark eyes on Wren. "You cannot dishonor us or Hawk this way. Who were you with?"

She stared at her brother. His steady gaze remained fixed on her. His playfulness and goofy smile no longer veiled his face with innocence. He stared at her, eyes unflinching, expression set in disapproval. He looked so much like their father she felt the reprimand twice fold.

"I would never dishonor my family or people. Tattle-Tale must have been seeing things. He has not had food or water for several suns." She turned to her mother. "I only sung of my love for the mountain."

Her father grunted and turned to Tattle-Tale. "Was she with a person of this band? I'll put a stop to this immediately."

Her brother shook his head. She folded her arms and watched him. He could not point a finger since he had seen no one.

"She stays on the mountain longer than any Nimiipuu except those who are hunting or gathering, yet, she does not bring back food. How could anyone spend that much time just singing?" Tattle-Tale crossed his arms and stared at her.

"You are discrediting your sister because you cannot sit still and you imagine no one else could." Proud and Tall sent Tattle-Tale a scathing look before motioning him to sit.

"She was not alone." Tattle-Tale did not sit, defying their father. She had never seen her brother do anything, but smile and be annoying. This was a side she had not seen and lessened her worries of him some day taking over the band. However, she feared for him as a spark of anger glowed in their father's eyes.

"You could not give me a name. How am I to believe she was not alone? There are no others on the mountain, our sentries would have told me."

"There was a white wolf." Tattle-Tale sent her a mocking grin. Her skin prickled. Did he know the white wolf was not what he seemed?

"A white wolf?" Her father turned to her, his eyes wide with interest. "Is that not your weyekin?"

Her mother and grandmother stared at her as though she had grown antlers. She studied each adult to see how far she could push the truth and not really lie to them. She did not wish to tell untruths, but if they found out about Himiin, she did not trust them to understand.

"Yes." Her heart fluttered with dread. Wren felt like the smallest of all creatures for telling half-truths. She had believed Himiin to be her weyekin when they first met.

"Is this who you have been running to the mountain to see?" Again, Proud and Tall watched her with distrusting eyes. Her heart grieved to see him question her, but she knew her behavior deserved the scrutiny.

"Yes." That was not a lie. She did go to the mountain to see the white wolf.

"Has he spoken to you?" Her father moved to her side. "Has he said anything of this union between the Blacklegs and Nimiipuu?"

She glanced around at the anxious faces staring across the campfire at her. A nudge from behind, caused her to peer over her shoulder. Silly One stood an arm's reach away. Her cousin nodded her head.

This was her chance to break off the marriage.

To stay with Himiin.

All she had to do was tell her father the white wolf was against her leaving the mountain. Himiin had expressed this. He was the white wolf, but, he was not her weyekin.

What should she say? Could she live with a selfish lie?

"My weyekin has not spoken." She had not spoken to her weyekin. Her heart beat fast. Would the Creator make her life with the Blackleg harder for the half-truths which slid so easily from her tongue this night?

Her father's lips curved into a smile. "If your weyekin has shown himself and said nothing, this must be the gift from your vision." He embraced her. "My daughter you will be fulfilling your fate by marrying Hawk. My heart is freer knowing I have made the right decision."

Tattle-Tale coughed then spoke, "Maybe the white wolf has shown himself because this marriage is not her gift?"

"What are you saying?" Her father narrowed his eyes on Tattle-Tale.

Wren's heart pounded in her chest. Could that be why Himiin was sent to her? To stop the marriage? He was not her weyekin.

"If the wolf has shown himself to her at this time, maybe he is telling her not to marry the Blackleg?" Tattle-Tale stated, looking from her to their father with a steady, unyielding gaze.

"No. He has shown himself to signify this is her gift, and she will follow through." Proud and Tall glared at his son. "There will be no more talk of the white wolf or a sign. Wren will marry the Blackleg."

Wren's heart lodged in her throat. How did one fulfill their fate when they had lied to their elders? Sadness overwhelmed her, blocking out the elation being with Himiin had restored. She rubbed her chest where the fang lay between her breasts. His gift would always be a reminder of her lies and her heartache.

"Are you not well?" her mother asked.

"I am fine. Just tired. I will go lie down now."

"Not here," her grandmother said, slowly rising from her place on a rock. "It is time for you to go to the old women's lodge."

Wren studied the people watching her. Now? She did not want to spend seven moons with the old women learning her duties as a wife, unable to roam the mountain or see Himiin. Panic gripped, rooting her feet as a strong desire to seek refuge on the mountain beset her.

"You must come now." Her grandmother's bird-like hand clenched her arm tightly as though she recognized her granddaughter's urge to bolt.

Wren stared at the ledge. The silhouette of a wolf stood out against the star-filled night. The sorrow and anger which besieged her at the news she would wed a Blackleg seemed trivial as desolation gnawed at her insides. The purification ceremony made the event a reality. Until this moment, the whole marriage and her leaving had been talk. Though she knew deep down it would happen, a small part of her had hoped it all a bad dream.

In her heart, she knew living among the Blacklegs would not be easy. She would mourn the mountain, lake, and people who loved her. And grieve for the spirit who held her heart.

Her feet slid along the ground like heavy boulders as her grandmother pulled her toward the old women's lodge. Silly One watched. Sympathy glistened in her eyes and unraveled Wren's nerve. Ducking her head to hide her tears, she kept walking.

Several of the old women stood at the opening of the lodge chanting. She knew each one. They were sisters and cousins of her grandmother. All had lost their men and families and now lived in the lodge together. Sharing meals of meat brought to them by the men of others and the roots they harvested.

The lodge brimmed over with the knowledge of life. Each woman had her own story which Wren would hear over the course of her seven-moon seclusion. She looked forward to learning from each of the wise women, but her heart clung to the mountain in search of a white wolf.

«»«»«»

Himiin stared at the activity in the village below. He had slept at night and stood looking over the ledge for the past three days. Ever since he witnessed Wren escorted to the old women's lodge. The knowledge she would be in the lodge for seven moons, did not change the fact he refused to miss a chance to walk with her should she sneak out.

Each night, he raised his nose to a sky filled with glittering, white stars and howled his misery to the moon which grew larger, brighter, and rounder. Before long the Blackleg would come to take Wren.

His body shook with rage. She belonged on his mountain. Not mistreated by a schemer. He wished he could walk into the village and tell her father the marriage was a mistake. The Blackleg would never make peace. They loved to kill and plunder. It had been a part of them since the Creator made each tribe.

To send Wren from the mountain would bring her death. Another death he would feel responsible for, yet, she must go to fulfill her weyekin. He did not want her in the arms of another, especially a Blackleg.

"Brother, we have not seen you in several days." Wewukiye stepped out onto the ledge, shaking branches from his great antlers. He glanced at the village. "You watch the village of the lake people. Why?"

The flap of wings was followed by, "He has let man's emotions take over." Sa-qan perched on a log at the far side of the ledge.

"You two did not need to seek me out. I am fine," Himiin growled, never taking his eyes off the village.

"But we did. You have been occupied by the Nimiipuu maiden and have neglected your duties."

He stared at Sa-qan. "What have I neglected?"

Spirit of the Mountain

"There are rumors among the animals a black wolf has been seen on this mountain. One with a tattered ear." Wewukiye stomped a hoof. "Does that not sound like the one you tangled with?"

The hair on his neck bristled. What was the schemer wolf doing back on his mountain? "Where was he last seen?"

"In the gorge on the side the sun sets." Sa-qan hopped to the edge of the ledge and nodded toward the old women's lodge. "She is content with her future. Forget about the woman and take care of your duties."

"She is hard to forget, but I will take care of the schemer on my mountain." He took one last look toward the village. She wasn't there, but his mind conjured up the sight of her in the clearing, chanting her love of the mountain. He could remember her scent and her touch. It would be a long time before he forgot the woman who made him neglect his duties.

"You and she can never be together. One of you would have to leave your world." Wewukiye shook his head, flailing the air with his great antlers. "Her duty is to her people as your duty is to The People. You cannot be together. Do your duty."

Himiin turned, leaving the ledge and the words floating out of his brother's mouth.

Paty Jager

Pú-timt wax ná-qt

(11)

Himiin smelled the stench of evil in the air. The moon sat high in the vibrant dark blue sky as he followed the trail of the schemer wolf. Why did the spirit come back? By all accounts of Sa-qan, the black wolf scouted this mountain for the Blacklegs. But why? The mountain was far from their territory with other Nimiipuu and Crow land to pass through.

Leaping a log, Himiin came down a short distance from his prey. The black wolf's eyes flashed disdain, but he didn't appear surprised by the encounter.

Snarling, moving back and forth, Himiin forced the dark wolf to retreat. "Why have you returned to my mountain?"

The wolf's upper lip lifted in a sneer. "It won't be your mountain long. It will be my pleasure to take it from you."

"Watch the words you choose. This will always be my mountain. The likes of you will not take it from me." Himiin leaped at the wolf, causing him to back into a log.

"I pick my words wisely. You and the people of this mountain will be nothing more than slaves." He showed his teeth as his eyes gleamed viciously. "Or dead."

"What you say will never happen. Not as long as I am of this mountain." Himiin launched his body at the intruder. His wide chest knocked the creature down to the forest floor. Pouncing quickly, he

106

pinned the dark wolf to the ground with his weight and paws.

"You may have the larger stronger body this time, but I will not leave until the mountain is mine." The wolf's eyes spit hatred. "I will do whatever it takes to have what I want." His lip curled, and his eyes sparkled. "The maiden, Wren, will help me get this mountain."

How did this vile wolf know of Wren? The lecherous gleam in his eyes proved more than Himiin could take. He growled deep and fierce before opening his jaws to show this wolf who he dealt with.

Frustration of not seeing Wren for days mixed with the fear this wolf was an omen to her destiny, unleashed Himiin's control. His jaws clamped around the black wolf's neck. He'd never wanted to kill as he did at this moment. The spirit not only threatened the mountain and the people, but he also had nefarious plans for Wren. Himiin would not stand for the maliciousness of this creature to come near her or her family.

Not when he had the power to stop the evil.

The spirit wolf thrashed about, lashing out with his claws. Himiin pinned him to the ground as the salty taste of blood stung his tongue. The taste repulsed him, as well as the thought of killing another. But he would never feel remorse over killing the black wolf in his jaws. The only thing which kept him from ending the wolf's life was to kill the vessel would not eliminate the evil within.

Himiin released his hold. Panting, he threatened, "You will—tell me all and leave this mountain—or die here this night."

The black wolf's eyes, dulled from pain, glared at him with hatred. The yellow eyes glimmered with the knowledge Himiin would not learn the truth from him. They both knew the portal the spirit lived in could be killed, but the spirit would be free to find another vessel and report to the Blacklegs.

Cautiously, Himiin rose. As much as he wanted to rid his mountain of the spirit, he would let the intruder go and call upon his brother and sister to help him track the schemer back to his kind. Perhaps by following, they could find out what the Blackleg plotted and save the Lake Nimiipuu.

The wolf remained still, his gaze darting in every direction, wary of an attack. Finally, he sat up. Blood trickled down his black fur, dropping onto the ground.

"Why did you not kill me?" he asked, standing on wobbly legs.

"I do not kill for the sake of killing. And you were not going to tell me anything. As a spirit you do not fear death."

The wolf walked away. Stopping as he entered thick brush, he looked back. "You will be sorry you let me go."

"I may, but my conscience will be clear." Himiin tilted his head. "Can you say the same?"

Dark Wolf sneered as he walked away from the white wolf. He would be the one controlling things soon. The vessel he chose to roam the mountain was no match for the larger white wolf, but that mattered little. Soon he would take another body, one the white wolf could not defeat. The great spirit of the mountain had shown his weakness tonight.

The Nimiipuu maiden.

He snickered as he crawled under a bush to soothe his wounds. He'd rest a while before heading to the meeting place. He Who Crawls would be pleased to hear the maiden prepared for her betrothed's arrival. The whole village would greet Hawk and his two escorts.

The escorts were hand-picked by He Who Crawls. His best scouts. They would find the most direct and less visible route to the village.

Dark Wolf's attitude improved thinking of besting the white wolf and living on this mountain. By the time the moon grew small and the nights were dark, they would be ready to strike.

Then the Lake Nimiipuu would no longer own the fastest horses, the lake, or the mountain.

He pushed the weakened body to a standing position and headed around the mountain. He could wait no longer if he wanted to stay ahead of the white wolf. The spirit may not kill, but he wasn't above following to search out Dark Wolf's plans.

《》《》《》

Himiin pointed his nose to the growing moon and howled a call to Sa-qan and Wewukiye. He'd barely thought about Wren in the old women's lodge when Sa-qan landed gracefully in front of him, and Weukiye charged into the open. He told them of the encounter with the Blackleg spirit.

"We will take turns following him to see who he speaks with in the Blacklegs." Himiin studied his siblings. "He said this would not be my mountain for long, and the Lake people will be slaves to the Blackleg. He also said Wren would help him." Himiin growled his disfavor and glared at his siblings. "This evil spirit can only know of Wren if he is part of the band who is taking her away."

His frustration mounted each time he thought of the Blackleg spirit using Wren for his schemes. He would have to keep her close by until she was safely in the Blackleg village. Even then she would not be safe from the Blackleg spirit. He should have killed the black wolf vessel and then went after the spirit.

"I do not like the glint in your eyes." Sa-qan walked up to him, her wings held out to her side for balance.

"He should not have brought Wren into this." The anger the black wolf brought out in him deepened his voice and narrowed his eyes. "I should have stopped him."

"You mean kill him," she snapped. "Why are you acting like a mortal? What have you done that has you forgetting the job of a spirit is to help the people and not harm?" She placed her beak inches from his nose. "You can ill afford another death on your hands."

He cringed. Surely the Creator would understand the death of the vessel carrying an evil spirit.

Wewukiye cleared his throat and shuffled his hooves. Himiin stared at his sister. Her neck feathers ruffled as her eyes bore into him like daggers. Very rarely did she show anger and usually at something other than himself or Wewukiye.

"He should not have threatened the mountain, the people, or Wren." Himiin stared at his sister. "I do not take such threats lightly."

"But to wish him dead—I do not understand you anymore. Why are you acting so—mortal?"

Wewukiye cleared his throat. "I will follow Dark Wolf, now." He looked at Himiin. "You should rest to be able to continue for me in the morning."

Himiin nodded his head, even though he wanted to go after the wolf himself. If he caught the spirit, there was no telling what he would do. One thing he did know, he didn't want his sister to be around when it happened.

Wewukiye headed off through the trees at a run. The click of his antlers against branches slowly faded as he headed around the mountain.

Himiin stepped away from his sister. He would tend his wounds and be ready to take over from Wewukiye when the sun warmed the mountain.

Sa-qan hopped in front of him. Her beady eyes stared into his.

"Wren will leave the old women's lodge in four moons." Her eyes narrowed to study him. "It is best for both of you if you do not see her when she comes out."

He knew his sister spoke with wisdom, but the ache in his heart overruled any wisdom bestowed upon him. Knowing Wren was safe for the next four moons, he was free to follow the schemer without fear of her safety.

But, he would see her one more time before she left the mountain. She had to know the Blackleg spirit and possibly the people of her future husband schemed to take over the Nimiipuu. She could not walk into the arms of her death unknowing. He had to warn her. No matter what his brother, sister, or the Creator wished.

《》《》《》

The seventh rising of the sun marked the last day of Wren's confinement in the old women's lodge. The ordeal would have been easier to bear if she had not spent every moment wishing to be on the mountain in Himiin's arms.

Many times the old women watched her and shook their heads, knowing she did not truly listen to what they told her. But how could Wren hear tales of child rearing and making a husband happy when her heart ached for a man she could not have?

Having listened half-heartedly to the stories, she wondered how she could become a good wife when her heart would be yearning for another. That subject had not been spoken of and she dared not ask for fear of being questioned.

On this last day of confinement, she would visit the sweat lodge and listen to the wisdom of the old man who sent the steam forth. She welcomed the trip.

Two old women escorted her to the mud-covered mound near the lake. Approaching the structure, she was stunned to see her grandmother and mother waiting beside the buffalo hide opening.

"Mother, Grandmother, this is a good surprise." She hugged them both before the three stepped to the side and undressed. Her mother stared at Wren's bare chest.

"Daughter, what is that about your neck?" Her mother pointed to the fang nestled between Wren's breasts.

Spirit of the Mountain

Her heart thudded. She had forgotten about the token it was so much a part of her. Every night, before she fell asleep, she held the fang and talked to Himiin as though he lay beside her. She could not bear to have it taken from her.

"It is something I found while walking the mountain." Her fingers started to caress the trinket out of habit. She dropped her hand to her side as her mother and grandmother studied her quietly. "I wish to wear it to keep the mountain and my people in my heart."

Her grandmother grunted and turned to step down into the buffalo hide covered structure. Her mother stared at her a moment and motioned for Wren to follow her grandmother.

She stepped into the structure relieved her mother did not pry. If her mother had insisted on her taking the fang off, she was unsure how she would have dealt with the command. The gift from Himiin would never leave her person.

The darkness in the sweat lodge hindered her sight. She stood, waiting for her eyes to adjust. Her mother pushed her to sit next to her grandmother and took a seat on a rock the other side of her daughter.

Why did they block her in? Did they feel she would run?

The old man of the sweat lodge chanted, thanking the Creator for the knowledge of the sweat lodge and the harmony it brought to those who entered.

Slowly, with great ceremony, the old man poured water onto the hot stones in the center of the structure.

The warm steam wrapped around Wren, a reminder of the heat that crept across her skin at Himiin's touch. She licked the sweat drizzling down her upper lip and thought of Himiin's soft lips when they kissed. The memories built a fire in her body, one to rival the steam and red glowing rocks in the center of the structure.

The chanting stopped. The graveled voice of the old man began a tale of duty and honor. He spoke of the importance to hold these in one's heart to make a person worthy.

Wren closed her eyes and thought of her visit by the weyekin. Her marriage to the Blackleg held duty and honor, making her worthy. But would she truly be worthy if her heart yearned for another? She fidgeted on the hard rock. Her mother's hand rested on her leg.

Trying to not appear churlish, she picked up her mother's hand, squeezed it reassuringly, and removed it from her leg. She did not need someone to hold her in the sweat lodge. Did they believe she would not listen to the old man? To not take in his wisdom would go against tradition and faith.

Shaking off the foreboding, she breathed the hot moist air and rose to pour water on the glowing rocks in the middle of the lodge. She chanted her belief in duty and honor as the water dripped slowly onto the sizzling stones.

Creator, hear my song of duty to my people and honor to myself and those who believe in me.
I will go to my betrothed fulfilling my gift and honor.
Living with the Blackleg, teaching them tolerance for the Nimiipuu and others, will be my duty to both the people of my heart and the people of my village.

The blistering steam washed impurities from her body and cleared her mind as her song came to an end. The old man's voice rolled into a melodic cadence and told a story of the longevity of the Lake Nimiipuu. Wren swayed before the rocks, listening, allowing her heart to fill with his words.

The old man told of the Creator giving their people this lake and mountain to grow great herds of horses and strong wise people.

The tone of the old man's voice changed. "All women are wise. It is this wisdom which keeps the men from killing others for sport."

Her eyes opened, and she stared into the steam. His words were directed at her and her plight.

"As mother earth feeds us and nurtures, our women must nurture and feed their men. A warrior needs many things to be strong. His woman can build his strength in food and companionship." The rocks in the center of the structure lost their glow; the steam gradually disappeared.

"Come." Morning Fawn took her by the arm, led her from the sweat lodge, across the grass, and over the dirt, toward the lake. They plunged into the icy water, shocking their hot sweaty bodies with the snow-melt water. She scrubbed away sweat and impurities just as the old man's stories washed away her selfish thoughts.

Once dressed, her grandmother led her back to the old women's lodge. She still had the rest of the day to learn more about being a wife.

The day lagged on as she pondered the old man's tales and rejected all the reasons why she should not see Himiin before Hawk took her away. Deep in her heart, she knew Hawk would never love her as strongly as Himiin. For that reason alone, she could not leave without saying good-bye.

When the old women opened the flap of the lodge to allow her to pass back into the village society, she refused to look at the faces of her family. They knew little of her fears and nothing of her heartbreak. She wished to be with the one who knew her heart. Her family did not realize how great the sacrifice she would make to follow her weyekin and live among the Blacklegs.

"Wren! Wren!" The calls of her family went unheeded. She zigzagged through the trees at a run, preventing anyone to follow. No one would keep her from spending her last night on the mountain with Himiin.

Moonlight faintly illuminated the tops of the tall pine and lodge pole when she started into the forest. She climbed the mountainside as the moon loomed overhead—bright, round, and mocking.

She rushed into the meadow, gasping for breath, and scanned the area for Himiin. Foolishly, she thought he would be waiting for her. Her heart told her, he would come.

She crossed her legs, sat in the grass, breathed in the sweet scent of the wildflowers, and waited for a man, not a spirit. They had to be together one last time before she rode away from the place of her heart to live among the enemy.

She clutched the wolf tooth Himiin gave her and sang the song which filled her heart. One of sorrow.

Her fears and concerns drifted into the air on a song to the Creator. Setting her thoughts free cleansed her mind of the ordeal she would soon face.

Tired from the sleepless nights listening to the old women wheeze and cough, she lay down in the meadow, cradled the wolf tooth in her hands, and fell asleep.

《》《》《》

Himiin could no longer track the black wolf. He was cunning. He'd known the Nimiipuu spirits tracked him. The creature had left the mountain. To set foot off the mountain, Himiin would no longer exist.

To no longer be the spirit of the mountain, he would lose the one thing he cherished most—caring for the mountain and people he loved.

Heading back over the peak, he heard the heartfelt song of a young maiden's broken heart. The sweet voice and song belonged to Wren. She was free of the old women's lodge and waited for him in the meadow. Hastening to the clearing, his heart beat not from the run, but the desire to see and touch her once more.

Nearing the meadow, all became silent. Worried she had been found by the dark spirit, he raced into the clearing.

The sight ripped the air from his chest and accelerated his heart.

Wildflowers, highlighted by the growing moon, swayed in the evening breeze and filled the air with their fragrance. That same breeze, tugged at loose strands of Wren's soot black hair, fluttering them about her serene face. Her dark lashes rested on smooth cheek bones, her soft lips curved at the corners in an innocent smile.

He stood in the middle of the clearing wanting her with every pulse of his blood and breath of air. Raising his muzzle to the moon, he closed his eyes. Smoke swirled around the wolf form, rose into the night sky, and returned to the earth, setting his spirit down in the form of a man.

He knelt beside Wren. Pushing the loose strands from her face, he grinned as she swat at the tickling hairs. His gaze drifted down to the spot between her breasts where she clasped his tooth in her hand. She had called to him with her heart.

He sat down, cross-legged, watching her sleep. His arms ached to hold her. He wished for the intimacy of a man and woman, but knew it was foolish. Tomorrow she would ride off the mountain with another. His head pounded with the turmoil between his good sense and his heart.

She murmured his name, and her smile grew.

He filled her dreams.

He wanted more.

The need to touch her and be a part of her last night on the mountain tore at his heart. He wished to capture memories to hold with him for the rest of the ages.

Reaching out, he touched her soft cheek with the back of his hand. Her head moved toward the touch.

"Wren, I am here," he whispered, leaning close to her ear. The sweetness of the flowers, her freshly washed hair, and her own unique scent shot a bolt of desire straight through him, lighting a fire.

He leaned closer, dropping a kiss on her cheek. Her eyes fluttered open. She smiled again.

"I knew you would come." Her low and throaty voice sent his body coursing with heat.

"You did?" He sat up, battling with what he wanted to do and what he should do. To touch her as he wished would go against all he'd been placed upon this mountain to do. Yet, he knew to not touch her and have these last moments of pleasure with her, he would cease to function.

"Yes." She rolled to her back, lifting her arms over her head and stretching. Her breasts pushed at the cloth pulled tight against them. The bottom of her skirt rested high on her thighs, the rest bunched about her waist. Long dark legs and her smile of welcome dissolved all of his control.

Pú-timt wax lepít

(12)

The drowsiness Wren felt moments before vanished as she peered into Himiin's blue eyes darkened with desire. Heat scorched her body, tremors awakened her lower regions, and excitement fluttered her heart.

He found her.

She knelt in front of him, touched his face, and traced the angular bones of his cheek and jaw. She wished to remember his face in her heart and her mind. It was a strong face, full of character and strength.

He covered her hand with his. "We should not," he said through clenched teeth as his eyes flashed otherwise.

"We will not see one another after tomorrow. I may never have contentment again." Tears stung her eyes. "I wish one night of happiness to cling to through my life with the Blackleg."

His hesitation sent spirals of dread piercing her heart. She did not wish to live her whole life wondering what she missed by not experiencing his touch.

"Please, tonight show me what it is to be loved." She grasped his hands, placing them above her beating heart.

"We must leave here. Your brother knows of this place." Himiin kissed her palm. His tenderness swept her breath away.

Nodding, she stood. Himiin led her through the forest, taking a path she'd never crossed in her wanderings. They climbed the mountain to an area shielded by many aspen trees, but open to the full moon shining down into a grassy area.

When they stopped, she heard the faint sound of water splashing. She looked around to find the source of the soothing sound, but found nothing.

"No one will disturb us here," Himiin said, drawing her into his arms. His embrace held the contentment of a sunny day; welcoming, warm, and cherished.

His body trembled as she slid her hand down his firm smooth chest. When she touched him this way in her dreams, she warmed with pleasure. Now, as she felt his hard body under her palms it brought waves of heat racing through her and a sense of power— a power that made her bold.

She ran both hands down his torso, savoring his solid muscles and contours. His breath hissed when her hands neared the top of his leggings. Reaching around to explore his back, she pressed her body against his and breathed in his scent. Forest, sky, and male.

He held her head in his hands, lifting her face to his. "You make me feel on fire," he whispered, before capturing her lips with his mouth.

Fire. Yes. Her body flamed with needs she'd never known. The old women said to lie still and let your man use you when he must. But she could not be still. Her body craved the nearness of his. Skimming her hands across his smooth skin and muscle, she wanted to feel every inch of him and taste all he would let her taste.

When his lips left hers, she ducked her head, dropping kisses along his chest, delighting in his salty maleness. He pressed his cheek against her head and groaned.

"Does this hurt?" she asked, pulling back, wondering how a kiss could cause him pain.

"Only in my heart, knowing this will be the only time we can touch this way." He folded her into his arms, clinging to her as though the Creator would strike them both with his great lightning stick.

"Let us not think of what is to come, but live in what is now." She wrapped her arms around him, breathing in his unique scent and savoring the strength of his body.

"I want you as a man wants a woman. Do you wish the same?" His dark blue eyes glistened with desire as he gazed upon her. His

Paty Jager

hand shook when he pushed a stray strand of her hair from her face.

Her breath caught. His need for her was strong. Her body yearned to be touched by him. If she did not spend this night in his arms, she would forever feel unfulfilled.

"It is what I wish." She smiled, knowing it meant he would make her a woman this night. Her heart fluttered in her chest. She would be his woman for life whether they were together or apart.

"Stand." Under the light of the moon, he grasped the bottom of her dress, drawing it up over her head. She stood before him with the coolness of the night and the moonlight flickering across her skin.

His fevered gaze moved from her face down the length of her body, causing a wave of heat to rage through her. When his gaze captured hers once more, a wide grin spread across his handsome face. "You are beautiful inside and out."

Stepping closer, yet staying at an arm's distance, he pulled the leather ties from her braids. His hands deftly loosened the braided strands, sending the fur adornments drifting to the ground at her feet. When her hair hung loose around her, he picked up her dress, spreading it out on the ground.

Without a word from him, she sat on the dress and watched with fascination as he untied the rawhide where his leggings rested on his hips. The leather garment dropped to the ground at his feet, revealing a magnificent body. The muscles in his legs were defined by the light and shadows of the strong moon.

His maleness pointed at her. She'd seen men naked many times in her life, but wondered at the appendage which normally lay slack. Himiin's was long, hard, and begging her to touch.

His groan of appreciation rent the air, when she took it in her hands. The soft skin reminded her of a horse's silky nose. Feeling the firmness, she shuddered with anticipation. This part of his body was unlike the muscles in his arms and legs. She delighted in the difference.

Himiin pulled her to stand before him. "You must not touch me that way if I am to bring you pleasure."

Her body tingled with the thought of him touching her in places only she had touched before. "And how do you do that?" she asked, kissing his chest.

He tipped her head to look at him. The brightness of his eyes stole

118

her breath as he leaned down, kissing her with need and passion. Her brisk heart beat kept time with the flutter of anticipation in her stomach. They would give themselves to one another this night.

And not regret it.

Her body molded to Himiin as his hands roamed across her backside and up her sides to her breasts, eliciting sparks and fire in their path.

Gently, he eased her onto her dress spread upon the sweet supple spring grass. He lay next to her, his mouth trailing kisses down her neck to her breasts. Her nipples tightened and puckered. His tongue flicked the erect nubs. Intense sensations pierced through her. The twittering of birds faded as her heart boomed in her head and her body.

His hand slid over her stomach and down to the juncture of her legs. His fingers ran through the hair and down. She jerked when he touched her. A flash of light scorched her body as she pushed her hips toward his hand. The sensations he evoked in her body were wild, wanton, and delightful. She wished to return the favor but could not lift her hands from where they gripped the dress under her.

Himiin planned to pleasure Wren. To make this night special. He wished for her to have their last time together in her thoughts always. He didn't care the consequences. This night was for her.

Her body responded to his touch like a butterfly to a fragrant flower. She drew away as her body trembled, only to return to his touch for more. His hand teased her lower regions in cadence with his lips teasing her mouth. When her moaning had his maleness throbbing, he spread her legs and lowered his body over hers.

Her smooth skin and taut muscles against his skin nearly brought him to completion. He lowered his forehead to hers and breathed in her scent, trying to stall his release. Her dark eyes shone glassy and bright. Her body quivered for more as her hungry mouth sought his. He kissed her long and lingering, stilling her fevered breathing.

When he'd gathered his control once more, she watched him with confusion filled eyes.

"I want you to remember me. Let me give you this night." He traced her lips with his tongue, coaxing her to allow him to taste. As the kiss deepened, he explored her body with his hands; kneading her breasts, rubbing his chest against her peaked nipples. When her hips moved under him and her center rubbed against his pulsing manhood, he groaned. He wanted her, hard and fast, but his edict to never hurt the Nimiipuu held him back.

Would this coupling bring her harm from the Blackleg Hawk? The thought chilled his ardor. His mind ticked off all the reasons he should stop. The least of which, the disfavor he was sure to feel from the Creator.

Wren pulled his lips to hers. Her passionate kisses and slick body writhing under him sent all his reservations away in a flash of need. The hurried rhythm of her movements rubbing against him flamed his desire.

Her body craved his.

He ignored everything, reveling in the feel of her. With thoughts of nothing other than pleasing her, he gently entered. Her breath caught, and her eyes widened. He held his upper body above her to watch her face when he brought her the joy she so deserved.

Entering more, Wren's face twisted in confusion, and he backed out, remembering she was a maiden. He would go as slow as it took to make this night one she would savor for seasons to come.

Kissing her and massaging her breasts, he ignited her passion once more. Again with patience he entered and was rewarded when her eyes sparkled like the distant stars, and her body convulsed around him.

Lowering his body, he wrapped her in his arms, breathing in her scent of wildflowers and female, feeling her heart beat with his. Moving with the rhythm of Wren's hips, she shuddered and whispered his name, causing him to lose control.

And lose his heart to something other than the mountain.

Wren smiled. She would carry a part of her mountain with her for all her life. Sated, she welcomed the sensations in her body and the glow in her heart. Himiin gave her something the Blackleg could never. A night of tenderness and love.

"You will always have my heart," she whispered, brushing his soft flaxen hair from her face.

He pushed himself up and looked into her eyes. "I will hold it with gentleness." The love staring back at her from his deep blue eyes told her should she ever need him, he would be there.

Rage balled in her throat. Why did she have to marry the Blackleg? In her heart she knew it would not bring peace to the Lake Nimiipuu.

"Come, you must clean up and go back before your family searches for you." Himiin helped her to her feet, snatching her dress from the ground. Still wobbly from their lovemaking, she staggered against him. He placed an arm under her knees and cradled her in his arms as though she weighed no more than a leaf.

She wrapped her arms around his neck and rested her head against his chest, breathing in the scent of their mating. It was a bouquet she would forever remember.

Himiin stepped through a tangle of willow brush and stood before a small waterfall spilling into a crystal clear pool. She stared at the water reflecting the light of the moon and defining the colorful rocks on the bottom of the pool. It was a beautiful spot. How could it be she had never found it on her wanderings over the mountain?

Without a word, he carried her into the lagoon. In the middle, the water came to his waist and touched her bare backside.

"Oh!" She grasped him tighter around the neck. "This is colder than the lake we bathe in."

"It is closer to the snow." He let her feet drop into the icy water.

"Brr. Why must we do this? I was warm and content." Her teeth chattered. Shivers ran the length of her body when he took a step back, taking away his body heat.

"Do you want your family to know what you have been about tonight when they are handing you over to another tomorrow?" The anger in his words told her of his distaste for what was expected of her. Did he now regret the intimate moments they shared?

"Are you sorry?" She was certain he had enjoyed their tryst.

"No." His eyes softened, and he cupped her breast. "I would pleasure you again and again until the moon left the sky." His eyes hardened. "But you must go to the Blackleg in the morning, and he would not like the gift of a woman who is exhausted from another."

"Will-he know?" She searched his face. He flinched and the anger in his eyes turned to guilt. She was to go to this Hawk as a maiden. After tonight; she no longer was one.

"He will know, but his pride will not allow him to voice it to others." He took her head in his hands. "My greatest fear is he will harm you when he learns the truth."

His concern took her breath away. It also caused panic to lodge in her throat, giving her one more reason to dread her future in the

Blackleg society. Her alarm must have shown in her eyes, for he bent and placed a chaste kiss on her lips. The tenderness he bestowed brought tears to her eyes.

"I would never do anything to cause you pain. But my actions tonight may very well." He placed his forehead on hers. Anguish marred his handsome face. Her belly ached. "Please forgive me my weakness. I only wished to bring you happiness."

"I know you would never knowingly harm me."

He placed a finger to her lips. "I will protect you all I can, but once you are off the mountain, I can do nothing but ask the Creator to watch over you." His hands slid to her neck, then down her shoulders and over her hips. A growl echoed across the lagoon as he dropped them from her and scooped water.

Himiin kept his head averted, but she saw the anger raging in his eyes. She knew it was not directed at her, but the situation that pulled them apart.

He poured water on her body and washed her. His attentiveness and the friction of his hands on her cold skin started a fire building in her once more. She wanted to wrap her arms and legs around him and never let go. To keep from clinging to him, she ran her fingers along his maleness to clean him as well.

Groaning, he captured her hands in his. "No more. We cannot do this again. You must go back to the village."

"I want to stay with you." She knew at that moment she would do whatever it took to stay with him—even fall out of favor with her father and the whole village.

"You cannot. Your destiny is to save your people. To be with me could cause them trouble should the Blackleg warrior become enraged to know you do not want him."

"How can you love me and send me into the arms of another?" Moments before they shared their bodies and their hearts, why did he not try harder to keep her with him?

"You are mortal. I am of the spirit world." He stepped back. "It cannot be."

"But, I can feel you. You are a man. Stay that way."

"I cannot. I can only stay in man form for short periods of time." He took her hands. "I would do anything for you, but I cannot abandon my purpose. The Creator gave me the mountain and expects me to carry on as protector. Just as your father and people expect you to do what is best for The People."

Her chest ached knowing what he spoke was true. Neither one could forsake their duties, even to be with each other. Wren stepped toward him. "Will I see you again?"

"I will follow you to the bottom of the mountain. But I cannot set foot on the flat land. If I do, my spirit will die, and I will be left with nothing but an empty vessel."

Taking his face in her hands, she gave him one last lingering kiss.

"You will never be a shell of a man to me," she whispered and stepped from the pool. He stood in the water, watching as she donned her dress. When her head popped out the top, he was gone.

Her heart splintered at the knowledge she would never again feel his hands upon her, nor know the taste of his lips. With dread and apprehension, she trudged down the mountain to the village. She knew not what her parents would say of her hasty departure from the old women's lodge.

At the moment it did not matter.

All she cared was placing this night in her heart along with all the other beautiful memories she had of the mountain. These would be all she had to get her through the rest of her life with a Blackleg.

Wren entered the village quietly, hoping everyone slept and would not see her return. She did not want to speak untruths to her family, but knew to tell them she lay with a man not her betrothed would hurt the peace her union with the Blackleg was to bring.

She dropped to her knees, crawling under the blanket flap. In slow, quiet movements, she made her way to her sleeping mat.

Proud and Tall stirred.

Her heart flew into her throat, beating wildly. She was not ashamed of her behavior this night, but to talk of it with anyone would ruin the goodness it brought to her and endanger peace with the Blackleg. She could not bring trouble to the band again.

When her father stilled and his breathing returned to an easy rhythm, she continued. As she placed her hand on her sleeping mat, Tattle-Tale turned to her.

"Where have you been, sister?" he whispered.

She jerked at the accusation in his voice. How did he always know when to goad her?

"Saying good-bye to the mountain." She lay down on her mat and hoped her brother would do the same.

He rose up on his elbow. "I am sure when you left here your hair was in braids. How is it that it hangs wet and unbraided?"

Instinctively, her hand shot to the wet strands of hair falling over her shoulder. Tattle-Tale's eyes lit with spite. How did she explain this?

"I was warm from climbing the mountain and bathed before coming to sleep"

"And the glow in your cheeks and spark in your eyes is from the bath?"

How could one so young accuse her of such things? True, she felt different after her mating with Himiin. She touched her cheek. Would her mother and father notice the difference in the morning? Her heart beat rapidly. Would they tell Hawk of this and ask her questions before the whole village?

"Go to sleep little brother," she whispered, trying to keep her voice even.

For the first time the consequences of what she did this night fell upon her with full force. She had once again thought of herself and not the band. Making a decision that could ultimately harm everyone she loved.

She turned from her brother's inquisitive eyes and stared at the wall of the lodge, waiting for the morning sun and the call of the Sun Herald.

With the breaking day she would be given to the Blackleg Hawk. She shivered.

Would her brother voice his concerns in the morning? And would her father and Hawk believe him or her? If they did not believe her brother and Hawk took her to be his wife, it would not be long before he knew her brother had spoken the truth.

She shuddered at the thought of Hawk punishing her for coming to him as a woman instead of a maiden. If he did, it was a beating she would gladly take, as she would have wanted no one but Himiin to have made her his.

However, if he decided to take her deception out on the band...

Pú-timt wax mita-t

(13)

Himiin spent the night pacing back and forth on the ledge above the village. Three riders entered the village shortly after daybreak. Their painted faces, feathers, and dark moccasins revealed they were the Blackleg who came to take Wren.

Anger and frustration seethed within him. No one should take Wren from the mountain.

From him.

To try and stop it was foolish. Wren must follow her weyekin, and do what her father believed best for the Lake Nimiipuu.

He growled. In his gut, he knew Wren's leaving would kill her. Either at the hands of the Blackleg or being away from the mountain she loved.

He sneered at the sick joke of her weyekin appearing to her as a white wolf. If he had not shown himself to her as a man, she would have believed him to be her weyekin, and he could have persuaded her to go against her father. But honor kept him from playing such a trick.

Her greatness would come from her sacrifice. The peace offering of the Blackleg would save many Nimiipuu. If they kept the treaty the schemers would no longer raid the village, killing indiscriminately. Or so the Lake Nimiipuu hoped.

Losing Wren, who had come to matter as much to him as the mountain, ripped at his guts. Her sacrifice diminished his role for the mountain. Those who said her gift the greatest ever bestowed on a maiden spoke the truth. He knew of no other warrior or maiden to have a vision of such greatness. Her courage and wisdom to fulfill her gift inspired many.

He looked down at the village once more. A string of ten horses stood at the edge of the encampment. Each horse carried at least three buffalo hides. Proud and Tall walked among the horses, inspecting each one and the bounty on their backs.

Himiin let out a sorrowful howl. He would give the entire mountain to have the woman standing between her father and the tall Blackleg warrior.

Wren glanced at the ledge. The sadness in Himiin's call pierced her heart. Torn between her love of the mountain spirit and her duty, she stared at the mountain longer than prudent with the village and her suitor watching. She must conceal her aching heart. To have anyone think she would not fulfill her gift would bring shame to herself and her family.

She turned her gaze to Hawk, the Blackleg warrior, before her. He stood a hand's width shorter than Himiin. His narrow shoulders proved no matched for the man she loved, and his black hair held the color of a moonless night.

Hawk raked her up and down with a dark unflinching gaze. Her hands shook, and the world around her turned fuzzy. Panic lodged in her throat. This man with his cold detached glower would rule her life for as long as she walked this earth.

He stepped forward. "I am Hawk."

Wren swallowed the lump in her throat. She did not like his intense stare or the coldness in his eyes.

The warriors who rode in with him sneered and elbowed one another. Hawk raised his hand, and they fell silent. The quick response from his actions told her he held their respect. This small act on his part stiffened her back and brought forth the strength she needed. From this day forward, everything she did was for her people.

"I am Wren." Her small ceremonial hat made of woven grasses threatened to topple to the ground at her courteous bow.

Tattle-Tale stepped between Wren and Hawk. "She is not worthy of such a great warrior."

Fear knotted in Wren's belly. Why was her brother doing this to

126

her?

Hawk glared at her brother while the corner of his lips twitched in a patronizing smile. "How would one so small know she is not worthy of me?"

"She hurried from the old women's lodge last night, not even acknowledging her family, and ran into the forest. When the moon was high and heading back to sleep, she crept into our lodge with her hair hanging wet and a glow to her cheeks." Tattle-Tale turned to her, his eyes alight with determination.

Wren felt her father stiffen behind her and heard the intake of air from her mother. Her brother had kept her secret until now. Why tell Hawk? And here in front of the whole village? It could endanger the peace her father grew desperate to secure. Had her selfishness once again brought trouble to her people? She stood frozen in front of Hawk, waiting for him to fly into a rage.

His eyes darkened. The cold untrusting gaze that scanned her face sent chills down Wren's back. "Your father assured me there was no one you coveted. What was so important on the mountain that you would hurry so and come back with wet hair?"

"My father was wrong."

Her mother moaned, and her father stepped forward. "What?" he asked through clenched teeth.

Tattle-Tale smiled, nodding his head knowingly to all those gathered in front of their lodge. He would soon wipe that smirk off his face. She would not say anything to prove his words.

"I covet the mountain of my people. After being in the old women's lodge for seven moons, I knew I must walk upon the mountain of my heart one more time and swim in the icy waters." She would not allow her time with Himiin to become an ugly event in her mind. The wonder and love experienced in the night were etched forever into the walls of her heart. He was the mountain—the spirit of the mountain.

A spark of arousal flashed in Hawk's eyes. "The next time you wish to swim in icy waters, I would like to be with you."

The heat in his gaze flushed her face and squeezed her heart. She did not wish to swim with anyone but Himiin. However, after this day, she was expected to do whatever this man, staring at her with lust in his eyes, asked her to do.

"Do not make light of this. My sister is unworthy of you and should remain here." Tattle-Tale grabbed Wren about the waist, pulling her toward the family lodge.

"Let go of my woman." Hawk took a menacing step toward Tattle-Tale. Eyes of Snake stepped between Wren and her brother and Hawk. His hand rested on the knife in the waistband of his leggings. The two warriors glared at one another. The tension in the village halted all movement and sound. The stench of hatred swirled between the two warriors as they gauged the other's strength.

"This is ridiculous! Let go of me!" Wren pried her brother's hands from her middle. She pushed him away and stepped between Eyes of Snake and Hawk.

"Stop this. I am going with Hawk to secure peace between our tribes, not cause a war." She turned to Eyes of Snake. "I know you do not believe the Blackleg will stay true to their word. But I am willing to stake my life on it. Is that not enough for you?"

She pivoted to face Hawk. "You say you want peace. Show us. Turn your back on this as if it did not happen."

Hawk swung his guarded gaze from the challenging warrior. He studied her. Wren's heart pounded in her chest, waiting for him to make a decision.

His gaze shifted from her, to Eyes of Snake, then back. "As you wish."

She breathed a sigh of relief and turned to face her brother. She did not want to leave the mountain but found her brother's behavior bizarre.

"Why are you acting this way? My weyekin is to go with Hawk and bring peace to our people. Do not disfavor yourself this way." She looked at Eyes of Snake and then the others gathered. "Or our people."

"But I fear for you to go with him." Tattle-Tale took a step toward Hawk.

"There is nothing to fear. I will make your sister my wife and we," he waved his arm to include the village, "will make strong children of the Nimiipuu and Blackleg."

Proud and Tall cleared his throat, bringing their attention to him. He placed a hand on Tattle-Tale, restricting the boy from voicing or doing anything else to upset the tone of the proceedings.

"Daughter, may the Great Spirit grant you peace, love, and good health." Proud and Tall smiled and kept a watchful eye on Hawk.

She held her face as smooth and solid as stone to hide the despair. The Great Spirit had granted her love and now yanked her from the arms of the man who filled her heart. The only peace she could hope for would be between the tribes—for there would never be peace in her as long as she lived away from the mountain.

"Little Bear, load Wren's things on her horse." Proud and Tall nodded to the Nimiipuu warrior in charge of her horse.

Tattle-Tale jerked from his father's grasp, snatching the rope from Little Bear. "She is not worthy of you," Tattle-Tale shouted at Hawk.

Little Bear grasped him around the waist and regained control of the horse.

Bewildered, she stared at her brother. Why did he act so strange and hurtful? It was as if he did not want her to bring peace to the tribes. What had happened to her carefree brother who liked to follow people around and be annoying? This went beyond annoying to the absurd.

"Enough, Tattle-Tale. Your sister will marry Hawk. They will bring our tribes together in friendship." Proud and Tall turned to Hawk, he grasped the warrior's wrist, and they shook once.

Hawk nodded to her father and grabbed her about the waist, lifting her onto his horse. The unexpected movement left her straddling the animal. Her antelope hide dress, made special for the occasion, hitched high on her legs. Her cheeks heated when Hawk touched her bare upper leg and jumped onto the horse.

He circled an arm around her middle and took off at a lope out of the village. His cry of triumph rang in her ears as the horse sprinted up the mountain, and her carefully woven ceremonial hat tumbled to the earth.

She grasped the arm around her to keep from falling. If they kept up this pace, they would be off the mountain before she could steal a glimpse of Himiin. Desolation crept into her heart with each lunge of the horse.

Hawk turned the animal to head around the side of the mountain and slowed the animal's pace.

"We will be alone until we reach my village. So we can come to know one another." His deep low voice held no warmth. His chest rumbled against her back and intensified the cold within her.

Since he started the conversation, she had many questions for him. "Why do you want peace with my people?" she asked.

His arm tightened around her. "For the same reason you do. I have heard there are people the color of the antelope coming this way. They kill anything that does not look as they. We need to be strong to stand up against these intruders."

"Why did you pick my father's band to start the peace keeping?"

"Do you always ask so many questions?" His irritation made the words come out in a growl.

"My father has said I seek knowledge like a bear seeks honey."

His body shook as though he laughed. Perhaps this Blackleg was not as mean as the ones who looted their village and killed her grandmother.

"He also says I have the tenacity of a badger when I wish to know something."

"You will find not many Blackleg warriors like answering the questions of a woman." He stopped the horse, grasped her chin, and tugged her head to the side. Leaning around her, he said, "You will keep your questions to yourself. If you cannot hold it in, you will ask only me. In the solitude of our lodge." His eyes shone dark and deadly. "Do you understand?"

She forced a slight nod. The fear in her belly spiraled into her heart. She thought at first he may be different than the others, however, the coldness in his eyes as he laid out the rules told her he was no different. She shuddered.

"Are you cold?" He rubbed her arm in quick, rough strokes.

"No." She shook her head and stared at the trees. To hold the tears burning at the back of her eyes from spilling, she bit her lip. How was she to let this man touch her so and not think of the gentleness of Himiin?

They continued over the mountain. The horse trudged through rocks, mud, and melting snow. One would think moving closer to the sun would be warmer, but the snow-covered peaks and the crunchy patches of snow brought bumps to her skin. They would spend one cold night before descending the other side of the mountain and into the warm weather again. She wished her belongings had not been loaded on another horse. A warm wrap would be welcome.

The sun faded behind the mountain when Hawk stopped his horse near a small stream. It was one of many they had walked the horse through and down. His actions reminded her of someone hiding his trail. He dismounted and grabbed her around the waist, hauling her to the ground unceremoniously. Hawk's hands remained on the curve of her waist as he studied her. Losing the warmth of his body against her back and the heat of the horse beneath her, she shivered when the brisk mountain air swirled around her arms and legs.

"You are pleasing. I was afraid you would be squat and hard to look at when they said you had seen sixteen summers and not taken a husband."

Wren stared at him. Was this his way of making her feel comfortable? She wanted to pull away from him, but knew she could not. He paid many horses and buffalo hides to own her. The only reason she held her tongue and rooted her feet was the knowledge being his wife would secure the safety of her family.

"I am pleased you are pleased." She stepped away, taking his hands from her waist, and scanned the area for a place to make a fire. "What are you providing for our meal?" she asked, circling rocks for a fire pit.

He stared at her as though she were daft.

"This is where we are sleeping?" she asked, walking toward the trees to find dry sticks and pine needles to start the fire.

"We will not make a fire."

"It is cold and I am hungry." She put her hands on her hips and stared at him. He may have bought her, but that did not mean she had to go frozen and hungry because he was too lazy to hunt.

"I do not wish anyone to know where we are." He drew the strap of a bag dangling down his back over his head. "We will eat what I have in here."

"That is fine, but how will I keep warm during the night?"

The glint of lust in his eyes made her chest squeeze. She did not want him holding her all night.

She turned her head to avoid his heated gaze. A streak of white in the trees behind Hawk caught her attention. Her heart thrummed with happiness.

Himiin!

Hiding her elation, she ducked her head and started into the trees. A rough hand grabbed her.

"Where are you going?" Hawk's eyes flashed with suspicion, making her wonder if he believed Tattle-Tale and not her own account of her disappearance the night before.

"I would like to relieve myself." She stared him straight in the eyes. He looked away, glancing around the area. Then pointed in the direction opposite of where she had seen Himiin.

"There, and stay where I can see you."

She glared at him. How was she to speak with Himiin if she had to remain where Hawk could see her? She stalked into the trees angry with the Blackleg and almost shrieked rounding a large bush. Himiin perched on a log smiling at her.

"Shh. Is he treating you well?" he asked in a whisper.

"Do not go any farther," Hawk called from the camp.

Wren waved and smiled, before squatting behind the bush. "He is rough, unlike your gentle touch." She reached out, taking Himiin's hand. "How am I going to live away from you and the mountain? Why did the weyekin have to give me such a great gift?" The tears she had kept from the Blackleg now trickled down her cheeks.

"You are strong." Himiin captured a tear. He raised it to his lips. "We will forever hold each other's heart. When you wish to talk, hold the wolf fang and speak to me with your heart. I will hear."

Brush rustled and Himiin disappeared in the bushes behind him. Her heart yearned to run after him. Live with him in the woods and forget all but him. However, her deep conviction to duty made her stand so Hawk could find her.

"Do you always take this long?" he asked, motioning for her to follow him.

"Only when I'm nervous." She glanced back over her shoulder and saw the flash of a white tail through the trees. Would she see him again? It was painful when they touched knowing they would soon no longer see one another. She should turn her back to Himiin and set her mind on the Blackleg. Their separation would come easier.

She studied Hawk when he stopped in front of her.

"You are my woman now. I will provide for you." He stood near a pile of pine boughs covered with a blanket. While she talked with Himiin, Hawk had made a bed.

Her cheeks heated. She did not want to lay with this man, not here in the forest of Himiin. But he had made only one bed. She rubbed her hands up and down her arms. The cold seeped clear to her bones.

Hawk frowned and walked to his horse. He pulled a fur wrap out of the pouch hanging across the animal's neck. Walking up to her, he placed the wrap around her shoulders.

"This should keep you warm until we are off the mountain." His hands lingered near her neck as he sniffed her hair. Shivers not from the cold shook her body.

"Sit, you must eat. We still have several suns travel to reach my village." Hawk pointed to a log. She sat, hands folded in her lap. He handed her dried meat. Taking the offering, she chewed and stared at the ground.

The sounds of the forest usually comforted her, but the awkward silence between them roared in her ears like an angry wind. Why did he not say something? Finally, she could stand it no longer.

"Tell me of your village." She glanced up and found him scanning the trees around them. The intensity of his stare made her edgy. "What do you watch for?"

"It is nothing of your concern." He looked at her and smiled, but the smile was forced, and his gaze went back to scouring the trees. His vigilance caused the hair on her arms to bristle.

"The Nimiipuu will not harm you. We have given our word in my marrying you. There will be peace." She picked at the dried meat.

"I do not fear the Nimiipuu." His voice was deep and growling, like a coyote defending a kill.

"But you fear someone, or you would not continue to stare into the trees." Trepidation crept up her spine like a shiver from a cold wind.

He looked at her. "I am Blackleg. We are strong and those who are frightened of us like to strike when we are unaware."

She turned from his cold stare.

Hawk watched the trees and continued. "You asked about my village. We near one hundred in size. Thirty strong warriors, the rest women, children, and elders." He broke off from his surveillance to look at her. "My mother is Nimiipuu."

Shocked, she studied his face to see if this was a ploy. "How?"

"She was taken on a raid many moons ago. My father liked her and bought her from my uncle who had brought her back from the raid." He looked at her. "She wishes to have someone of her people to be with in her ending years. That is why I wished a Nimiipuu wife."

"And for peace," Wren stated, making sure he did not lose sight of that once she became trapped at the Blackleg village.

"Of course," he said, but did not meet her eyes. He glanced out into the trees. "There are others in my village who would like a Nimiipuu bride. Your women are more giving and complacent than our own. Many Blackleg covet Nimiipuu maidens. Those are the ones I watch for."

"But you are on our mountain. No Blackleg would come here." This was the mountain of the Nimiipuu. It was ridiculous to think Blackleg or any other tribe would set foot in Nimiipuu territory.

"We will go wherever we desire to get what we want." He motioned with his hand to the trees around them. "You are mine. I paid with good horses and buffalo hides from many hunts. I do not wish to have you taken. By anyone." The ominous tone of his last statement, made her wonder if Tattle-Tale's words had left doubts in Hawk's head.

She would always be a possession to this man. For her people she would endure a grueling future. She sucked in her breath and rubbed the wolf fang hanging between her breasts. Hawk's gaze followed her hand as she caressed the talisman. The light in his eyes unsettled her. She quickly dropped her hand into her lap, refusing to give him any encouragement or ideas.

"I am tired." Wren lay down on the horse blanket Hawk had placed over the pine boughs. She curled into a ball, pulling the wrap tight around her and drawing the other edge of the blanket over her. If Hawk wished to lie next to her, she would not share the blanket. He was the one foolish enough to travel over the mountain without proper provisions.

Wren closed her eyes only enough to feign sleep and watched Hawk. He stood, glanced at her, and took a spot under a pine tree where he could view the area.

She shivered not from cold, but the anger of the young warriors in her village over the peace with the Blackleg. The knowledge many in Hawk's village felt the same did nothing to help her believe her sacrifice would change things. She grasped the fang and whispered her fears to Himiin. He could only keep her safe as long as she remained on his mountain. After that, she would be in the hands of the Blackleg

Hawk.

The thought did not lend her any comfort.

Pú-timt wax pí-lept

(14)

Himiin snarled and fought back the urge to take what was his.
Wren.

When the Blackleg warrior held her against him as they rode,
jealousy roiled in his gut. Seeing the man didn't lie with Wren eased
his mind. Their conversation left him wondering at the man's wisdom
to put both himself and Wren at risk by forcing peace between the
Nimiipuu and Blackleg.

He ground his teeth watching the Blackleg escort Wren back to
the camp. The warrior treated her like a prize horse, leading her around
and ordering her every move. He may have paid horses and buffalo
hides for her, but they were merely material goods.

He had given much more—his heart. Wren belonged to the
mountain and him. She became his when they made love. It took all
his restraint to not barge into the camp, scoop her into his arms, and
carry her back to the mountain where she belonged.

Her future could never be with him. Their ill-fated attraction was
doomed from the start with him a spirit and her a mortal.

And neither could shirk their duty to the Nimiipuu.

But it didn't make watching her with someone else any easier. If
he could walk away and let the Blackleg take her, it would spare both
their emotions. But his gut told him trouble was coming, and he
couldn't walk away when Wren was headed toward danger. He would

do whatever it took to keep her safe, even if it included the torture of watching her with another.

The Blackleg sat at the base of a pine, leaning against the tree with his weapons at the ready. A sign he expected conflict.

Himiin glanced at Wren curled up like a coyote pup under the blanket. Nothing in the bushes around her moved. The sounds of nightfall rustled around him as birds perched and the animals of the dark came out.

Although he didn't sense any trouble, he began another vigilant circle around the camp. He would keep this up all night, if need be, to make sure nothing happened to Wren.

The wind shifted and a familiar scent flared his nostrils and lifted his lip in distaste. Crouching down, he crept through the underbrush toward his quarry. His body quivered with rage as the scent of his prey exuded exhilaration and confidence.

Peering through the undergrowth, he saw the black wolf with the tattered ear stealthily approaching the Blackleg warrior from behind. Why would he attack the man before the woman? There was little time to wonder. He had to stop the creature.

He covered the distance between he and the dark wolf in a flash, pouncing without warning.

The black wolf growled as Himiin landed in the middle of him. They rolled through the brush, snapping limbs and snarling. A blur of fangs, fur, and yellow glowing eyes barely registered as every muscle in Himiin flexed to kill. It didn't matter the wolf viciously fighting back was a spirit and would take another form. Or the fact he would fall in disfavor once more for killing. If he could stop the wolf form, it would prevent anything bad happening until the spirit found another willing vessel.

His love for the woman this animal seemed bent on harming, overrode Sa-qan's lectures and his vow to not kill. He must protect Wren. Not only for the peace of The People, but for himself. To be the one to allow her death, another mortal, would shrivel his heart and make him useless to the mountain and mortals depending on him.

He grasped the black wolf's neck, sinking his teeth in. The warm salty blood trickled into his mouth. This time he didn't find the taste repulsive. It heightened his fury, making his goal of destroying the wolf inescapable.

Growling his anger, he shook the animal viciously. The sound of bones snapping penetrated his wrath.

He stopped.

The body in his mouth went limp. The yellow eyes lost their glow.

Dropping the lifeless form to the ground, he stepped back as a wisp of smoke curled out of the body, bunched into a cloud, and swirled up into the sky.

Malicious laughter taunted him until the smoke dissipated.

The Blackleg spirit would be back. In what form, he didn't know, but he doubted the dark spirit would return this night.

He looked down at the dead wolf and grieved for the innocent animal. Now, he had the blood of two on his hands. His stomach squeezed with revulsion. How had he let it go this far? Had he sealed the fate of his siblings?

The spirit had to be stopped. Killing the vessel was the only way. His anger renewed at the thought of the dark spirit taking another body. Possibly getting that innocent killed as well.

The sound of approaching feet broke into his musings. He scurried away from the body and closer to Wren. Hawk approached the dead wolf. He scanned the area, then leaned down to look at the footprints and blood in the snow before poking at the animal with his bow.

Himiin froze, hidden in the brush. At the height of the battle, he'd given little thought to the warrior or Wren attempting to see what caused the noise. Watching the warrior inspect the footprints made him nervous. What if the man decided to follow the tracks? It had been stupid to attack so near the camp and flee without thought to the trail he might leave behind.

Once Hawk determined the animal dead, he knelt beside the wolf and skinned the body. After every stroke of the knife, he looked around and listened. The warrior's vigilance helped to ease the fear he had about Wren when she would no longer be in his sight.

Himiin slipped under a large bush a short distance behind where Wren slept. The spot was close to the woman he wished to protect and a good vantage point to keep an eye on the warrior.

When the warrior finished the task of skinning the wolf, he rolled up the pelt and stuffed it in the pouch hanging from his horse. He walked the perimeter of the camp, peering into the woods before returning to sit at the base of the tree. The Blackleg resumed his sleepy scan of the trees beyond the camp.

Himiin placed his head upon his paws and watched the rhythmic motion of Wren's sleeping body. So peaceful and beautiful, the sight of her made his heart ache. He wished more than anything they were on the other side of mountain wrapped in one another's arms.

《》《》《》

Wren stretched and tentatively slipped a leg from under the blanket. The brisk air curled her toes, but the early morning sun seeped through the branches, touching her face and warming her skin. Hawk slept under a tree on the far side of the clearing. His body slumped over his bow. The position looked uncomfortable, but she refused to wake him and spoil her few moments of private time.

She followed the trickling stream down around a bend and found a small copse of dogwood. Looking back toward the camp, she could not see Hawk, which meant he would definitely not be able to see her once she stepped in the stream.

Wren slipped the wrap off her shoulders, dropping it on a rock. The cold air sent bumps popping up on her arms, but the cold would not keep her from missing a chance to bathe. Slipping off her moccasins and pulling the antelope hide dress over her head, she parted the dogwood limbs. She placed her clothing on the edge of the stream and stepped into the cold water.

Shivers vibrated her body. Her nipples puckered and stood out reminding her of the night Himiin made love to her. The memory of the night his hands roamed her body sent a flash of heat scorching her center. The pleasure of their joining under the moon lightened her heart. She closed her eyes, allowing her body to relive the sensations.

Water splashed behind her. Fear spiraled in her belly. She did not want Hawk to think she was for touching—not yet. Opening her eyes, she braced herself and turned to confront her soon-to-be husband.

Her breath caught, and her heart pattered with anticipation.

"You should not stand in the middle of this stream. It is not safe." Himiin's voice floated over her like caressing hands.

"Why is it not safe?" She stepped closer to him to touch his magnificent body.

"There is trouble afoot." When her hands slid down his inviting chest to the top of his breeches, he sucked in his breath, taking her hands in his. "This needs to be discussed."

139

"Talk." She leaned forward, kissing his chest and drawing the tip of her tongue across the smooth skin and hard curves of muscle.

He held her head in his hands like a cherished keepsake. He leaned forward, touching her lips with his and sending the heat already swirling in her body into an out-of-control blaze.

She wrapped her arms around his neck and her legs around his middle. His hands slid down her body to cup her bottom, holding her against his belly. The heat and need building with each deepening kiss made her head buzz and her heart pound.

Himiin gradually pulled his head back. His dark blue eyes sparkled like tiny stars twinkled within their depths.

"We must talk. And be careful. The Blackleg could come looking for you. Finish your bath and join me there." He pointed to the opposite side of the stream. "We will hear his approach."

She was reluctant to leave Himiin's warm body and smoldering kisses. He squeezed her bottom and pried her legs from around him. She could see in his eyes, this was not how he would have liked to end their meeting. However, he thought with a clearer head than she.

When he stepped away from her, she sat down in the stream. Rubbing the numbing water over her body cooled the fire which only a moment before had been all-consuming. She watched him walk into the trees, his leggings shedding the water of the stream. Hurrying to her clothing, she grabbed her dress and moccasins, and ran back through the stream, ducking into the trees where Himiin disappeared.

As soon as the branches closed behind her, hiding the stream, Himiin tugged her into his arms. Her naked body pressed against him as her hands grasped his shoulders, pulling his mouth down to hers. The desperation in his kiss matched her urgency. This was the last time she would feel his arms around her. By the end of the day, she would leave the mountain she loved and the spirit who captured her heart.

Fighting back the tears, she clung to him like the moss she picked from the trees. He was her source of strength—of life.

"I will never forget you." She held his head and stared into his sad eyes. "You will forever be in my heart."

"What we have done is wrong, but I would not change a thing. You have given me love and strength. Always remember I hold you in my heart as well." Himiin slid his hands down her body and up under her arms. He raised her like a weightless feather and whispered a chant.

Forever we will hold the heart of the other.
Committed to the truth of our hearts and duty to the Creator and The
People.
We will live for the day we meet again and become one. And The
People can rejoice in peace and prosperity.
Forever our hearts will be one.

Tears burned her eyes as the poignancy of the words and their separation settled in her heart.

When the words faded on his lips, he lowered her, placing gentle kisses the length of her body. Flames of desire lapped at her confused senses. When his lips touched hers, he placed her feet on the ground and bent, kissing her deep and lingering. She sagged against him when her knees weakened, and her body cried to be under his.

Wren pushed at the leggings riding low on his hips. At first he pulled away, but she refused to miss out on this last chance to feel him inside of her. Latching on to the string, she tugged, loosening the rawhide. His wet leggings clung to his legs. Pushing her hands between the clothing and his legs, she shoved the garment down, exposing him.

"We should not do this. What if—"

She stopped his words by taking him in her hands.

A low moan escaped his lips before he raised her in the air and eased her over his maleness.

She wrapped her legs around him as she had in the stream, rubbing against him. He grasped her bottom, moving her up and down his length. She wanted to watch his face, and see the joy she gave him, but a body wracking bolt of light shot through her, blinding her. When the light returned, she shook the dizziness from her head and peered at Himiin.

A satisfied smile tipped the corners of his lips, and his eyes shone a deep, contented blue.

"We will forever have this time in our hearts," she whispered, kissing his salty shoulder.

He shook his head, and the serious Himiin she loved stared at her with remorse. "I will hold what you have given me for all time, but

141

you must get clean before you go back to the Blackleg." He slowly
lowered her feet to the frozen ground. "He will know you have been
with another."

Wren did not want to leave. She wanted to be held in this man's
arms and loved again. But the urgency of his plea, and the fear in his
eyes for her, set her in motion.

She hurried back to the stream and sat down in the middle,
scrubbing her body to rid it of Himiin's scent and their lovemaking. It
grieved her to have to wash away the mark of their love for one
another, but her life was not her own.

Not since her vision quest.

Himiin stood on the far side of the stream. Having his dark eyes
watch her every move, sent shivers of delight pulsing through her
body. Those same eyes, had only moments before, shown her the
magnitude of his love.

"Hurry," he said, turning his head and listening. Irritation flared in
his eyes.

"Come. Get dressed," he whispered roughly and motioned for her
to come to him.

She stood, shook the water from her body, and ran into the trees
where Himiin had disappeared. He grabbed her dress, helping her pull
it over her head.

"I will be with you to the bottom of the mountain. If you need me
after that, speak to the wolf tooth, and I will hear."

When he kissed her lightly on the forehead, she closed her eyes to
hide how it pained her for him to leave.

His breath whispered across her face. "*Donadagohvi.*" *Until we
meet again.*

She opened her eyes, he was gone. Splashing in the creek drew
her attention away from his departure. She bounced on one foot,
pulling her moccasins over her icy feet. When she finally had the
coverings on, she walked out of the trees, brushing at the tears
trickling down her cheeks.

"Where have you been?" Hawk demanded. He glared at her with
suspicion.

"I took a bath and then thought I saw a bush with berries. She
looked back the way she had come. "I was wrong." Her heart fluttered
hoping for one last sight of Himiin.

Hawk held the wrap in one hand as he walked through the stream toward her. "Why do you have tears?"

She peered into his accusing eyes. "You are taking me from my family, my people, and after today, my mountain."

"Your people have wandered for many moons. You will find peace at my village as well." He grasped her hand, dragging her through the stream and stalked back to the clearing where his horse stood ready to travel.

Her stomach rumbled. Hawk pivoted and glared at her.

"You should have eaten more last night." He scanned the area as if at a loss of how to feed her.

"Did you not bring enough food to get us to your village?" She placed her hands on her hips and glared at him. It was one thing to be taken away from all she loved, but to starve when he was capable of hunting was another.

"I did not want the others to know how long I planned to take getting back to the village."

"Why?" She stepped closer to him, making him unable to avoid her eyes seeking beyond his words.

"There are some who did not wish to make peace. Who think our marriage should not happen." He looked away.

Rage and fear thundered through her. Without thinking, she struck him in the chest with her fists. "You are taking me to people who do not even want me? Are you so full of yourself, you believe you can protect me from-from who knows how many people?" How could he be so arrogant to think he alone could change the attitude of a whole village?

He stared down at her with anger-filled eyes. His hands fisted at his side.

What had she done? To hit him in such a manner would not be tolerated. This she was sure.

She waited, clenching her eyes and steeling herself for pain.

When he did not hit her, she glanced up and found him fighting for control. He wanted to hit her; she saw it on his rigid face. What kept him from doing so? The knowledge he for some reason would not harm her, gave her strength.

"How many in your village are for the marriage and peace?" She grabbed his chin, making him look at her. His dark eyes glazed over, showing no emotion. "I want an answer," she said through grinding teeth. "It is my life you have put in peril."

"I will protect you."

"How? What is one against a whole band, perhaps a whole tribe?" His arrogance fueled her anger, sweeping fear away. She left all she loved to be in the middle of a dispute in which she could easily end up being killed and no peace coming from it.

When he would not answer, she dropped her hand from his face and paced. What should she do?

Continue, and hope they could make the village see the good to come from peace? That would be the way of her weyekin. *And her duty*. Or should she run, tell her father no one but Hawk had wanted the peace? And have her family and band believe she once again disobeyed and put them in peril?

Her gut clenched. Death would be better than bringing the wrath of the Blackleg down on her people.

A rough hand grabbed her, stopping her thoughts and pacing. Before she could make the decision, Hawk set her on his horse and swung up behind her.

"We will continue. All will be good." Hawk placed the wrap around her shoulders and jabbed his heels into the horse. The animal bolted out of the clearing.

"If you are the only one who wishes peace, what good will my living in your village do? I will only be looked upon as a slave," she snapped back, not ready to go down without a fight.

"Many want you to come to our village."

"Who? Your mother. She is Nimiipuu. Who will listen to her?"

His arm tightened around her. She hit a wound. How many in his village actually wanted peace? Maybe a handful of elders who no longer wished to plunder and raid, but she was sure all the younger warriors were against this union. She and Hawk would be targets of every Blackleg they encountered. A shiver of apprehension snaked up her back, causing more doubts.

How could she fulfill her gift if she were dead? And if this was her gift from her weyekin, would there be this much peril involved? Some warriors had gifts which helped determine battles, but she had never known of one to be so perilous.

Her head spun with thoughts while her stomach growled and

twisted with hunger and unease.

Hawk continued to scan the trees and underbrush along their way. He had a feeling someone watched. Who, he did not know. Not Blackleg. They would have attacked by now. The only explanation he could come up with had to be Nimiipuu making sure they made it safely. That was why he used all his control to not hit the insolent woman. If they saw him lay a hand on her before he was off their mountain, he would never make it to meet the rest of his group. Once the woman was out of Nimiipuu territory, he would teach her to never hit him again. He would mate with her, making her his wife. And no one else would touch her.

Then if the plan did not go as he wished, he would use her love of her people to get back to the village of the Lake Nimiipuu. Before the cold winds came he would have Chief Proud and Tall's herd of horses. And he would be the most influential Blackleg, making him the leader of all the bands.

During the night, he followed the sounds of animals fighting and found a dead wolf. The incident raised his vigilance and worries. What would kill a wolf so viciously? The neck had been torn to shreds and the bones had fallen apart. Why had the animals fought so close to camp? He spotted the largest wolf prints he had ever seen not far from the body. Proud and Tall had told him Wren's weyekin was a white wolf. Could he be watching over her? But why would he attack another wolf?

He shook his head. Foolishness. Why would a weyekin need to watch over her? He would get her to the village and keep all others away from her. She would believe her gift to her people was fulfilled. All this good news she would hear from him, and he would be rewarded with her body. Hawk smiled. The wolf pelt he took from the dead animal would make a nice gift for his mother. And keep her telling Wren only what he wanted her to know.

The hair on the back of his neck tingled. Just as it had this morning when he woke and found Wren gone. At first he thought his enemies had stolen in while he slept. But after searching the area, he had found only her footprints leading to the stream and the wrap he gave her on a rock. She had a penchant for bathing. He liked a sweet-smelling woman and would not curtail her need to bathe. His only wish was to be with her on one of her daily rituals.

The sorrow on her face when he found her proved more than missing her family. She had secrets, his woman. He would learn those secrets one way or the other.

Going up a small rise, she slid against him. Her small backside rubbed his belly and lower regions. Had there not been a need to watch for enemies, he would have made her his woman last night. The idea made his maleness throb.

She moved forward, putting distance between them.

"How is it you know of my desire for you?" he asked. As a maiden she should have no knowledge of a man's needs.

"I spent seven moons in the purification lodge. The tales the old woman tell would make you blush," she said, moving nearly up on the horse's neck.

"I do not know what they said, but I do not wish you to move away from me." Using the arm wrapped around her, he slid her against his belly. "We will soon become man and wife. You will find pleasure with me." Her back went rigid as he moved against her.

She was feisty. He would have to move his mother out of the lodge for a time. His new wife would take some training to have her come to accept him into her body.

He would use her belief in peace and keeping the Nimiipuu safe to secure her continuing the marriage and bearing them many children.

Pú-timt wax pá-xat

(15)

Himiin's feet crunched through the top crust of snow, slowing his pace as he ran down the mountain. Not long after Wren and the Blackleg left camp, they topped one of the lower peaks and headed downward. Hurrying to not only get below snow level, but to catch glimpses of the two on horseback, he zigzagged in and out of the fir and pine trees, boulders, and budding bushes.

Whatever Wren and the warrior discussed caused Wren's posture to slump in defeat. Himiin had feared for her when she struck the warrior. When the warrior's hands balled into fists, he was sure the man would hit her. But the Blackleg stood stone still, never lifting a hand. Any other Blackleg he knew would have slapped the woman for her insolence. Could this Blackleg be different from all the rest? Or did he control his temper until he had Wren far away from all she knew?

His heart squeezed as each step brought them closer to the bottom of the mountain. Once they no longer traveled down the rocky, tree-lined slopes, he would be useless to protect her. He also would not have to endure the Blackleg's hands upon her. The man touched her at every opportunity.

Wren's back had stiffened at the Blackleg's contact. This made his heart sing, even though he knew she would have to give in eventually and mate.

His head throbbed with rage at the thought of the man touching her intimately. Yet, it was her fate, and he would never see her again except in his dreams. He'd given her hope to converse with him through the wolf fang, when, in fact, he would not listen to her words. Her musings would pain him, while it brought her comfort.

The snow no longer crunched about his feet and the trees and boulders grew sparser with each step that drew him toward the bottom of the mountain. His mind wandered to the wolf lying dead where he'd battled with the Blackleg spirit. What form would his enemy take next? If that form attacked Wren, he, Himiin would not be there to save her. This weighed heavily on his mind and heart with each step he watched the horse and riders take through the trees.

Agony seized him, freezing his muscles and rooting him in place. What good did it do to follow her all the way to the end of his territory knowing once she left the mountain her life would cease?

Her death was imminent. He knew it in his heart.

The ache gnawing inside him had nothing to do with their separation and everything to do with the knowledge she would perish. When she came to her end, he would know.

He'd be consumed by emptiness.

The horse walked on. He stared after it and the woman who held his heart. The horse's backside and the back of the warrior hid Wren from his sight.

Urgency to see her one last time overcame him. His paws shuffled in impatience while his heart thrummed with anticipation. He had to warn her about the Blackleg spirit. He'd failed this morning. Lust caused him to think of things less important than her life.

She had to be warned. But how?

He loped after the horse, dried pine needles and decayed leaves kicked up in his wake. He had to find a way to stop the warrior and get Wren to himself. Scheming, he darted around bushes and stared at the horse ahead of him.

Hoof beats gaining behind him stuttered his stride and his heart. Were Wren's enemies catching them? He sent a furtive look over his back.

Wewukiye's regal form raced through the trees in his direction. The sight of the large creature rushing toward him relieved the tension of his tightened muscles and slowed his gait. When his brother came abreast, they both stopped.

"I have been looking for you, my brother." Wewukiye's eyes slanted. "Your scent and footprints were found near the carcass of a wolf." The censure in his brother's eyes did little to expel the triumph he felt at stopping the dark spirit.

"It was the Blackleg spirit. He left the vessel once it was lifeless." He sent his brother a challenging look, daring him to mention it was he, Himiin, who took the life. "I fear for the Nimiipuu maiden. The spirit and others want her dead before she weds the warrior Hawk. We must stop Wren and the Blackleg warrior, so I can warn her."

"It was foolish to take a life. You cannot continue to ignore the Creators decree." Wewukiye studied him as though he'd eaten the wrong mushroom.

"As much as I dislike Wren living among the Blackleg, it is my duty to make sure she gets there." He glared at his brother, "I will do whatever I must to help her achieve her weyekin."

Wewukiye shook his head. "I do not want to be you when the Creator discovers the change in you.

"Will you help me stop the Blackleg and Wren?" Himiin would worry about his consequences later. Right now he had to warn Wren.

"How are we to stop them?"

"I had hoped one with your wisdom would have an idea." Such praise was bound to put him in favor with his brother and gain his help. He stared in the direction the horse and riders had disappeared. "We must do it soon. Once they leave the mountain I'll no longer be able to warn her."

Wewukiye looked in the same direction as Himiin with a glint of mischief in his eye. "I could show myself, and see if the hunter in him cannot resist such a fine creature."

Himiin hid a smile as his brother preened, licking his ruffed hair.

"It is better than no plan, I suppose." Himiin bumped the elk's leg with his head to get the animal's attention. "We will have to run to catch up, and then hope he is a hunter."

"I barely had a run looking for you. Come on." Wewukiye tipped his head back to allow the tree branches to glance off his great antlers. He charged in and out of the trees. His antlers hit and slid along tree branches with a resounding 'thwack' echoing through the forest.

Himiin grinned at his impressive brother and chased after him.

When they caught up and passed the riders, Wewukiye stopped. He planted his front feet on either side of a medium-sized fir tree and rattled his antlers against the trunk. The loud clacking of antler against the hard wood could be heard for some distance.

Himiin peered through the trees to catch sight of the Blackleg and Wren. "I hope he hears you and takes on your challenge."

Wewukiye stopped, looked around, then rubbed again. "A good hunter will know I am a big bull."

Himiin nodded to his overconfident brother and traveled around behind the horse and riders. The warrior had stopped the horse. Hawk craned his neck. He listened and peered into the trees where Wewukiye shined his antlers. The Blackleg's hand gripped his bow. Wren sat uninterested in front of the warrior.

She glanced Himiin's direction, and he stepped out from the break of trees. The glum expression on her face brightened. She shifted and spoke to the warrior. Hawk seemed hesitant. She rubbed her stomach. After a brief exchange, the Blackleg slid off the back of the horse.

Himiin grinned as Wren sprawled on her belly across the horse's back. She watched the Blackleg walk into the trees toward Wewukiye. When the warrior vanished in the trees, she dropped off the horse, landing on her feet, and ran toward Himiin.

He backed into the woods and stepped behind a bush. The change from wolf to man became easier with each transformation. Now, man form fit more comfortable than any other. The soft shuffle of Wren's steps approached. When he stepped from behind the bush, her searching eyes brightened.

"Why do you wish to see me?" She stopped in front of him, her eyes darkened with worry. Her beautiful face should never be marred by concern. She was young and should carry a light heart. What he had to tell her would not take away her anxiety. Only make it worse. He groaned inside, there was no way he could take away the misfortune and pain she would experience once she left the mountain.

"This morning you distracted me with your beauty." He touched her cheek. The warmth and softness against his fingers, reminded him of other soft, warm areas of her body. He mentally shook away the thoughts and dropped his hand to his side. He could not let his body get in the way of what he had to tell her.

Like this morning.

Taking her hand, he drew her farther into the woods. A fallen log offered the perfect seat. He tugged on her hand, drawing her down beside him. Her scent triggered heat in his nether regions. He exhaled, taking control of those thoughts.

"What have you followed me to say?" She placed her small hand over their clasped hands. The sight clenched his gut. They belonged together. Yet, it was not possible. He needed to warn her and disappear. She didn't deserve his possessiveness to keep her from her duty.

"Be careful. Last night while you slept, I killed a black wolf carrying a Blackleg spirit. He is set on stopping the marriage."

"It seems there are many who feel that way."

It shocked him to hear the words uttered with no emotion. Her eyes gave little away.

"I have found only a handful of the Blackleg wish for peace with the Nimiipuu. Hawk is stubborn. He believes he can keep me safe, and his people will come to treat me as one of them."

The sudden droop to her shoulders and sadness in her voice showed signs of defeat.

"You know you could be killed before you even reach the village and yet you travel on?" He put his hands on her shoulders. Duty to the mountain and the Nimiipuu people and his honor to help her fulfill her weyekin battled with his desire to protect Wren. He wanted her safe with him, but knew neither one could live with themselves should her gift to her people not be accomplished.

If she didn't fulfill her gift, he was as good as killing her. He would not kill another mortal. Yet, he couldn't let her continue and know she would perish at the hands of the Blackleg.

He gripped her tighter than necessary and blurted, "Come back with me, now. We will find another way for you to fulfill your gift."

She placed her hand on his cheek, tears trickled down her face. "I cannot run away. I cannot be the one to cause the death of many. What if all goes well? And my marriage to Hawk will bring peace? I could never turn my back on the possibility, even when my heart is breaking for you and my people." Sorrow and regret dulled the confidence in her eyes.

Himiin's heart squeezed with helplessness and pride. She was strong in her convictions; despite walking into a life of unknown conflict and loneliness. The foreshadowing of her death plagued him as strongly as the pain of her leaving.

He gathered her in his arms and embraced her to his aching heart. Her body molded to his. He ran his hands down her curves and back up. Wren's body shivered under his hands. He didn't want to let her go.

Ever.

Lowering his head, he watched the surprise in her eyes turn to desire. He touched his lips to hers and tasted her tears. He revealed his desperation by deepening the kiss.

Wren surrendered to the fervor of his kiss, knowing she would never feel his arms around her again, nor experience the urgency of his desire. Clasping her hands behind his strong neck, she pressed against his muscled body. She immersed herself in the feel and taste of him. His hands eagerly roamed her body, gently squeezing and caressing.

Her body did not become inflamed like when they made love. A sweet, sad yearning burned in her, knowing this was the last time they would be in each other's arms. She did not wish to mate, but to remember the pureness of his love.

Sighing, she melted in his embrace and wished they never had to part. The tranquil trill of birds and swoosh of limbs dancing in the breeze lulled her senses, sinking her deeper into his arms and kiss.

The brush next to them popped and snapped, squeezing her heart with panic.

She gasped and clung to Himiin when a great set of antlers and the head of a bull elk emerged from the flying sticks and leaves. The massive animal's hooves dug into the ground as he slid to a stop within arm's reach. He shook his head and pinned his gaze on Himiin.

"The Blackleg is not far behind. Get her back to the horse, I'm leaving." The elk took in the full length of her and smiled, then returned his gaze to Himiin. "I see why you're having problems letting her go. But you must."

In great, quick strides the magnificent animal disappeared in a thunder of hooves and crackling brush. She stared at the flattened bush where he had stood.

"Come." Himiin grabbed her hand. Together they hurried in the direction of the horse. When she stumbled on a rock, he swung her up into his arms and continued at a run.

"Did I really hear an elk speak?" She looked at the man carrying her through the forest. Could his kisses make her hallucinate?

"He is my brother, Wewukiye, the spirit of the lake." Himiin stopped at the horse.

"How is it I could hear him talk, yet when as a wolf I cannot hear you?" She clung to him, searching his eyes for an answer.

"I did not wish to speak to you in wolf form. The Creator does not like us to speak to mortals while as an animal."

"But, your brother—,"

"Now you know about spirits." He released her legs, allowing her feet to touch the ground. "I cannot remain. If the warrior should see me, it will bring you trouble."

The steady rhythm of his heart pressed tight against hers gave her strength. Beyond the horse, brush snapped and moved. Himiin pulled away. The sadness in his eyes tore at her heart.

He placed her on the horse, his voice husky with emotion. "May you always find happiness and live a prosperous life." He squeezed her hand and hurried away.

Tears burned her eyes as she watched his broad, strong back disappear between the pine trees. It would be her last glimpse of him. Her heart ached and loneliness gathered in her chest.

Knowing the man she loved roamed the mountain and held her heart would be hard to ignore when her life with the Blackleg became difficult. Her stubborn streak to see her weyekin through and keep peace between the Nimiipuu and Blackleg would be the only thing to keep her from returning to the mountain and her love.

If she lived long enough to marry and fulfill her gift.

A shiver of fear prickled her skin. If the evil spirit Himiin spoke of was after her, could Hawk keep her alive before and after the wedding? Of this she was not certain. He may have strength and wisdom over mortals, but what power would he have against a spirit?

She had only Hawk's word there were others who wished for peace. He had yet to show her any dishonor. But that did not mean he would be above telling untruths. Look at how she had dishonored herself, by the half-truths she told her family. Queasiness settled in her belly.

Would things go wrong because she had not been true to her weyekin? She should have stayed off the mountain once she knew of the marriage and the peace it would bring between her people and the

Blackleg. Her selfish need to walk the mountain of her heart had brought about the lies and perhaps damaged her chance to fulfill her gift.

She watched Hawk return. He was a strong warrior, but she did not think he could protect her as well as he presumed. She would have to keep a watchful eye on everything around them once they left the mountain. Until then she knew Himiin would do whatever it took to keep her safe.

Hawk did not look at her as he grasped her waist and swung up behind her on the horse. His body reeked of sweat and he breathed hard. Himiin's brother took him on a lengthy chase.

Smiling, she whispered thanks to Wewukiye. With the poor sleep Hawk had the night before and now this strenuous hunt, he would sleep like a child this night.

Tremors of excitement coursed through her body remembering Himiin coming to her at the stream in the morning light. If they lingered on the mountain this night, he may make another appearance. Her heart thrummed expectantly, giving her something to look forward to when they made camp.

Her excitement died by late afternoon. The horse walked out of a stand of trees. Swells and valleys spotted with trees and swaying with tall grass spread out before them. The mountain had come to an end.

She glanced back, scanning the edge of the brush. The hope of one last glimpse of Himiin started to fade when she spotted a white animal hovering inside the tree line. She made out the silhouette of a wolf. The animal paced—a show of agitation. Her heart ached at her last vision of him.

Hawk pulled her upright when she would have stared at the trees until they became a blur.

She sat tall, staring forward, setting her mind to her future. The need to see Himiin one last time overruled her good sense. With little thought to what Hawk might think, she leaned around him and used hand signals to tell Himiin he held her heart.

Hawk pulled her back around.

"What are you looking at in the trees?" Hawk looked over his shoulder. "Were your people following us?"

Wren did not bother to answer. She stared forward and listened to the forlorn call of a wolf pierce the air. She tucked the cry into her

Spirit of the Mountain

broken heart along with her sorrow and despair.

Pú-timt wax `oylá-qc

(16)

The mountain behind them grew smaller as the horse moved steadily away from all she knew and loved. Topping yet another small hill, Wren peered around Hawk. Each time they climbed a treed hill and moved across a rise, she glanced at the snow-covered peak diminishing in the distance. With each glimpse, fear and dread took a tighter hold.

"Tell me of your village." She wished to keep her mind busy rather than relive Himiin's forlorn call over and over.

"It is a village of strong Blackleg." Hawk's answer did little to help her nerves. "I have heard your father has fast horses."

Suspicion crept into her head at his tone.

"His horses did well at the Weippe races." She did not plan to tell the warrior any more than he already knew.

"He has many I am told. How many?"

"I am sure as a woman it is not something I am told." Hawk's arm tightened around her, his body became rigid.

"Can you not guess?" His voice held a tremor of impatience.

"I have not seen them all together in a meadow, so it is hard to say."

"Ah, so they are kept in the high meadows?" His questions set off waves of distrust. He searched for answers. But why? He had no reason to wonder where the horses grazed.

"High, low, it means little to me. It is the job of the boys to tend the horses not mine." She let her voice sound disinterested while her whole body remained alert.

"When I first met you your intelligence appeared keen. I see now, you are no different from every other woman. You must be told what to do for you cannot think on your own."

She caught the surliness of his words and worked hard to not spout off. He baited her, trying to make her spill about the horses. He believed himself smarter than she. Fury shook her as she witnessed what she would battle the rest of her life.

They stopped long after dark. Without a word, she lay down the blanket and feigned sleep to keep the man from prying any further information from her.

Sleep proved elusive. She wavered back and forth between fear and outrage. The cruelty of life made her fume. That she should find a man who moved her and have to leave him to fulfill her gift to her people absurd. The fate which made her great among her people could also be her demise. Fear of being tortured and mutilated by the Blackleg, should Hawk not be able to protect her, made her jump at every unfamiliar sound.

She shivered not from the cold, early morning air, but her fate. Hawk had lain beside her during the night, giving his body heat to keep her warm. She had not feared his trying to mate with her. The fatigue from his vigilance the night before and his chase after Wewukiye was evident on his face and in his slow movements. But once he lay down next to her, she did not dare move for fear he would take it as a message to do more than sleep.

Now, as the sun peeked over the tree tops, she slipped out from under his heavy arm. She rolled away and stood, making sure her shadow did not fall across the warrior.

Glancing around, she was astonished to find they camped in a ravine. The stark, rocky terrain of the deep narrow gorge reminded her of their winter home on the Imnaha. In the opposite direction of the rising sun, she spotted the snow-covered mountain peaking above the edge of the ravine. From the size, they had traveled a great distance from Himiin's mountain.

Many times Hawk's actions made her wonder if he was aware of the love she left behind on the mountain. He had pushed the horse at a

Paty Jager

fast pace once they left the mountainside, loping over wooded rises and through small valleys. In the valleys, he walked great distances in streams and made the horse walk stretches of rocky terrain. His actions aroused her suspicions. Who did he fear would follow them? Surely not the Nimiipuu.

Moving with stealth, to not disturb the sleeping man, she walked away. The stillness of the ravine unnerved her. No breeze evoked the musical sounds of rustling leaves and limbs, babbling streams, and bird songs. Mother Earth's voice. The only sounds in the gorge came from Hawk's breathing, the horse shifting from foot to foot, and the soft scuffle of her feet on the hard ground.

She craved a bath and a drink of cool water. Tilting her head, she listened for a stream. Moving farther and farther down the ravine from Hawk and the horse, she searched for food. The small rocky canyon sprouted new clumps of spring grass and delicate yellow flowers among the old dried plant life littered along the sides and bottom.

The thrum of wings drew her attention to a quail escaping a pile of brush as big as her favorite rock on the mountain. She dropped to her hands and knees to peer into the tangle of sticks. Deep in the middle of the mound sat a nest with eggs.

She wove her hand through the sticks. Her finger tips wiggled in the air above the dry grass nest. The sight of food just out of her reach, along with a fitful night, brought forth all her anger and frustration. She uttered a vicious growl and stretched her arm once again. Her fingers barely skimmed the grassy nest. Her stomach rumbled and her mouth watered. Food was so close, yet, her arms too short. Was this a test of the Creator? Just like her fate at the hands of the Blackleg?

Backing out of the brush pile, she sat a moment and gathered her emotions. Holding her hands skyward to the Creator, she swayed back and forth and sang a song of forgiveness.

When the urge to scream had passed and tranquility filled her, she resumed the task of foraging food.

She hummed a song of thanks for showing her the nest and one by one, pulled out sticks until she could reach the eggs. Plucking the gifts of nature from the nest, she laughed with pleasure at her accomplishment and brushed stray strands of hair out of her face.

Hurried footsteps accelerated her heartbeat. There could only be one reason for someone to run.

158

The Blacklegs had found them.

Wren clutched the eggs and turned her back to the pile of brush. She pushed with her feet, shoving her body into the mound of sticks to hide. The sticks scratched her arms and legs as she pushed deeper.

"Wren. Wren!" Hawk's stern voice stopped her feet. She waited until he came into view, and she could witness the expression on his face. It would tell her whether or not to give up her hiding spot.

The lines of annoyance on his face eased her mind. He only looked for her. No one chased him. She scooted out of the brush. He rushed forward, yanking her to her feet. Her first nourishing food in two days nearly dropped to the ground.

"What are you doing? Were my warnings not enough for you to stay close?" His eyes scanned her face, the anger in them made her wish she had remained hidden in the brush pile.

"I was hungry." She held out the eggs.

He glanced from her face to the eggs and back again. "It was foolish to leave. I can provide for you." His stomach grumbled.

"I have yet to have a full stomach since leaving my village. You are a warrior, why do you not hunt something for us to eat?" She offered him six eggs, keeping the rest.

He took the food without any shame. "I do not have time to hunt."

"I think you are not such a good hunter. You did not come back with the elk we heard yesterday." When the words touched the air, she wished to pluck them back.

Anger flashed in his eyes. She took a step back. Hawk's empty hand raised as though to strike her. She dug into the ground with her feet. If he hit her, she would not go down. She would not give him the satisfaction.

Her conviction not to be a victim must have shown in her eyes. He grabbed her free hand and dragged her back through the scrub brush. "Come, we are to meet my friends tonight. We must hurry to get there before dark."

Back at the small camp, he motioned her to sit on a log and eat her eggs. He pierced the ends with his knife, but not before making a show of the sharpness of his weapon. After witnessing Hawk's anger, her hungry stomach did not accept her offering as eagerly as she had hoped. She would have to watch her tongue if she wished to not get struck.

However her curiosity had to be sated. "What friends are we meeting?"

"Warriors who wish to be my friends." He threw the last empty egg shell away from him and stood. "We must go."

Wren tossed her shells to the ground. He pulled her to her feet before she could stand. The farther they traveled from the mountain the sadder her heart became. Her feet dragged along the ground like large stones, with the realization this day brought them closer to the Blackleg territory and her new home. Hawk grasped her hand, towing her over to the horse. She looked back toward the mountain—the peak nothing more than a small white bump in the distance.

"Someday you will return," Hawk said, placing his hands on her waist.

His words sparked hope in her heart. "When?" Would she still yearn for the spirit of the mountain when she returned, and would he seek her?

"When I have accomplished my goal." He squeezed her sides, making her look up at him. "We will make strong children. They will be the ones who carry on and make the Blackleg strong."

Wren averted her gaze. The fire burning in his eyes sent a shiver down her spine. He wanted to make children with her, but she could think of only one man whom she wished to have that honor.

She would not be able to keep him from touching her as was his privilege. He placed her on the horse and swung up behind her. His arm wrapped around her possessively, drawing her back against his hard body as the horse set off.

Hawk liked the feel of Wren's body. She would be a challenge. The distant look in her eyes told him she had thoughts of another. Who, he did not know. Her father had said she had no suitors, but a father does not always know his children.

He sneered. His own father had no hint his son plotted to be the strongest, most influential of all the Blacklegs. The raids on villages had brought Hawk much wealth and admiration. The blood on his hands worth the looks he received from the other warriors. Capturing the Lake Nimiipuu horses would make him wealthy enough to become head chief. A dream he had coveted for many seasons.

Wren's head dropped back against his chest. He looked down at her peaceful, sleeping face. Her body was small, but she struck him as a strong woman. One who took on more burdens than one so young should be allowed. Proud and Tall told of his daughter's gift to her people, and how this union fulfilled her gift. If not for her vision, she would never have gone through with the marriage. She had a deep affection for the mountain and her people.

His lips curled in a wicked smile. He could use her love of what she left behind to make her a willing or unwilling mother of his children. Her stout character and strong body combined with his cunning would make offspring full of wisdom and physically able to guide the Blacklegs into a path of growth and strength.

One Ear was to meet him this night at the hidden valley. It was the perfect spot for a gathering with his followers. There was a small cave not far from the location where he could hide Wren while he discussed matters. He didn't want her to overhear the conversation.

He smiled and his body throbbed. She would be his mate tonight; he would make sure of it before his friends arrived.

A whisper of cold wind tapped on his shoulder. Hawk scanned the horizon. He sensed trouble the moment he awoke this morning. Wren missing started his anxiousness. Later in the day, he thought he saw a flash of color on a rise. After that, he could not shake the feeling someone watched his every move. He must stay alert again this night. There were those within the Blacklegs, if they knew of his plans, would wish to stop him.

He glanced down at the woman sleeping in his arms. They would take her from him and use her to get into the village.

He snorted.

She stirred, but did not wake.

From what he had witnessed so far, she would die rather than take a group of bloodthirsty Blackleg into her village. But he had the plan. With his words of peace, she would do anything he asked, even lead his group into her village unaware they intended to plunder and seize the horses.

His aging mother had finally come up with something good. When she first brought up the idea of him marrying a Nimiipuu, he had pushed it out of his mind. The rest of the band would have mocked him for such thoughts.

But as the idea bounced around in his head, he realized it was the only way to get to the prized horses. Use the Nimiipuu's weakness;

their desire for peace.

《》《》《》

Himiin couldn't leave the spot on the mountain where he last saw Wren. He paced back and forth, every muscle twitched, his temper volatile. Why had she come along and opened him up to emotions?

The worst part—after touching Wren, he yearned for a mate. Something he'd not even considered before. The problem—he wanted only one, and she would never return to his mountain.

He'd spent the first night howling forlornly to the Creator for the trick he played on him. To have the woman dance into his life and back out after opening up emotions he'd never known existed.

"Creator, how could I have been a spirit for so long and not known the power of another's touch?" He stared into the clear blue sky.

"Brother, are you talking to yourself?" Wewukiye stepped up beside him.

"Not myself, the Creator." Himiin peered at the sturdy elk standing beside him. "Have you ever crossed paths with someone who lightened your day, and who you thought about every moment?"

Wewukiye shook his head. "I have not, nor do I wish it to happen. You have neglected the mountain while mooning over this woman. She is gone. She is not coming back. You must leave this spot and continue."

"I cannot continue until Wren has reached the village, is wed, and no one has killed her." Himiin growled at his brother.

"How do you plan to learn of this?"

"I have called our sister. I will ask her to fly to the village of the Blackleg, He Who Crawls, and see that all is well."

"All is not well." Wewukiye stared at him, his eyes unflinching.

"What is not well, besides Wren being taken from this mountain?"

"I heard Wren's brother took one of his father's horses and has been missing since the day the Blackleg left with Wren. The women spoke of how he was against Wren leaving and caused a scene, even accusing her of being unworthy of the Blackleg."

Himiin flinched. How had her brother known she lay with another the night before she went with the Blackleg?

"Have you seen him following you?" Wewukiye asked.

"I have not seen the boy. But I will watch for him."

162

Sa-qan landed gracefully on a branch above their heads.

"You have summoned me, my heart-sick brother."

Wewukiye laughed until Himiin sent him a scathing glare. "Yes, Sa-qan. I would like you to fly to the Blackleg village and make certain Wren arrives safely and the Blackleg takes her for his wife. Then I will be content she is safe."

"Why do you fear for her safety?" Sa-qan peered at him with beady yellow eyes.

"The Blackleg spirit tried to kill the warrior with her, and I believe he would have killed her as well."

"Tried?"

"I stopped him." He glowered at her, defying his sister to reprimand him for killing.

"It was only his vessel you killed." Her stern tone told him she did not condone his killing, even to save a mortal. "An innocent vessel." She shook her head. "You cannot kill when you think someone is being threatened. Did you not learn your lesson the last time?"

He stared into her eyes. "I will forever work to wipe out the wrong I committed so many seasons ago."

"How can you say that? Killing is killing, no matter the reason." She ruffled her feathers, walked away and then came back. "You are no better than the Blackleg you scorn."

Embarrassed and enraged by her assessment, he cleared his throat and tamped his anger.

"I do not indiscriminately kill. The dark spirit had to be stopped or it would have killed both the Blackleg and Wren. You were not there to see the hatred in his eyes." His heart squeezed. "I fear he will try again. Not all the Blacklegs wish for peace with the Nimiipuu."

"I see. And you will kill another innocent animal because the dark spirit is in it?" The disdain she harbored for his actions was minor to the hatred he had for the spirit and what he must do to save Wren.

"I do not make the spirit take over the innocent animals. But I cannot have him win. He will not have Wren or this mountain." He glared at his sister.

Sa-qan bowed her head. "I do see where this could go if the dark spirit is not stopped. I just feel no loss of life, especially at your hands, is right."

"I agree, but it cannot be helped." Himiin softened his gaze. "Will you watch for Wren and see that she makes it to the Blackleg village?"

"If this will set your mind at ease, I will fly to the Blackleg village and see if they prepare for a wedding." She looked at Wewukiye and then back at Himiin. "Where will I find you when I have answers?"

"On this side of the mountain."

They both stared at him.

"You cannot possibly stay on this side of the mountain for that long." Wewukiye rolled his eyes.

"You have said Wren's brother is following her. I will search for him and remain close to Wren until I know she is safe."

Himiin acknowledged to stand around was foolish. Since Wewukiye revealed Wren's brother followed her, he believed it would not take him long to find the boy. From all Wren had said of Tattle-Tale, he most likely had become lost.

"It is true you should find the brother, but you are foolish to remain here for a mortal." Wewukiye walked away, his antlers held high.

"Is this woman worth the anger of the Creator and possibly your spirit?" Sa-qan asked.

"She is worth the very breath I breathe." Himiin looked into his sister's eyes. "I hope a day comes when you will meet someone who brings joy and life to your heart." His heart hammered as he thought of Wren's touch and soft lips. "There is no better feeling."

His sister shook her head and opened her wings. "I find that hard to believe, but I will search for this woman who has changed my brother."

"Thank you. If she is safe, I will be content."

"Will you ever be content, if you feel this way for her and yet you may never be with her?" Sa-qan flapped her wings and disappeared.

Himiin watched his sister fly gracefully away and wondered the same.

《》《》《》

Tattle-Tale spotted the gathering of a white wolf, a bald eagle, and an elk. Anger filled him at the sight of the wolf. This and the sensation the creature looked familiar puzzled him. He watched the three. It seemed odd they were together and even seemed to be communicating. But he had other things to think about besides animals.

His sister rode away from Nimiipuu territory. The farther she went, the harder it would be for him to prevent her marriage and fulfill his weyekin. He was not sure how to interfere. If the Blackleg warrior had already mated with her, he would fail and could not return to his people.

He had taken one of his father's horses and left right after Proud and Tall finished lecturing him on his behavior before the Blackleg Hawk. The whole village would look for him soon, and his father would not be pleased to realize his horse had disappeared.

Why had his weyekin bestowed such a hard and disagreeable task on him? He had tried his best to stop the pair at the village. Discrediting his sister made him feel small, but it had been necessary to stop the Blackleg warrior from taking her.

He sighed and slumped over the neck of his horse. His plan had not worked.

Father had talked to him of honor and speaking wrongfully of others. Saying his new brother, Hawk, would think less of him for his words and actions. Tattle-Tale did not care what the warrior thought of him. If he put doubts in the man's head about his sister, and she lived up to her reputation of being stubborn, then he, Tattle-Tale, had a chance to get her away from the Blackleg.

It bothered him that to stop the marriage could ruin the peace it was to bring, but he would not question his weyekin, only follow his orders.

Trailing the two over the mountain had proved difficult. The first night he had felt lost and uncertain until passing through a puff of smoke. Then all became clear. He sensed his sister and the Blackleg even when he lost their trail. Had his weyekin sought him to help with the task?

Due to his age, he had never traveled the country beyond the Nimiipuu borders. Logic told him the Blackleg did not head to his village. If he had knowledge of the land, he could cut them off. Instead he must follow, hoping to gain ground by not sleeping and keeping his horse at a steady pace.

He wiped a hand across his face as fatigue set in. He had not eaten or slept since he left the village. This was more of an ordeal than his vision quest. His head bobbed, and he sagged to the side of the horse. A strange sensation warmed his body, holding him erect on the horse, and slipping him into darkness.

Dark Wolf had run out of time when the boy came along. He'd quickly made the decision to slip into the human instead of the horse. After a short time, he realized the body was the brother of the woman he sought.

When they passed by the white wolf, he couldn't keep his sentiments from entering the boy. Luckily, the mortal didn't find the experience unusual, which surprised Dark Wolf. The boy had taken several commands easily and not seemed unnerved he was making decisions not his own.

With little effort he slipped the boy in a deep sleep. This vessel proved as simple to control as a stupid animal. And to think this was the son of an important Chief. Dark Wolf laughed at the thought. He'd entered a witless boy who would grow into a witless man. The Blackleg did the Nimiipuu a favor taking them over. Otherwise, they would be led by a weak warrior.

With the boy asleep, he could make decisions to put him closer to He Who Crawls. Dark Wolf knew Hawk headed to a meeting with his followers. He chuckled. Hawk's followers had been detained. Followers of He Who Crawls would show the insolent whelp what happens to those who try to outwit their leader.

Dark Wolf turned the horse and headed north. The Blackleg raiding party expected him with a report. The boy would be in the midst of Blackleg warriors when he woke and never realize what happened. Dark Wolf laughed and jabbed the tired horse in the ribs.

Pú-timt wax `uyné-pt

(17)

Wren raised a hand to shield her eyes from the low evening rays of the sun. Hawk stopped the horse at the foot of a small wooded hill. She scanned the area, peering through the trees for the people they were to meet.

"We will stay the night here." Hawk slipped from the horse and roughly dragged her down beside him. When she tried to pull away, his hands clutched her sides.

"I thought we were meeting your friends?" She tried to keep her voice normal as panic seized her throat.

"They will be here when the moon is directly overhead. Until then, we will make our marriage binding." The glint of lust in his eyes, made her shudder. She knew he felt the tremors when his lips curved up in a lecherous smile. "Show me what you learned in the old women's lodge to make your man happy." He lowered his head to kiss her.

He had paid a handsome price for her. That and the peace their union would bring were the reasons she should remain obedient and give him what he wanted. But the painful grip he had on her sides and the memories of Himiin's gentle touch, kept her from raising her lips to his.

She turned her head, and he kissed her hair.

"You will not turn from me." He grabbed her face hard and

167

yanked her head around. His dark eyes glinted with anger. The ugliness of his face twisted in rage made her stomach churn. He held her face so she could not turn away and smashed his lips against hers.

When she refused to respond, he scraped and nipped her lips with his teeth, drawing blood. Repulsed, she pushed her hands against him in an attempt to break free, but his arm banded around her like drying leather. With the other arm, he held her head and licked the blood.

Wren hiccupped back a sob. She had never encountered this type of cruelty and forcefulness growing up in a peaceful band. How was she to give herself to a man who treated her with such disrespect? She could never tolerate this brutality. Her heart shattered. She had to. If she refused him, she could put her family in peril. To live with the guilt would be harder than the violence she now faced.

"Stay." Hawk moved away from her and pulled at a pile of dried brush. Tossing the dead plants to the side, he revealed an opening in the side of the hill. The hole was not large enough for a person to walk through, but plenty of room to crawl.

"Get in there." He forced her toward the mouth of the cave. She hesitated; fearful an animal might use it for a den.

"Get in." The force of his foot shoving her backside sent her head first into the dark earthen hole.

She fell, scraping her hands and knees on a hard dirt floor. The cave dug in far enough for two people to stretch out side by side. The scent of musty dirt and animal droppings pinched her nostrils as she remained on her hands and knees. Sunlight streaming through the doorway dimly lit the interior. The cave darkened.

He entered.

She was trapped.

The small area left her little chance to ward off his advances. Her body shook with fear and anger. How dare he behave toward her this way? Did he not think she would get word to her father of this? She rose up on her knees to try and stand. A strong arm grabbed around her middle. He hauled her to her feet and spun her to face him. Even in the dim light, she could see the cruelness in his eyes. She could not control the tremor which shook her body. His eyes glistened with the knowledge he had frightened her.

She swallowed the panic gathering in her throat. How did one handle such a man? To show fear delighted him, to fight him would be useless.

She had to give in. Her family depended on it. But she would not meekly let him take what he wanted. In all her summers, she had never been submissive. One of her flaws, according to her father.

Hawk grabbed her head, drawing her up onto her toes and forced his lips against hers. She struggled for breath as he smashed their faces together. In a desperate attempt to get free, she punched both her hands just below his ribs.

He dropped her like a burning stick and sucked for air. Thinking of the horse just outside the cave, she dove for the fading light at the entrance. When the warmth of the sun's evening rays touched her hands and face, an arm snaked around her middle, and her back hit the hard body of the warrior.

"You are mine. You will never leave me." He grabbed her breast and squeezed while his other hand pulled her head back by one of her braids. His teeth nipped and scraped the tender skin of her neck. The hand on her breast pinched so hard she cried out. He laughed against her neck.

"You will be begging soon."

His hardness rubbed against her. The pain from his hand and the rawness of her neck made her think of the old woman's words. Lie down and spread your legs for your man, it will be over quicker. That was all she wanted. For him to spill his evil seed and leave her alone.

She found nothing wondrous or fascinating in this man's touch. Her heart yearned for the love and gentleness of Himiin and ached with the knowledge she would never experience it again.

She stopped struggling. His hand moved to her belly, and his hold on her braid loosened. She'd discovered how to keep it less painful.

Pushing deep into her mind, she forgot the onslaught of the warrior's hands. Reveling, instead, in memories of her walks in the pungent forest and basking in the warmth of the sun with Himiin's tender voice.

"Take it off."

Hawk's request shattered her thoughts. Brusquely, he grabbed the bottom of her dress and peeled it from her body. The rough motion of pulling it up, threw her arms over her head, and nearly ripped her braids out by the roots.

He tossed her clothes to the back of the cave. She thought of

Himiin spreading her dress on the soft grass for her to lie upon. Grief for a time she would never share again brought tears to her eyes and heaviness to her heart.

Being this man's mate, she would never feel a gentle touch again.

A satisfied chuckle brought her back to the cave and the cruel man who would make the rest of her days a walking nightmare.

He grasped her shoulders, turning her to face him. His gaze stopped at the spot between her breasts where Himiin's wolf fang rested.

"What is this?" He grabbed the fang, ripping the leather from her neck, and burning her skin.

She reached out to snatch her keepsake of Himiin and the love they shared from the offensive man. He tossed it to the back of the cave.

"Where did you get that thing?" He grasped her chin in his hand and nearly raised her off the ground.

The pressure of his fingers made it hard for her to speak. "I-I found it in the forest."

"Why would anyone keep a wolf's tooth and wear it around their neck?"

"It reminds me of the mountain." She worked hard to keep her fear of him from showing.

He stared into her eyes, searching. "You do not need to think of the mountain any more. You will be Blackleg. You will think only of me." When her neck felt as though it would snap, he finally dropped her back onto her feet.

"You are a beautiful woman. My beautiful woman." He ran his hands down her sides, squeezing her hips, and pulling her hard against him. "You are built to produce many babies." He licked his lips. "I will enjoy making them with you."

His hips gyrated against her, the leather of his leggings rough against her skin. Placing her upper arms against his naked chest, she tried to put distance between them. He stepped back giving her space. Elated at his retreat, she glanced his way as Hawk dropped his leggings to the floor.

She turned her head. The sight of his pulsing manhood and his leering gaze shattered her faith in her weyekin. She did not care how many buffalo hides or horses he paid for her, she was not allowing him to enter her. Her stomach churned with revulsion. No one would touch her there, but Himiin.

"Look at me!" Hawk ordered and stepped close, grasping her chin once more. He yanked her head around.

She closed her eyes. He could turn her, but he could not make her look upon him.

Pain shot from her breast to her stomach. She yelped and opened her eyes. Glancing down at her breast, her head buzzed. He'd bit her nipple. The tip hung sideways as droplets of blood dripped onto her belly. A wave of nausea swept through her, buckling her knees.

She fell to the hard cold dirt floor, hitting her head. Dizziness and confusion roiled her stomach. Gently shaking her head, she pushed to remember what had happened. Something caressed the skin below her breasts. She looked down. Fear spiraled into her heart. Hawk straddled her hips as he licked the blood from her skin.

Shoving with her hands, she pushed his head away from her and tried to scramble out from under him. He grabbed her hands, pressing them above her head.

"You are mine. I will do with you what I wish."

The hardness of his manhood rubbed on her belly. She froze. It would not be long before he entered her. Pressing her legs together, she called to the Creator for forgiveness. She could never be this man's wife, even to bring peace to her people and fulfill her gift.

His hands slid between her thighs.

She squeezed with all her might.

He laughed. "You are a weak woman. I will win." He pried her legs apart with his hands and used his legs to spread them wide.

《》《》《》

Hawk crawled off the woman, stripped her maiden blood from his shaft, and ventured out into the moonlight to show the Creator they were mated. He stared at his hand. There was no blood. *He had been tricked!* They were to provide him with a maiden. Rage burned in his gut and pounded in his head. She would die and her lover would die.

He crawled back in the cave and straddled her enticing body. Her curves and warmth ignited his need. Her body trembled and he smiled. No, he would enjoy her body and seek revenge. He entered her again, pouring forth his seed. She stopped fighting the third time he entered. Her body quivered with exhaustion as she turned away from him. It would take more time, but she would soon come to crave him.

He needed her alive. She would get him and his men back into the Nimiipuu summer camp. He smiled; glad he had not killed her. She may be repulsed by him, but her strong body would take all the mating he wanted. With her body, it would be a lot. He already hardened thinking of their next time.

Hawk peered out the cave entrance. His followers would arrive soon. He pulled on his leggings and glanced down at the woman. The strip of moonlight filtering through the entrance washed over her body. Her bruises would be a reminder for her to not disobey him again.

"My friends will arrive soon. I will meet them not far from here." He leaned over her to see the fear in her eyes. "If you should yell to them or try to get away, I will let them each have you." He snickered. "And they are not as gentle." She would do nothing to give away her hiding. The panic in her eyes reassured him.

He reached up and removed the rock from her hands. He would be back long before her arms and hands worked well enough for her to try to escape.

"Heed my words. One sound and I will give you to my friends. If you believe you can get away before I come back, you are wrong. Do not try to leave. I will hunt you down and do worse to you than this night."

She curled into a small ball with her back to him. The bruises on her bottom matched his hands. His brand. Pride made him smile. Hawk scanned his new property one more time and crawled out of the cave.

Mounting his horse, he headed to the area where he would meet his followers. With loyal warriors around him, he could relax his vigilance the rest of the way to the village. Once there he would leave Wren in the care of his mother and work out his plans to raid the Nimiipuu village.

His heart pounded with giddiness. The Nimiipuu horses would make him the most influential Blackleg. Along with his riches, he will have the feisty Nimiipuu woman to give him strong male children, who will become fierce warriors.

He smiled, enjoying his thoughts as he rode through a rocky area, down a gully, and up again. Wariness and covering his tracks had become second nature to him. He did not want anyone to find his new wife. She would be his only wife until she provided several children, then he could take another more willing wife. To make Wren agreeable to mating with him might take their whole lifetime.

He stopped his horse in the middle of a clearing and studied the moon. It was time. His group would join him soon.

The thunder of several horses running toward Hawk made him nod. He'd picked his followers well. They would not let him down.

His jaw clenched as Red Dog, a strong supporter of He Who Crawls, rode into the meadow followed by six warriors. He searched the area for his followers. Why was this group here?

"We have come to have a look at your woman." Red Dog motioned for two of the warriors to dismount. One looped a leather strap about the neck of Hawk's horse, handing the end to Red Dog while the other studied the ground.

"You are wasting your time. She is being escorted back to the village by men I trust." He did not want these men to have his woman or anything he owned.

"I know the woman was with you today. We have been watching you for some time." Red Dog scanned the area. "You must have bedded with her somewhere around here." His large arm circled in the air. The two men on the ground widened their circle in search of tracks and signs.

"She is not here. Your information is false." Hawk's uneasiness during the day, now made sense. He should have heeded it rather than letting his thoughts about the woman and what he planned for her this night distract him. Those thoughts could bring their deaths.

"It is not false," Red Dog pushed his horse up next to Hawk's. The loathing in the warrior's eyes set the hair on Hawk's neck bristling. "I also do not need the woman to own Nimiipuu horses."

Hawk stared at the hatred and greed in the man's eyes. Red Dog was one of He Who Crawls most trusted confidantes. Had the chief accepted Hawk's proposal of marriage to the Nimiipuu woman as a trick to get his hands on Chief Proud and Tall's horses?

Hawk had trusted only a few warriors to his plan. Who had betrayed him? He knew someone did. He could tell by the insolence on Red Dog's face.

"Why are you here?" Hawk kept his voice controlled even when he wanted to kill every one of the men circled around him. It would come down to either them or him.

"We were told you plan to take the horses He Who Crawls is already set to take." Red Dog stared at him. "And we are not going to allow it."

"I would not talk big so fast." Hawk scanned the area. Where were his warriors?

"Are you looking for your men?" Red Dog raised his arms and the warriors around him let out ear-shattering whoops. "They will not be coming." One of the warriors held up a long, black-haired scalp. "We have intercepted your men."

Fear meant nothing. An outraged cry ripped from him and he lunged at Red Dog. He would take down at least one of them before they killed him.

His hands squeezed Red Dog's great neck, silencing his oaths and taking his breath before the others fell upon him, bludgeoning his body.

Hawk did not feel the blows. He reveled in the sickening snap of Red Dog's neck and the power at having taken away one of He Who Crawls' men.

They both fell to the ground. He landed on Red Dog and rolled ready to fight the others coming at him.

The wait was short. The warriors kicked, bludgeoned, and stabbed him. He fought back. Elation, each time he landed a blow, helped him survive the onslaught, until he could no longer defend himself and lost consciousness.

The sense of floating made him wonder if he would see the Creator. The steady loping motion under him told him he rode a horse. All went black.

Pú-timt wax `oymátat

(18)

Himiin had only one more section of the mountain to cover in his search for Wren's brother. The boy had vanished. Even Wewukiye, who had covered a lot of ground, was at a loss for where the boy had disappeared.

As the sun faded, casting dark shadows in the trees, he heard the skittering of small rocks and the clomp of many horse's hooves on rocky terrain. He hurried toward the sound and moved as close as he dare without the animals catching his scent. Frightening the horses would alert the riders to his presence. Twenty painted Blackleg warriors with decorated ponies rode by. It was a raiding party.

The last two horses in the group were led. He moved closer and found Wren's brother on one horse and Hawk flopped over the other. This explained Tattle-Tale's disappearance. But why did the Blacklegs have Hawk stretched over a horse as if he were dead?

Where was Wren?

His heart squeezed with fear. Was she dead? She couldn't be. His heart would stop beating.

She hadn't used the fang to call to him. Could that mean she was spared whatever fate the Blackleg planned for Hawk?

Why did a raiding party have these two? Captives slowed the

group down. Was Hawk a trophy? His desire for peace with the
Nimiipuu may have angered many in his band. Himiin studied the
group. Yes, it was his band.

He glanced at Tattle-Tale. Why did a raiding party bother with a
boy?

Whatever their reasons, he would have to get the two away. For
their protection and to ask Hawk about Wren.

He raced ahead, stopping on a ledge above the trail the Blackleg
traveled. From this vantage point, he could watch the group's
approach. Tipping his muzzle to the sky, he called Sa-qan and
Wewukiye.

The two appeared at his side as the Blackleg raiding party made
their way into a narrow canyon.

"What are they doing here?" Wewukiye stomped his foot and
curled his lip with contempt.

"I have yet to find out. They have two hostages. See." Himiin
tipped his muzzle to the end of the line.

"That is why I could not find Hawk or Wren." Sa-qan stared at the
body hanging over the last horse. "But where is Wren?"

Himiin's fur bristled in displeasure. "That is what I wonder. How
is it the Blackleg have Hawk and not her? She must not be dead, I
would know. But she hasn't called to me."

"Is Hawk alive?" Wewukiye asked.

"He has not moved since I discovered them. I will soon find out,
when I take over his vessel to get Wren's brother to safety." The plan
he had formulated while waiting for his siblings required their help.

"How do you plan to do this?" Sa-qan watched him intently.

"I will use his vessel to talk with Tattle-Tale and deliver him to a
safe place until the Blackleg have been dealt with. Inside Hawk's
vessel, I hope to learn where to find Wren. You and Wewukiye will
enter the two Blackleg leading Tattle-Tale and Hawk's horses. Stay in
their vessels and keep them distracted until the boy and Hawk can slip
away."

"Where do you plan to go once you are away from the Blackleg?"
Wewukiye watched the approaching group.

"We must get in the vessels soon." Himiin's heart raced. The
raiding party neared the point he intended to use for their escape. "My
plan is to slip off the horses at the rock wall canyon. There is a trail

used by the mountain goats which leads to a rock overhang. The animals stay out of the rain and snow under this." He studied his siblings. They both nodded their heads in agreement.

"I will leave the two there with instructions to stay hidden until either Hawk, if he is not dead, is healed enough to get Tattle-Tale to the village of his people or I return."

Sa-qan spread her wings. "Your plan is good." She narrowed her eyes. "You will do nothing to harm the Blackleg Hawk while you are in his body."

"If he has not harmed Wren, he will live." He returned his sister's intense stare. "If Hawk has harmed her, I cannot say what I will do."

"You cannot harm another mortal." Sa-qan glared at him.

"If his body is beyond mortal healing…" He shrugged, "I will not exert myself to save him. That is not killing." If the Blackleg warrior hurt Wren in any way, he would only use the vessel to save Tattle-Tale. If the warrior had good thoughts of Wren, Himiin would see what he could do to help the man.

Sa-qan rolled her eyes. "You do not act as a spirit since meeting that mortal woman. You will have to counsel with the Creator soon." A wisp of smoke swirled out of her body and curled toward the Blackleg party.

Wewukiye winked and closed his eyes. A wisp of smoke shot skyward before rushing after Sa-qan.

Himiin took a deep breath, turned into smoke, and hoped he found the Blackleg vessel salvageable.

《》《》《》

Warmth spread from Hawk's chest to this dangling legs and arms. His mouth felt dry as a handful of dirt and salty. He spit, leaving a blob of red on the ground before the horse's hooves trod over it.

His head and body throbbed, but he was alive.

A horse walked alongside the one he hung over. Tilting his head, he saw a small foot, short leg, looking higher—he found Wren's trouble-making brother.

His gut clenched. This was why Red Dog proclaimed he would have the horses. They planned to use the boy to enter the village. Anger rushed through him. Not for He Who Crawls besting him, rather for them using Wren's brother. He shook his head and became dizzy. Why should he feel remorse about the boy's capture? He held no opinion for the impudent youngster.

Though now, he realized what the boy had tried to tell him the day he took Wren. Her brother had known she had a lover. She regretted that now. As he played their mating over in his head, anger gripped him, and pain shot through his body like a knife twisting.

Panting to push through the ache, he chased away thoughts of Wren and wondered at the fate his own people planned for him. He would never show them the way to the village. If he could not have Proud and Tall's horses, he was not about to let He Who Crawls. He knew if the jostling on the horse did not kill him, the raiding party would not hesitate to finish the job.

He shifted his weight to lessen the jostling he received as the horse plodded along. How long had he been on this horse? How far was he from Wren? The cunning woman went to him proclaiming to be innocent. He sneered. There was nothing innocent about the woman, especially now.

He thought of his last glimpse of her rolled into a ball, covered with bruises. Recalling the mating, the fear in her eyes, and her screams, anger pulsed his blood, breaking open the stab wounds. He weakened as pain ripped through his body and took his breath away.

Himiin shook with rage from the vivid scenes of Hawk desecrating Wren's bruised and naked body. His heart ached for her, knowing she lay all alone, battered and rejected. Devastation recoiled in his gut and shattered his heart. He'd inflicted injury to another mortal. Perhaps even death. His actions, his selfishness, had caused the Blackleg to brutalize her.

His body shook with anger at himself and the Blackleg. Loathing himself for his weakness and loathing the Blackleg for his dishonor, he fought the impulse to bolt from the vessel. Battling the mixed emotions, he settled on his next actions.

He had to make this right; for Wren and for the Lake Nimiipuu.

He shut down Hawk's spirit and prepared to use the vessel. The man had brutally taken his sweet Wren. Refusing to help another would bring him in disfavor with the Creator. But the vessel of the Blackleg Hawk could not be salvaged. Too much of Himiin's power would be needed to bring Hawk back. The Lake Nimiipuu were his main concern. Hawk would remain a victim of his own people. Before letting the Blackleg's spirit go, Himiin revisited the path to the cave where he hoped to find Wren.

It was imperative he get Tattle-Tale away from the Blackleg party and get to Wren. He had to save her and her people. It was the only way to redeem himself for his selfishness.

He touched the boy's foot. Tattle-Tale yelped with surprise.

Himiin flinched even though he knew the two warriors leading the horses would not turn around. With Wewukiye and Sa-qan in the Blackleg bodies their escape would go unnoticed.

He twisted his head, bringing the boy into his view.

"I thought you were dead. You have not moved or said anything for a sun and a moon." The worry on Tattle-Tale's young face eased.

"I too thought I was dead, but I am feeling stronger." Himiin tried to scan the area from his downward position. "Are we coming to a passage through tall rock cliffs?"

The boy stretched his body, peering to the front of the line of horses. "Yes, I see the cliffs."

"When we enter the passage, I will tell you when to slip from your horse. Wait for me behind a boulder on your side of the trail."

Tattle-Tale nodded.

"Where is my sister?" His young eyes implored Himiin for good news.

"I do not know." He wished to comfort Wren's brother, but to give him false hope when he wasn't even sure what he would find, was something he could not do.

The boy's usually jovial face turned dark with disapproval. "Was she not with you when this happened?" He indicated the bruises and wounds on Hawk's body. "She could be dead or hurt badly like you."

"Someone kind will find her. This I am sure." He could say nothing more without giving away his existence to the boy.

"We are in the canyon." Tattle-Tale eyed him with skepticism.

Himiin shook away the thoughts of the vicious-looking marks he'd seen on Wren while Hawk thought of her. If the man were not already dead, he would have gladly killed him with his bare hands. The Blackleg deserved a thousand deaths for harming a Nimiipuu maiden. Especially Wren. Anyone who would treat the sweet woman of his heart so badly did not deserve to walk this earth. He ground his teeth against the anger boiling in him and watched closely for the spot to drop from the horses.

"Now."

Tattle-Tale dropped off his horse. Himiin watched the boy scramble behind a large boulder. He glanced forward. The two Blacklegs leading the horses remained unaware of the escape. Smiling smugly, he slipped from the moving horse. His feet touched the ground, and he rolled behind a mound of rocks. Kneeling, he peered over the rocks at the departing horses. The last two warriors never looked back. He sent up thanks to his siblings and tried standing. The legs of the vessel wobbled and pain shot through the stiff, battered limbs.

Ignoring the pain, he moved to the boulder where Tattle-Tale huddled, waiting for him.

"Come," he took the boy's arm, pulling him to his feet.

"How do I know you are not taking me some place to get rid of me?" The boy stubbornly planted his feet.

"I am taking you where the Blackleg will not look for you. You must stay there until it is safe to travel to your village."

"How do I know you did not kill my sister and plan to do the same to me?" Tattle-Tale crossed his arms.

"I do not have the time or patience for your little boy games." He moved passed the boy and headed up the narrow path carved in the rock cliff by tiny mountain goat hooves.

He didn't glance back, but soon heard the labored breathing and skittering of rock behind him as the boy followed. He had to stop and rest the fatigued vessel when he would have rather pushed on. Though the essence of the man was dead, his battered vessel would carry Himiin only if he did not push too hard.

They continued up the rock cliff to a large area with a flat rock extension, protecting the back of the ledge from sun, rain, and snow. The boy would wait here.

"You must stay here for three suns." Himiin waved his arm. "Then go over that ridge and down through the ravine. It will put you on a spot where you can look down upon the lake and see how to get to your village." He turned to leave.

"Where are you going, and how do you know a Nimiipuu mountain so well?" Tattle-Tale grabbed his arm, making Himiin face him. His young eyes, though skeptical, were also scared.

"Your sister told me of this place when we rode by." He placed a hand on the boy's head. "I will find your sister. Do as I say. Wait three suns, giving the Blackleg time to leave the mountain. They will not carry out their plan without you. But if you wander the mountain, they may find you again."

He looked to the south. "There is a small stream not far that way. You may drink of the sweet water and catch fish. But do not make a fire. Dry the fish in the sun or eat the root of the keeh-koot which grows not far past the stream." He squeezed the boy's shoulder. "You must stay here three suns to be sure all is well. Then head for the village the way I told you."

"My sister?"

"I will find her and bring her to your village."

Tattle-Tale nodded.

Himiin smiled encouragement and left the boy standing on the ledge watching his departure.

Half way down the mountain, he slipped from the Blackleg body, leaving it for the animals to feast upon. Back inside the wolf form, he loped through the trees thinking of Wren. He must get to her before an animal or another Blackleg. He had to save her, so she could fulfill her gift to her people. The visions he'd witnessed inside Hawk made his body quake with rage.

He caught a scent on the wind, every nerve bunched. Cautiously, he moved toward the vile odor. He knew not what form the dark spirit had taken and did not wish to be caught unaware.

He rounded a boulder and discovered a cougar with dark coloring on its legs standing in his path. The narrowing, yellow eyes told him it was the Blackleg spirit, and he waited for the spirit of the mountain.

"You are on my mountain. Do you not remember what I did the last time you were here?" Himiin never took his gaze from the creature. The large cougar equaled him in size, but possessed more agility. The spirit would be more determined than ever to take this mountain in a vessel with such power.

"You think you have bested the Blackleg. You are no match for me and my people." The cougar swished his long tail. The black tip quivered.

"We shall see." He circled the cougar, calculating the best form of attack.

The only way to stop this creature from following and discovering

Wren meant he had to kill the beautiful animal. An outcome destined to anger Sa-qan and the Creator. He cringed at the idea, but knew no other alternative. The vessel must be stopped, even though the spirit would again go free. Without a vessel, the spirit had to find another to continue his evil.

He worried the spirit might enter Tattle-Tale. The boy was not far away. Even though he had discovered long ago, the Blackleg spirit did not like to take man form. Something, he had always found interesting.

"Why is it you are never in man form?" Himiin hoped his curiosity bewildered the creature.

The cougar looked at him. His tail swished once, hard and fast, then stopped. His eyes gleamed. "I have been in man form. And it reestablished my claim man is the weakest of all creatures."

Himiin stared at the great mountain lion. "Why do you say that? Man can do things animals cannot."

"But a man has emotions. More than animals. Emotions which cause him more pain than a flesh wound." The cougar lunged as his words flashed the visions of Wren's bruised body before Himiin.

He recovered with barely time to skip to the side. The conversation ignited his emotions rather than his reactions. He needed to keep his wits about him. The cougar could kill the wolf body, but not him. Doing so would give the evil spirit the advantage of traveling faster. Himiin didn't know if this spirit knew where to find Wren, but he must make sure the creature he possessed could not help him.

The thought of the cougar coming upon Wren shook him to his claws. He would not let that happen. Fury pushed him forward. He charged the cougar, taking the animal to the ground.

They rolled, growled, screamed, and lashed out. The heavy body of the cougar fought harder than the previous vessel the dark spirit had taken.

Himiin shot to his paws when he broke free of the snarling animal. He barely registered the ledge and loose rock at the edge before the cat pounced at him. The large white fangs slashed at his shoulder and neck. The warmth of blood matted his hair and stirred him into action. The cougar could not win.

He must complete his duties. Wren needed him and her people had to be warned of the renegade band of Blacklegs.

The cougar backed him onto a rock ledge. Himiin glanced down.

182

It was a long fall to the bottom. One he did not wish to take.

He charged the cougar, knocking him against a boulder. The cat screamed in pain and lunged.

Himiin leaped to the side, and the cougar sailed over the edge. An eerie, outraged cry pierced through the silent forest as a wisp of smoke swirled out of the body before the animal hit the bottom.

《》《》《》

The Nimiipuu spirit won this round, but he would not win the next one. Dark Wolf watched the white wolf lick his wounds. The woman held the key. He would find a way to get her and destroy them both. It was the only way he could reside over the mountain.

As his spirit drifted to the ground, Dark Wolf searched for another vessel. A large buck stood under a fir tree, nibbling tender spring grass.

A perfect vessel. He could travel over the countryside unobserved and swiftly. Floating through the air, he entered the body. It was a shame he couldn't move about and take care of business as the wisp of smoke. There were times he found it hard to find a regal vessel.

He scowled. The Creator had made his existence harder to bear. He could not switch forms when he wished; first he had to find a vessel to take over.

Dark Wolf flicked the buck's antlers against the tree trunk and flexed the legs. This vessel would carry him across the mountain quickly.

The white wolf would go to the woman. He, Dark Wolf, would follow the spirit and get the woman. Now that the boy had been taken from the Blackleg raiding party, the woman was his best hope to get rid of the Nimiipuu once and for all.

Pú-timt wax kúyc

(19)

The morning sun spilled through the cave entrance, warming the small area and Wren's aching body. She remained awake the entire night fearing Hawk's return. Fatigue and terror battled as she curled in a tight ball on the ground to keep warm and listened for sounds of another in the cave. She could not take treatment like the night before again anytime soon.

The joyful songs of birds outside the cave nearly drove her to scream. How could everything go on as if nothing had happened? Her body had been savagely abused. She would never experience hatred for another as she did for the man who violated her and walked away, leaving behind vicious threats.

Neither anger nor her strength would defend her from the vile man. Her husband. A sob shook her body. As this warrior's wife, she would endure this treatment for years. The thought nearly stopped her heart.

She had to get away.

Go back to her people.

But how?

She listened harder. A slight breeze whistled in the cave followed by the trill of the early morning birds. There was no thump of hooves or snorting of a horse. Hawk had not returned. Or was this a trick? Had he left his horse a distance from the entrance, and once she stepped outside the cave would he attack her again? She shuddered, remembering his cruelty the night before.

She would not allow him to touch her again.

With great effort, she uncurled and winced at the pain. The juncture of her legs throbbed. She wished for a bath in a cold mountain stream to ease her aches and wash away the stench of the cave and her assailant.

Lifting her bound hands to her mouth, she chewed on the leather straps digging into her wrists. Her stomach ached from hunger. She swallowed the spit her chewing induced and managed to stop the gnawing pain in her belly. What would fill the hollow in her heart?

When her hands were free, she groped around the back of the cave for her dress. She tried twice to lift her arms before managing to hold the garment over her head. Her shoulders cried out in pain, and her arms shook with fatigue as she dropped the dress over her body. The leather garment lay heavy on her torn nipple, reminding her of the man's brutality.

A noise outside the cave stopped her heart and panic squeezed her throat. Was he back? How could she keep him from hurting her again? His size and cruelty outweighed her. She hid in the darkest area of the cave.

Crouching down, she pressed her back to the wall and used her hands to balance. Her fingers touched something familiar.

The wolf fang.

She clutched it in both hands and called to the one man she trusted with her heart.

Himiin, I need your strength to guide me. All is not what we were led to believe.

Flashes of the night before ran through her mind, she halted her plea to Himiin. Hawk had said no one would want her after his defilement. The pain the man inflicted left a scar in her memory. The breast with the hanging nipple would forever be a visible reminder. No man, no matter how much he professed to love her, could look beyond such damage.

Tears spilled down her face as she leaned against the hard dirt wall and wept. She would rather die in this cave than have the man who held her heart look upon her with disgust.

《》《》《》

Himiin paced at the edge of the tree line. Wren was in trouble. He'd heard her call. And though he'd told himself he wouldn't listen, her pleading voice had pierced his heart and opened his ears. He had to get to her. If he stepped off the mountain he would lose his spirit and be nothing more than a hollow vessel. How could he help her in that state? But she needed him. He sensed it with every breath he took.

"Oh Great Creator, grant me the privilege of traveling off the mountain to help Wren. She is a Nimiipuu woman worthy of my guidance. She was willing to sacrifice all she loved to help her people, but she has faced cruelty and possibly death without my aid. If she is given to the earth, she will never fulfill her vision. I ask you to show me the way to help her."

He stared at the sky. Wren's pleas penetrated his thoughts, squeezing his heart with fear, and flaring his anger.

He had to leave the mountain.

He had to save her.

She was his redemption.

"Creator, I have done things in the past that put me in disfavor in your eyes. This woman, Wren, has done nothing but wish to save her people. Do not let my bad decisions sway you from allowing me to help her. She is the future of the Nimiipuu."

Himiin stalked inside the tree line, his vision blurred with images of Wren. The Creator had to let him help. He was the only one who could.

Sa-qan landed beside him. "Brother, what is troubling you?"

"Hawk is dead." He glanced at is sister. The knowledge of the man's death did little to ease his wrath.

"By your deeds?" She watched him, her eyes barely revealing her thoughts.

"His vessel was nearly gone when I entered. But his thoughts—" Himiin shook with rage. "He harmed Wren in a way she may never recover."

"She is alive?"

"If that monster didn't do too much damage." He pushed by his sister to pace. "I have to get to her. I know where she is. I saw this while in his vessel."

He stared at his sister. The ache he felt over Wren's pain and loneliness proved more agony than anything he'd ever experienced. "I have asked the Creator to give me leave of the mountain."

"He has spoken to me and granted you three suns. You must hurry." The sympathy in her eyes let him know he would not be alone on his travels.

"We must hurry. Wren hasn't called to me for some time," he said, running from the mountain and straight toward the rising sun.

He followed the images he'd witnessed while in Hawk's body. They traveled up and down wooded hills, winding in and out of canyons, and crossing through streams until the sun began its descent toward the mountain behind them.

Sa-qan landed on the ground in front of him. "Let me fly ahead to scout for trouble and locate her. We are a long distance from Nimiipuu country."

"Hawk left her in a cave on the side of a hill." Himiin stared at the rise before him. Helplessness engulfed him at the knowledge the woman he loved was a short distance away scared and waiting for him.

"Stay here. I will hurry." Sa-qan jumped, spreading her great wings. Effortlessly, she soared into the sky, circling to the other side of the small hill.

His head pounded with frustration. Wren was out there somewhere; frightened and hurt. He wanted to run over the hill and find her. Kiss her worries away and take her back to the mountain.

With Hawk dead, she could remain with her people. His heart raced. They would spend her lifetime walking the mountain together. He could hold her in his arms and breathe in her sweet scent. Once she was back with the Nimiipuu he would do whatever it took to keep her there. Close to him.

Sa-qan returned. "I have found the cave. There was no sign of anyone."

"I will go to her."

"As a man or a wolf?" Sa-qan tipped her head toward him.

"As a man." Himiin closed his eyes, thought of holding Wren in his arms, and made the transformation from wolf to man.

"I think you would be less frightening to her as a wolf from what you have told me." Sa-qan waved her wing toward the hill. "Go to her, but go slow. She has not been treated well by a man."

He nodded and headed over the hill. Sa-qan flew ahead, leading him to a cave on the far side of a small valley. His heart raced with anticipation. He would soon hold Wren in his arms.

Listening at the entrance of the cave, he heard a painful whimpering. Surely that could not be Wren? Had she left and an animal taken over the cave?

Sa-qan landed near him and whispered, "If that is the woman, she is badly hurt."

His heart squeezed. The visions from Hawk had torn at him. The violence hard for him to fathom. How could his sweet Wren have withstood such torture?

He crawled into the cave. "Wren. Little bird. I am here to take you home."

A scuffling sound in the back of the cave drew his attention. He peered into the dark corner, and his stomach twisted with hate for the man who would do this to a woman. Her small body crouched in the dark recesses of the den. She gripped her bottom lip between her teeth as angry eyes stared back at him.

The carefree maiden with conviction no longer existed.

Stepping forward to take her in his arms, he stopped when her eyes enlarged and flashed with fear. She pressed against the wall so hard, dirt fell on her head.

The pain and anguish in her eyes nearly doubled him over as if someone had struck him in the stomach with a club.

"Wren, I won't harm you. And I promise no one will hurt you again." He sat down cross-legged in front of her, not wanting to loom over her. The wide eyes of a cornered animal stared at him. Her shaking hands clutched the wolf's fang.

"Hawk is dead. He will never hurt you again." He spoke in a soothing tone while the fury within buffeted him like angry storm clouds.

Hatred for the warrior shone in her eyes like a blazing forest fire. Her lips curled in distaste.

Her bruised and bloodied lips made him cringe. Trailing his gaze down her neck, he found bruised and scraped skin and bite marks. An ugly red welt ringed her neck. The man had tried to strangle her with a piece of leather. Himiin shot to his feet and banged his head on the ceiling of the cave.

How dare the man do this to a woman? Any woman, especially Wren. *His woman.*

His impetuous actions startled Wren. He gulped down the rage blazing in him and dropped to his knees. The more he saw of her injuries the harder it became to contain the anger he felt for a man who should have died a much more violent death.

"Wren, let me take you home." He held out his hand.

"No." She shook her head and twisted to avoid eye contact.

"You don't want to go home? To the mountain?" After all she'd been through; he'd expect her to run back to her sanctuary.

"I am no good for anyone anymore." Tears trickled down her face. "It is best to leave me here."

The bluntness of her statement hurt him more than the sight of her bruises and welts. The man had led her to believe she was now worthless as dust.

"You are good for me and your people. I wish you to come back to the mountain with me." He wanted to grab her up in his arms and head for the mountain. If she struggled, he would hang onto her until she realized he would never let go. But the fear and agony in her eyes kept him from attempting anything so impulsive and stupid.

"You will not want me once you have laid eyes on me in the light. Go away." Wren wanted to jump into his arms and believe nothing would ever hurt her again, but she could not. Once he saw the damage Hawk had done to her, the man she desired would shun her. His rejection she could not take. She wished to die right here—where her body was taken from her.

"You do not know how I will react. Step outside the cave and let me see for myself." He stood and offered her a hand.

"You do not want to see. You do not want me. Not now. Not ever. This I know."

The indignation that flared in his eyes surprised her.

"Do not tell me you know my emotions. Only I know the greatness of my passion for you, not you or anyone else." He moved his hand. "Come out into the light, and let me see."

She wanted to believe he loved her as deeply as she loved him. But he was a spirit; he had a long lifetime ahead of him. He would find another who could bring him joy. She would waste away to a hideous old woman.

The daylight receded. If she stalled, it would be dark soon, and he would not be able to see her. Even though she wished to die in this cave, she did not want to spend a night alone. These conflicting sentiments confused her. Her whole existence confused her.

"Are you stalling?" He smiled and his eyes lit up with humor. The color of his eyes warmed her.

She looked away. Her treacherous heart could not stop her from what must be done. She had to get him to leave—without her.

"How is it you are off the mountain and could not be here to stop Hawk?" She stared at his face. Remorse dulled his eyes and wilted his smile. "I thought you could not leave."

"When I learned of Hawk's evil and heard your plea, I asked the Creator to allow me off the mountain to find you." He crouched in front of her. The warmth his body radiated did little to warm her cold skin.

"You-you know what he did?" The terror of Hawk's assault came back in haunting clarity. Her body wanted to curl as her fists clenched.

"Yes. I took over Hawk's body to get your brother away from the Blackleg raiding party."

"My brother? Blackleg raiding party? On our mountain?" She searched his face, confused. Had the whole Nimiipuu world gone wrong since she went willingly with the Blackleg warrior? What of her weyekin? Why did this all happen?

"I'm not sure how Tattle-Tale became caught, but he is now safe. While using Hawk's body to help him escape, I learned of the Blackleg's viciousness." His eyes dulled with remorse. "I caused his actions and your pain. Can you forgive me?"

She stared at the man in disbelief. How could he even think he was the cause of her torment? "You did nothing to make that man hurt me."

"It was because you did not come to him as a maiden he hurt you." His voice cracked with emotion.

"He was vicious to me before he found out I had been with another. His cruelty had nothing to do with you or me. He never intended to keep the peace."

Himiin's eyes glinted with hatred as his lips grimaced with remorse. "Had I known he would not honor you, I would have taken you from him on the mountain and done battle with your weyekin."

He touched her cheek so gently, tears burned in her eyes. Her heart hummed.

"You are too precious to let anyone destroy. Come back to the mountain with me. I promise no one will hurt you again." He took her hand, studied the red welts ringing her wrist and softly placed kisses all the way around the mark. "Let me help you heal."

Where his lips touched, her wounds no longer stung. Her breath caught. This man would never cause her harm or allow it to happen if he could.

"I wish a bath very badly," she said, sniffling back tears of joy.

"I know the perfect spot, but we will not get there until the morning. Can you wait?" His eyes watched her wistfully.

"If it is a far distance, I do not think I can make it. I tried standing earlier." Her face heated with embarrassment. "It is painful."

The flare of anger in his eyes quickly turned to tenderness. "You do not have to walk. I will carry you."

"But, you cannot carry me so far."

He took her hands, helping her to her feet. She winced as the pain in her thighs and between her legs responded from the movement.

"Can you crawl out of the cave?"

"I will try."

He motioned for her to go ahead of him.

She dropped to her knees and slowly crawled out. Her whole body ached when she tried to stand. Himiin carefully bent, placed an arm under her knees and behind her back. He stood, cradling her in his arms.

"Does this hurt you anywhere?" His breath warmed her ear.

"No."

"Then this is how I will carry you." He walked toward a large bald eagle who stood a short distance away.

"She is well?" the eagle asked, walking toward them. Her yellow eyes stared at Wren intently.

"She is well enough to travel to the mountain," Himiin said, holding her as if she weighed no more than a pine needle.

"And you are?" Wren asked, watching the interplay between the eagle and Himiin.

"I am Sa-qan, Himiin's sister. He has asked a lot of the Creator to allow him to come to you. You have captured my brother's heart. If you love him, do not dishonor him." The eagle spread her wings as Himiin cleared his throat.

"My sister does not think it is good I formed such a strong bond with a mortal." He winked at the eagle. "But she is just jealous."

The eagle snorted. "I have looked around while you were in the cave. There does not seem to be any Blackleg for a great distance. I did find some bodies over the hill in a clearing."

Wren gasped. "Hawk left to meet his friends at a clearing." Her heart pounded from the memory of his parting words.

"Shh, he cannot harm you now." Himiin must have sensed her panic. He held her closer and kissed her hair. She rested her head against his chest. Peace slipped through her, relaxing and soothing, for the first time since Hawk flung her on his horse and raced away from her village.

"I will fly ahead and make certain you do not run into any trouble." Sa-qan spread her wings and jumped into the air. With hardly a sound, she disappeared into the star-filled night sky.

"Hold on." Himiin snuggled her closer to his chest and started off at a run.

They traveled along the top of a ravine. The cool evening air fluttered across her cheeks before she folded her arms and buried her head against his chest, clinging to his strength and safety. She marveled at his even breathing as the wind rushed past them. Once they were a good distance away from the cave and hidden in a grove of cottonwood trees, he stopped.

His breathing barely labored when he set her feet on the ground. As much as she longed to linger in his powerful arms and the intimacy in his beautiful eyes, she could not allow herself such fantasies. No matter how he talked, there was still the chance he would turn from her when he knew the extent of her abuse. She must keep her heart distant or be crushed.

"Thank you, for coming to my aid." Her breath caught when his arms embraced her, pulling her tight against him. She bit her lip when the embrace pinched her injured breast.

He placed his cheek upon her head. "I thought I would never see you again. Then you called, and I feared I would not be able to help you."

Her heart stopped when small wet droplets touched her scalp. She slipped from his embrace. Placing her hands on either side of his face, she gazed at him in the light of a partial moon. Tears glistened in his eyes. His fear for her moved her beyond words. Gently, she pulled his head down and kissed the tears at the corners of his eyes.

"The feelings you have for me are strong—now. They may not remain so when you have looked upon me in the light."

"Again, you think you know me. And I thought I knew you. Where is the woman willing to sacrifice all for her people?"

"That woman has sacrificed all, and yet, her people will find no peace. The man who proclaimed to help build that peace did not speak the truth." She spat on the ground. "He used me to get my father's horses, and he used me till I wanted to die." Tears burned her eyes at the humiliation the man put her through.

Himiin tipped her chin up with one finger. "I am glad you did not die." He could not hide the glint of anger changing the color in his eyes as he consoled her.

"But what good is surviving if my chance to give my gift to the people is gone?" She had many hours waiting and wondering when Hawk would return and torture her more to think about her bleak future and the future of the Nimiipuu.

"Was that really my gift? Or some test of the Creator?" She glared at him. "If he is testing me in this way, he is as cruel as the Blackleg."

"I do not think it was meant to happen this way. He would not have allowed me to come to you if you followed the words of your weyekin." Himiin took her hand. "I do not think it was your gift to bring peace between the Blackleg and the Nimiipuu."

"That is good. I will never accept peace with the Blackleg." Her heart weighed heavy and cold. Her experience at the hands of a Blackleg would never leave her.

"I believe if this had truly been the gift to your people, it would have happened. Another opportunity to fulfill your gift will come along." He grasped her shoulders. She winced and the pain it brought to his eyes made her suffer more.

"This I believe as strongly as I believe you and I are meant to be together." The love he professed for her shone in the deep blue emotion of his eyes. If only she believed she deserved that love.

Her stomach growled.

"You need food." Himiin turned the conversation from Wren's burdensome problems to something easier to handle. Right now he wanted her focused on his attentiveness and love. She'd been through

Paty Jager

a harrowing experience, one which would take a lot of work to overshadow. His sister might disapprove of his infatuation for a mortal, but he could not tell his heart whom he should care for. Nor did he want to. Not if loving Wren made his life complete.

"Come, we must find you food and keep moving if we are to reach your village before the Blackleg." He gathered her in his arms once more.

"What do you mean before the Blacklegs?" She peered at him with anxious eyes.

"When Sa-qan and Wewukiye helped me free your brother, they overheard the group talking about raiding the village and taking Proud and Tall's horses." He glanced down. Her face had gone white. "We will get there before the raiding party and warn your father. All will be fine."

She rested her head on his chest. His words comforted her. Words were all he had to buffer the truth. There would be a battle before the Blackleg left Nimiipuu territory and lives would be lost. He hoped by warning the Nimiipuu there would be fewer deaths than from a surprise attack.

Le'éptit

(20)

Himiin stopped in a meadow. The purple flowers of the *kehmmes* bobbed in the slight breeze. Mixed in among the taller plants were the fringed, pink blossoms of the *thlee-tahn*.

He placed his lips against Wren's ear and whispered. "I have found food to sustain you until we are on the mountain."

Her head slowly lifted from his chest. The sleepy droop to her eyes made her appear younger than her eighteen summers. The suffering in the depths, made him grieve for the woman she was before taken from the mountain.

"Where are we?" She wiggled her feet toward the ground. He set her down and motioned.

"We are surrounded by kehmmes and thlee-tahn. I will dig the roots for you." He searched for a stick suitable for the task. These two plants were the earliest of the roots gathered by the Nimiipuu. Luck had brought him to a meadow with both.

"I can help," Wren said, grimacing as she walked to a clump of kehmmes.

"Sit. I will bring the root to you." He lowered her to the ground and dug in the earth with his stick near a clump of purple flowers. Wren chanted a song to Mother Earth for her giving this child of the earth to them for nourishment.

When he had several bulbs dug, he handed them to Wren. She

cleaned the dirt and outside layer from the bulbs and took a bite.

He watched her with fascination. Her eyes closed while her lips curved in a satisfied smile.

"It is good?" he asked.

"Yes. My empty stomach welcomes this treat."

"How does it taste?" He sat down beside her, watching the motion of her jaw as she chewed.

"You have never eaten a kehmmes?" She stared at him as if he'd changed into a wolf before her eyes.

"As a spirit I do not require nourishment."

"You do not eat?" She scanned his arms and broad chest. "How did you grow so big?"

"This is the body I had before…" He stopped before uttering the failings of his father.

"Before what?" She placed a hand upon his arm and searched his face with her gaze.

"Before I became a spirit."

"You have not always been a spirit?" Her curiosity echoed in her voice. "How can that be?"

He glanced into the surrounding trees.

"You know all that is in my heart. You should return the favor." She grasped his chin, drawing his gaze to her face.

The empathy in her eyes and the encouraging smile on her lips, straightened his shoulders.

"My family lived in the land closer to the cold. My father was weak of spirit. He followed the wrong people and believed in those who would make him a fool. One day, he listened to coyote and wishing to bring back more food from a hunting party to impress my grandfather, he led the party, all the bands best warriors, into an ambush. He was the only survivor, because of his cowardice. He bolted at the first sign of danger." Himiin hung his head. He still found it hard to believe he came from the loins of such a man.

"Then what happened?"

"When he came into the village bragging of his escape and generously giving the meat others had killed to the grieving families, the Creator turned him to stone and whisked Wewukiye, Sa-qan, and myself away, making us spirits." He glanced at her, expecting to see the same hateful gleam the members of the band had exacted upon them.

She sat quietly for a long time and munched on the root as her forehead wrinkled in thought. Finally, she swallowed the last of the bulb and smiled at him.

"I do not think the Creator made you a spirit for punishment. I think he whisked you away to save you from the hatred your father put in the rest of your people." She touched his arm. "Why would he make someone he felt as weak as your father a spirit? Spirits must be strong and of good judgment."

Himiin studied her. He had not reasoned the matter. He'd believed being a spirit was punishment.

He picked up a bulb from her lap. "Eat."

She took the offering and wiped it clean. "What else do you not do that a mortal does?"

"I do not sleep." He shrugged. He'd never thought of how this would be strange to a mortal.

"Your body does not get tired?" She placed the last bit of the root in her mouth and licked her fingers.

Need sliced through Himiin as he watched her pink tongue touch each fingertip. He wished to taste her fingers as well. Not so much to taste the root, but to savor the intimacy with the woman. It was odd he did not require the other things which kept a mortal alive, yet since meeting Wren, his body ached and hungered for her. How could this be?

She picked up another root, sliding it between her soft lips. "Are you sure you do not want to at least taste it?" She held out the root with the pattern of her small teeth marks. His groin ached. If she knew the thoughts raging in him she would skitter away.

Swallowing the lump of passion in his throat, he turned his head. "Eat faster. The moon is heading downward."

The crunch as she bit into the root and the smacking of her lips suggested she ate the last one. He glanced at her. The roots had vanished. Her eyes sagged half-closed in satisfaction.

"Come, we must leave." He held out his hand and helped Wren to her feet. He scooped her up into his arms and hurried across the meadow.

She dozed, cradled in his arms as he kept a steady pace toward the mountain which loomed ever closer. The moon disappeared, and the sun gradually climbed higher. When the sun blazed directly overhead in the blue sky, he finally stopped.

He stood Wren on the ground, holding her until her legs became stable.

Himiin dropped to his knees. "I have returned," he said, raising his arms to the sky and chanting.

Wren knelt beside Himiin. His strong voice thanked the Creator for allowing him to go to her. She squeezed her eyes shut, holding the tears back. The man beside her had saved her and now thanked the Creator for her very existence. How could he hold her so dear, knowing the evil that had touched her? Did he believe she was no different than when she left?

If so, he would be greatly disturb to know the battle going on within. She had lost faith in the Creator and herself as a Nimiipuu. She had failed her people, once again, and her weyekin. There would be no peace with the Blackleg. A raiding party was on its way to ambush her family. All because of her.

A tear slipped from her eye. She and Himiin could return to find nothing but the charred remains of her village.

When Himiin finished chanting, he turned to her. "We may take some time for you to rest."

"I do not need rest. I slept in your arms and am ready to continue on." She touched his arm. "We must arrive to warn my people before the Blackleg."

"We will." He took a step back. "Would you like a bath?"

His action and words hit her like a slap. "Do you smell the vileness of the Blackleg on me?" The shame of her ordeal reminded her Himiin would never feel the same for her as before.

"No!" He stepped close and drew her against his side. His arm encircled her shoulders in a comforting embrace. "I am not suggesting you need to bathe. You requested it back in the cave." He continued to hold her. "Would you rather have more to eat first?"

She scanned the area. "I would prefer a bath. But where is the stream?"

His arm slid from her shoulder and clasped her hand. "Come with me. I have better."

The charm of his excitement to show her something caused her to smile and follow willingly. She knew they must hurry to warn her people, but being with Himiin and seeing his happiness, made her wish they never had to return to the village. Never had to face her family and tell them of her shame and failure to her weyekin.

They climbed up around the side of the mountain. During the climb, Himiin stopped often to ease her steps and allow her sore body a respite.

The sound of splashing water became louder. Before long, they stood halfway between the top and bottom of a spectacular waterfall. The sparkling liquid spilled down over the edge of a cliff, splashing into a deep lagoon before cascading over colorful round boulders and through the trees.

"Beautiful." She stared at the shimmering water. Birds flew in and out of the spray, while a doe stood at the pool of water, drinking.

Himiin tugged on her hand, carefully navigating down the rocks to get to the pool. "This is a nice spot to bathe," he said, glancing at the water then back at her. A sly smile tipped the corners of his full lips. Passion burned in his eyes. A shiver crept up her spine even though she knew deep down he would never do anything to hurt her.

"What will you do while I bathe?" she asked, taking a step toward the shimmering, crystal lagoon. She did not need to see into his eyes to know her question wounded him. However, after her ordeal with the Blackleg, she did not wish Himiin or anyone to see her or touch her intimately.

"I could catch you a fish to eat." The words warmed the back of her neck, he stood so close. She spun and nearly bumped her nose into his chest. "But I believe you will need my assistance with your bath."

"I can manage." She backed up and stepped into the icy water. The chill was nothing compared to the trepidation snaking up her spine.

"Then take off your dress and go in." He stood before her, his arms crossed, waiting.

"Turn around. You do not want to see me." She motioned with her finger for him to spin.

"No."

The finality of his one word squeezed her chest as panic lodged in her throat. He could not see her battered body. She had not even seen it. In the dark, she had donned her dress and had no idea what hideous sights she would find when she took it off. By the throbbing in her

199

Paty Jager

breast, she was certain no one should witness such a sight. Not even her.

"You cannot see my body." She refused to look at him.

Himiin tipped her chin up. His compassion-filled eyes stared into hers, making her view the depth of his concern.

"I know what Hawk did. I was in his body seeking knowledge of you." His throat bobbed as he swallowed the anger she heard in his voice. "I saw the vile things."

She stared at the ground between their feet. Ashamed he witnessed the acts she endured.

"Do not feel shame for someone else's actions." He touched her cheek with the back of his hand. "You are strong and brave. Do not let this man's evil make you meek. Do not give him the power to take away who you are." His words spoke what she feared: to become scared of men and live her life never knowing the joys of companionship. Gazing into Himiin's eyes, she knew he would never let her become weak.

"Let me help you bathe." He spoke quietly as he crouched before her and grasped the bottom of her dress.

She watched him. His eyes glistened with sincerity. She'd trusted this man before.

"May I take off your dress?"

Battling mortification and the need to feel someone care, she barely nodded.

He raised her dress carefully, lifting it over her head. She tried to help, but her arms did not cooperate. They ached from being stretched and felt heavy as logs. One by one, he helped her arms through the sleeves. She winced at every movement.

He tossed the dress to the grass. She averted her eyes, refusing to view his face as he gazed upon her violated body.

Himiin scanned the full length of her.

His heart stopped at the sight of one nipple hanging askew and the dried blood marring her skin. What kind of torture must she have endured? He forced back the rage that boiled in his chest and untied his leggings, letting them fall to the ground at his feet.

He had to suppress his anger. To show it would only upset Wren. Telling himself to think only of the woman and not the schemer who tortured her, he pulled his moccasins off. He stood naked before her, and she still did not look at him.

He walked passed her and into the lagoon. Diving, he swam underwater before breaking the surface.

"Come in. I promise to do nothing you do not approve."

She watched him bobbing in the water. The longing in her eyes, proved she would soon join him.

Himiin dove under again and swam over to where the waterfall splashed into the lagoon. He popped up and glanced back at the water's edge. Wren's head and shoulders poked out of the water. She vigorously scrubbed at her arms. He knew she would not be able to clean her whole body by herself. He ducked under the water and swam to where she stood.

The cold water caressing Wren's bruises eased her discomfort. The weightlessness of her body in the deep water took the strain from her battered muscles.

Himiin paddled up close to her, but did not touch. "Would you like help with your hair?"

Ridding her body of the stench and dirt from the cave lifted her spirits. Without hesitation she answered, "Yes."

"Turn," he said, indicating with a twirl of his finger.

She obediently turned. His hands went to work, loosening her braids. The strong fingers massaged her head and weakened her knees.

"Relax, lean back." He held her head, drawing her body up to float near the top of the water. He cleaned her hair, rubbing it in his hands. The strands floated in the water around her, tickling her shoulders.

His gentle hands traveled to her neck, skimming over her raw skin, massaging and scrubbing. The trail of his hands down her shoulders and arms and over to her breasts, soothed. At the injured nipple, he lovingly caressed the base, working his hands up to the wound.

Her breath hitched as he touched the offending tip. How could he react with kindness when she was ugly?

"There is filth which needs to be cleaned or you will become sick." His eyes reflected his concern and caring. "Will you allow me to clean this?"

How could he, after seeing her battered, ugly body and knowing what had been done to her, still care so deeply? She swallowed a lump of emotion and nodded her head.

"If it hurts, tell me." He grasped her hand and squeezed gently.

Wren nodded and shut her eyes. She did not want to see her wound nor watch him touching it. The way it had come about was vile and hideous to her. How he could even look at it, let alone touch it, was something she did not understand.

Thankfully the coldness of the water had numbed her body. His touch was soft, never once causing her discomfort as he administered to her wound.

Floating in the water, eyes closed, the sun beating warm upon her face, she could almost forget what happened to her. Almost.

The warm path of his hands caressing her body and moving down over her hips let her know he had finished cleansing her breast.

The whole time his hands soothed and massaged, his soft, deep voice murmured endearments.

"Do not be alarmed," he cooed when his hands slipped between her legs, spreading them only enough to run his hands across her skin and cleanse the juncture of her legs. His movements did not invade her body. His calm voice and tender touch relaxed her.

By the time he finished rubbing her feet, it felt as if the water around her boiled like a basket of soup. Her body hummed and throbbed with desire for the man standing at her feet, grinning. As she drifted in the water, he aroused every inch of her body with his gentle touch and caring.

After her assault, she believed she could never harbor emotions for any man again.

Himiin smiled at the desire shining in Wren's eyes. It would be some time before they could make love with the injuries she had sustained. But it was good to see she still had the craving.

"You are now clean." He pulled her feet, and then her knees drawing her over to stand in front of him.

"I feel more than clean." Her eyes sparkled.

He couldn't wait any longer. He had to kiss her. Taking her head in his hands and sliding his fingers into her hair, he bent to her lips. She hesitated, but soon her lips opened, and he tasted her. Sighing, he took a breath and deepened the kiss. He reveled in her sweetness and savored her lips.

Her arms wrapped around his waist, hugging him to her. Her

breasts pressed against his chest. He worried about her injuries and tried to pull back.

Her arms fell to her side. Dejection dulled her eyes. Her response nearly buckled his knees.

"What is wrong?" He tipped her chin up to gaze into her face.

"You pulled away." Large tears formed in her eyes. "I knew you could not forget what has happened to me."

"I will never forget, but that is not why I pulled back." He placed a hand under her injured breast, lifting it for her to see. "I did not want you hurting yourself." He bent, kissing the wound, her breast, collarbone, neck, jaw, and finally resting his lips upon hers. Holding his mouth slightly above her lips he whispered, "There will never be anything that could make me not love you." He kissed her long and slow before carrying her out of the lake.

Placing her on her feet, he ran his hands over her body, stripping the water from her skin. He spread her dress under a tree and led her to it. "Rest while I find you more nourishment."

"I am not tired." She sat on the dress and smiled up at him. Himiin had never seen anything as lovely. Her lips curved in a beguiling smile. Only remnants of her harrowing ordeal flickered in her brown eyes. With more loving and encouragement, she would be her fighting self in no time.

"Then make a fire. I will catch you a fish to eat." He bent, kissed the top of her head, and wandered along the stream away from the waterfall.

He slipped and tripped around in the water, splashing and making all kinds of noise. Himiin glanced toward the waterfall frequently to make sure she didn't have problems starting a fire.

At peace, he concentrated on the fat, speckled fish darting into yet another hiding spot. The creature was fast and slippery, making the job of catching him harder than he had anticipated.

The trout re-emerged from under a rock. Watching the sleek sides shimmer in the sunlight, Himiin moved slowly up behind the fish, barely picking his feet up so as not to disturb the creature nor the silt on the bottom.

The trout hovered near a rock, his tail swishing back and forth. Himiin bent and cupped the fish in his hand, swinging it up and out of the water. The trout flew through the air, landing on the grass beside the stream, flopping and gasping.

He grinned and proudly looked around. He accomplished a feat he had only ever witnessed. As a spirit he required no food. Therefore, he had not hunted or gathered. His chest expanded with pride to know he not only dug roots, but caught food for Wren. Now he knew the gratification and triumph of warriors who brought back bounties to feed their families.

He sloshed out of the water and up to the flailing fish. The acrid scent of smoke burned his nostrils. He glanced back toward the lagoon. Wren was dressed and huddled over a small pile of sticks. She waved her hands and coughed at the gray spirals rising out of the mound.

Himiin hurried to where she knelt. He held out his catch. "Will this feed you?"

"It should fill me well." She banked more sticks in the hole she had dug. "Go find some large leaves." She shooed him away and picked up the trout.

Leaving her to take care of the fish, he walked through a grove of cottonwood trees, gathering the largest green leaves he could find. He wasn't sure what she planned to do with them, but he'd witnessed the Nimiipuu warriors take leaf-wrapped packets out of their quivers and eat what was inside.

When he returned to the fire, white hot rocks lined the bottom of the hole. The burning sticks were pushed to one side.

"Thank you." Wren took the leaves and spread them on the ground in several layers. She placed the trout in the leaves, wrapping the layers around the fish. Carefully, she set the leaf-wrapped trout on the white rocks and covered it with more rocks before pulling the burning sticks over the top.

She smiled when she finished the task. His heart thudded with happiness. The high-spirited woman he first met was slowly coming back to him.

"You have much confidence and wisdom for one so young." Himiin sat next to her on a log he had pulled up to the fire. He never wanted to be away from her side again.

"We learn at a young age how to take care of ourselves and others." She glanced at him. Her eyes held the haunted look of one who has seen too many horrors. "I did not feel confident at the hands of Hawk. I tried to stop him." She wrapped her arms about her body. "It only made him worse."

She fingered the fang hanging around her neck. "When he saw this he ripped it from my neck." Her gaze sought his face. "He demanded to know who gave it to me. I said I found it." She shuddered. "He became enraged at the discovery I was not a maiden." Her eyes enlarged with fear. "I would have rather he hit me with his fists than what he did to me."

Himiin put his arm around her shoulders, pulling her to his chest and the beating of his suffering heart. His actions brought about the Blackleg's wrath.

"I should have been the one punished. It was my selfish need to make love." He seethed with remorse. "I should have been stronger."

"You are not to blame. I seduced you that night. I wanted to have experienced love." She grasped his face between her hands.

"Through my selfish actions, I harmed you. I failed. I am unworthy of both the Nimiipuu and you." He would forever hold the blame for her ordeal. He would return her to her father and then take whatever retribution the Creator doled out.

"No! You tried to tell me I should not go with the Blackleg. I refused to listen. I felt to disobey this time would bring worse fates for my people than my foolish behaviors in the past." Wren smoothed her finger back and forth across his cheeks. "We both knew in here," she touched her stomach, "it did not feel right, yet, we listened to everyone else. Hoping it was my gift and would be well."

She spoke the truth. If he hadn't felt honor bound to not talk her out of marrying the Blackleg, she would not have left the mountain.

She shook her head. "You, nor I, had any way of knowing things would turn out this way."

"Yes, we did. We know the Blackleg. They have always been untrustworthy." He pulled her closer. "I should have gone against my duty and persuaded you and your family it was not good to send you to the Blackleg."

"I would have gone. I believed my weyekin had shown me my gift." She stared into his eyes. The conviction he saw humbled him. He'd never felt as strong about anything. Until now. He would do whatever it took to keep the woman in his arms alive.

"When you have eaten, we must keep going." The Blackleg

raiding party could be on its way to the village even though they no longer had Tattle-Tale to get them through unscathed.

"After swimming and building the fire, I feel too weak to continue without resting."

"Eat your fish and rest." He kissed the top of her head. "I will scout while you sleep."

She scraped back the ashes, lifted the rocks with the sticks, and plucked the wrapped fish off the rocks. Placing the package on a flat rock, she pushed the leaves aside. Steam and the smell of cooked fish rose in the air.

She ate eagerly. When her stomach was full and her eye lids drooped, he settled her in an aspen grove. After placing a kiss on her forehead, he headed up the mountain.

Glancing back, he smiled. Wren had moved into the sun. Her arms were flung out to her sides where she sprawled in the grass under the warm rays.

He continued up the side of the mountain, searching for a spot where he could see for a great distance. A buck deer wandered by. The hair on the back of his neck quivered. The buck showed no fear, aimlessly walking out of sight. Himiin raised his face to the sky. His body warmed and glowed as he changed into wolf form.

Sniffing, his hair bristled. The tang of evil hung in the air.

The Blackleg spirit hid in the buck.

He took off through the trees, following the scent. From the easy trail, the spirit knew he followed. Why was the Blackleg spirit leading him this way?

Wren.

She was alone by the waterfall. Did the spirit know this? What was his plan for her? Wondering if he should continue the chase or go back to Wren, Himiin leaped up on a rock and surveyed the area.

The course the buck took did not circle back to Wren. Could he be meeting the Blackleg raiding party? Himiin watched the waterfall crash over the cliff and down to the quiet lagoon below. He could see Wren sleeping in the sun. If he could see her, could the blackleg spirit as well? Would the spirit turn from his goal to harm her?

His body twitched, ready to sprint to Wren. Indecision battled within. He decided to follow the spirit. If he met up with the Blackleg raiding party it would be good to know their location. If the spirit circled back to the waterfall and Wren—he would deal with the Blackleg spirit.

Paty Jager

Le'éptit wax ná-qt

(21)

Wren woke as the sun disappeared over the mountain. Stretching, she sat up and called to Himiin. Her voice floated to a whisper beyond the thundering of the waterfall and twitter of birds in the trees.

What kept him so long? He knew the urgency to get to the village to warn of the Blackleg attack.

A twinge in her stomach made her anxious. In her dreams she had been with child. When the child arrived, he had the look and viciousness of the Blackleg Hawk. During Hawk's assault on her, his seed had spilled in her many times. So many times, she was certain she would become with child.

Wren shuddered. She would not bring something which would remind her of her torturous night into this world or another Blackleg. There were ways to make sure his seed did not take root. If Hawk had not pulled her onto his horse so hastily, leaving all her belongings behind, she would have her herb pouch. Without her herbs she would have to find more.

As she and Himiin made their way down to the lagoon, Wren had noticed a patch of dogbane. Boiling the root would give her the medicine she wished. Smoke from the smoldering fire tickled her nose. If she replenished the fire and found a hollow rock or piece of wood, she could boil water to make the drink.

Gathering small twigs, she searched for the needed items. She could find nothing to hold enough water, but found a large armful of twigs to add to the smoldering ashes.

She climbed up the side of the canyon they had followed to the lagoon. Several times she stopped and rested her sore legs. The fragrant scent of dogbane caught her attention before she spotted the small, pink blossoms. Using a stick and her hands, she dug around the plant, extracting enough of the root to make a drink for this day.

Glancing at the lagoon far below, spray from the water cascading over the edge of the cliff misted her face. She should remain nearby. When Himiin returned, he would be upset to find her missing. However, she desired to find something to use to hold the drink and walked deeper into the woods.

She squinted into the growing dusk and scanned the undergrowth for an object to boil her water. Her gaze also scanned the area for signs of Himiin.

A log caught on her dress. Reaching down to release its hold, she spied a bowl-shaped rock. With the rock and root clutched to her chest, she hurried back to the lagoon, sliding part of the way down the incline, adding more bruises to her battered body.

The lure of the shiny, smooth pool drew her to the edge of the water. She stared into the sparkling liquid that tumbled over the cliff and splashed into the pool. The water droplets glittered in the light of the new moon.

The beauty of the water and a yearning to slide into its glistening depths, enticed her to forget about the rock and the roots. She pulled her dress over her head, dropping it to the ground and stepped into the pool. Chills raced up her body, standing her hair on end. Slowly, she walked deeper and deeper, until she had to paddle with her hands and feet.

Her body grew used to the cold, and she swam to where the waterfall fell into the pool. She dove, swimming under the pressure of the falling water and surfacing on the back side of the waterfall. The wall of water distorted the world beyond, making her laugh with delight. The echo of her laughter filled her with happiness and wonder. How could she have thought, only a day ago, she wished to leave this world? There was still so much of the mountain she had yet to see and experience.

She stared at the shimmering wall of water, allowing the steady cadence of the thundering roar to seep into her. The sound vibrated her body, bringing forth a song of beauty and strength. As the words floated from her, the pain in her body and heaviness in her heart lessened. The miracle of the moment lifted her burdens and helped her to see she had yet to give her gift to her people. All was not lost. As she cowered in the cave waiting for the Blackleg to return, she had believed her gift would never be fulfilled. Being back on the mountain, she realized there was much she could do to put her in favor with her people, her father, and her weyekin.

Her song ended, and she spun to see what the earth looked like behind the waterfall. The jagged cliff had a large gaping hole just above the surface of the water. She started toward the opening. Anxiety fluttered in her belly. She should not explore without Himiin.

Scanning the cave entrance, the falling water, and dazzling light display beyond the curtain of shimmering liquid, she thought of the wondrousness of the Creator to make beautiful things and the glorious days filled with sunshine and warmth.

And the cave behind her which beckoned.

She glanced over her shoulder at the dark hole in the earth, speculating what could be in the cave and where it led. As she peered and wondered, her name fluttered gently around her. Could Himiin be in the cave? How else would she hear her name above the roar of the falling water unless it was the person of her heart who called to her?

She swam to the shallow water and stood. Someone whispered her name. She took a step toward the cave opening, anxious to see both the inside of the mountain and Himiin.

Apprehension slithered up her spine.

Who or what called to her from the darkness? If it were Himiin, he would show himself. She ignored the beckoning and looked through the veil of water. Someone stood by her dress and picked it up. The flaxen hair made her heart trill with happiness.

Himiin was back.

She dove under the falls once more, bobbing up in the middle of the lagoon. The water streamed from her head and face when she paddled to keep afloat.

"Are you a woman or an otter?" Himiin asked, holding her dress and watching her swim.

"A woman," she answered and swam toward him.

"Then why do you dive and bob like an otter?" He stepped into the water. "Why is there a hollow rock and dogbane root beside your dress?" He motioned toward the items on the grass at the edge of the lagoon.

Embarrassment heated her face. Should she tell him her fears? The concern in his eyes and his gentleness earlier gave her the courage to speak her heart.

"I do not wish to bring a child of the Blackleg into this world."

His eyebrow arched, but his eyes held no censure.

"As many times as Hawk spilled his seed in me, I fear I may become with child." Tears of humiliation slid down her cheeks. "I do not wish to carry his child within me or bring a Blackleg into this world. What he did was too horrible to relive every time I see what his seed has produced."

Himiin took a step toward her and held out his hand. "Come, we will make the drink, but we must hurry."

Fear tickled the hair on her arms. "You have seen the Blackleg?"

"Yes, they are headed to your village. We must hurry to warn your father."

Wren grasped his hand and followed him out of the lagoon. Not even bothering to dress, she picked up the rock bowl and filled it with water. Himiin carried the roots to a flat stone and smashed them with another round stone.

She placed the rock bowl next to the fire and added a red hot stone along with the smashed roots. The liquid fizzed and steamed. When the water no longer moved, she removed the stone, swirled the contents and held the bowl to her lips, drinking all of the bitter liquid.

While she drank, Himiin chanted for the elixir to chase away her worries and bring her good health. She set the bowl down, and he took her hands in his, continuing to chant. Her mouth filled with spit from the bitter drink, but relief flowed through her, soothing her stomach and lightening her heart.

His voice trailed off. He placed her hands upon his chest. The warmth and hardness of his muscles under her palms gave her strength.

He cleared his throat, drawing her gaze to his face. "It is my wish to keep you always with me." His eyes sparkled with love. "I do not know how to do this, but my wish is to keep you with me on the mountain during the cold time. Do you wish the same?"

How could he look upon her with such love in his eyes knowing what the Blackleg had done and not knowing how her people would react to her return?

"We do not know if my people will accept my failure to bring peace." She bowed her head. "How am I to tell them my weyekin meant something other than marrying a Blackleg?"

"We will find a way." He kissed her hand and led her to the lagoon.

"I thought we must hurry?" Wren asked as Himiin walked into the water.

"We are."

"Why are you bathing?" She stood at the water's edge, her gaze soaking in his powerful body. "And why do you still carry my clothes?"

"Come." He held out his hand beckoning her forward. The mischief gleaming in his eyes made him hard to resist.

She walked out to where he stood with the water touching either end of her dress draped over his shoulder. "You are getting my dress wet," she said, trying to hold one end out of the water.

"It will become wetter." Holding her chin in his hand, he kissed her. "Do you trust me?" He brushed his lips against hers, sending a wave of heat rushing through her.

"Yes." She leaned into him as he deepened the kissed.

He drew away slowly. "We will swim under the waterfall." He glanced at the spray of the water where it splashed into the lagoon.

"Are we going into the cave?" Elation hummed through her when his puzzled gaze studied her face.

"You know of the tunnel?"

"I found it while swimming." Her body tingled with excitement. She would explore the cave with him.

"So you have found our way." He grabbed her about the middle with his free arm, lifting her out of the water enough to nuzzle her neck. "You are brave and wise."

His touch warmed her to her toes and sent a spiral of heat to her core. Wrapping her arms around his neck, she clung to him, sighing. To spend every day just like this, with his arms around her giving her warmth and security, she would leave this earth a satisfied woman.

"Our way? So we will go into the cave?"

"It is a shortcut to the village." He released her. "When I dive, grab hold of my feet, I will pull you to the other side." His flaxen hair drifted behind him as he dove into the water.

Wren grabbed his feet and held on. His strong arms pulled them under the pressure of the waterfall and up into the area behind the curtain of water. On the other side, she sat on a rock. The roar once again reminded her of ceremonial drums. After wiping the water from her face, she squeezed her hair.

The place held a special appeal to her. She sang of its beauty. During her song, Himiin walked up beside the rock where she sat and watched her. His eyes shone like the sparkling droplets of water in the moonlight. At the end of her song, he leaned forward, kissing her.

"Your voice is so beautiful, I feel blessed to hold you in my arms and hear the sweetness."

Tears of joy spilled down her cheeks.

"Did I hurt you?" he asked, immediately drawing her into his arms.

"No, you have made me very happy." She wiped at the tears and smiled into his confused face.

"You mortals are hard to understand. Why do you cry when you are happy?"

She shrugged her shoulders. "I do not know, we just do. And those were definitely tears of joy, not sorrow." She touched his cheek. "I am happy to be back on the mountain and to spend my time with you."

He kissed her palm and grasped her around the waist, standing her on the rock. Himiin wrung her soaked dress. When water no longer spilled from the garment, he pulled it over her head. The dress clung to her. If the garment had been an everyday dress of woven grass and hemp, instead of her marriage dress made of antelope hide, it would have slid on easier and dried faster.

Wren cringed.

Had the Blackleg who assaulted her not died at the hands of his own people, she would be on her way to his village and more torture. And warriors who killed their own were headed to her village. Tremors reverberated through her body.

Himiin must have sensed the shivers were not just from the cold garment. He tipped her face up.

"We will get there before the Blackleg. This cave goes through the side of the mountain. It is dark, but will get us to your people ahead of the raiding party."

"Are you sure we can warn my father in time?" She feared arriving at the village and finding everyone dead. Her chest ached with dread.

"Yes. We will be there before the Blackleg. I worry more about the Blackleg spirit." The anger in his eyes reflected his scorn for the spirit. "I followed him to the raiding party before losing his scent." He tenderly touched her cheek. "He will be at the village when the Blackleg attack. Of this I am sure."

A shiver crept up her spine. It had nothing to do with the cold dress.

"Come." Himiin witnessed her shiver and pulled her close, rubbing her arms and body to make her warm. He knelt, running his hands up and down her legs. Her shivers were from more than cold. Her tense muscles revealed the truth. What had her nervous? The avenging Blacklegs? Her father's wrath? He sighed. She had many things to worry about. He had one. To get her back to her people safely.

"Even traveling through this cave, the Blackleg have an advantage because they are on horseback. We must hurry," he said, standing.

"I will warm as we walk," she said with conviction, heading toward the cave entrance. Her feet faltered a moment, and her head tilted to the side.

"Do you fear the cave?"

"It is as if it calls to me." She watched him with bewilderment in her eyes. "I heard my name called earlier when I was here. Right before I saw you."

"You must have heard me calling to you." He kissed her to allay her fears and warm her body. Her eyes remained closed when he stepped away.

When they opened, he saw acceptance of what they were about to do, and courage.

"I must lead," he said, touching her cheek. "I can see in the dark. Hold my hand and walk beside me. It will be very dark for a long time. Do not be frightened, I have traveled this way before. Nothing lives in the cave, and only a few creatures travel this way."

He smiled when she held out her hand and placed it confidently in his. Her eyes shone with excitement as he led her into the darkness of the cave.

Halfway through the tunnel, his nerves vibrated from the crackling noises in the air.

They were not alone.

He scanned the cave ahead, but saw nothing suspicious. Still, the hair on the back of his neck tingled. He stopped, drawing Wren to his side. Through the long walk, she had not uttered a word.

He protectively tucked her under his arm and kissed the top of her head. It was good she was resilient. He feared he knew the intruder. Their battle would be something most mortals had never witnessed.

Wishing to shield her, but knowing she must know the truth, he whispered, "Something is not right."

Her body stiffened in his embrace.

"Hold tight to my hand. If I say sit, do it immediately. Do not worry. I will come back for you. But you must remain quiet and wait for me." He kissed her cheek. She silently nodded as alarm tensed her face.

"Do not be afraid. Nothing will harm you. Nor will I let anything keep me from you."

The darkness pressed in as they walked farther.

The air crackled. A slight hiss vibrated in his ears. The dark spirit was near. Peering ahead, he searched the tunnel wall to wall. There it was.

Glowing red eyes.

The blackleg spirit was here.

"Sit," he whispered, squeezing her hand and quickly letting go. He never took his sight off the eyes coming toward him. He refused to battle on top of Wren. Sprinting toward the oncoming dark spirit, he wondered how he could conceivably defeat the apparition and what form it had taken this time.

He scanned the tunnel as he ran and hunted for his enemy. A glimmer of red caught his attention as it started to pass him.

Reaching out, his arm and hand grew warm from the spirit's energy. The dark spirit had yet to take a form. How could this be? The Creator had given dark spirits the ability to be out of a body for a short time to travel to another. Where was his vessel, and why did the dark spirit ignore him?

Himiin frantically searched the darkness for the glowing eyes. Fear clutched at his throat, the Blackleg spirit traveled toward Wren.

He had to be stopped.

Himiin ran through the darkness, keeping his eyes trained on the red glow. His foot caught. He stretched his arms forward, toward Wren. The hard earth slammed into his body, and his head hit the wall.

He pushed up, tried to lever his body to a sitting position.

Wren.

The dark spirit could not harm the woman he loved.

His head pounded and darkness wrapped around. *Keep-her-safe. Not-fail-again.*

Heat seared through him like a rabbit on a spit. A voice he knew chuckled in his head.

"I will stop you, and she will be mine," said the voice as darkness closed in on Himiin.

《》《》《》

"Yes, go to sleep White Wolf. I'll no longer need your body once I have passed into your woman's." The dark spirit gradually raised Himiin's body to a standing position. It took more energy using an unwilling body, but it would get him close to his target. He desired the woman's vessel next.

As the daughter of the Chief, he would enter the village and cause havoc when the Blackleg attacked. Many more, and perhaps all the Lake Nimiipuu, could be wiped out—including the woman. He chuckled. Killing the woman would also kill the spirit of the mountain.

He Who Crawls would reward him highly with his help in capturing the village and all the horses.

Approaching the woman sitting on the floor where White Wolf left her, his feet faltered. He found this vessel hard to conquer. The power of the white spirit's vessel was stronger than a mortal vessel. The passion this spirit held for the woman proved more intense than anything the Creator bestowed upon him.

He couldn't let the goodness of this woman's emotions touch him. His spirit lived off greed, pain, and suffering. To feel anything other than that would be his demise.

《》《》《》

Wren heard an "oof" and thud of a body hitting the ground.

"Himiin? Himiin, is that you?" She stared into the darkness, but it

216

was as if her eyes were not open. The cold damp floor she sat on penetrated her wet dress. She shivered and exhaled, hoping to never again have to smell the dank mustiness of wet earth.

Something moved to her left. She turned her head. A flicker of light—then two.

Himiin's blue eyes.

"Oh!" She stood, throwing her arms around his neck. "I feared you were hurt when I heard the sound of someone falling." She leaned back, gazing into his eyes. Something was different. His body stiffened, and his arms did not close around her, returning her embrace. Where had the warmth that usually lit his eyes gone?

"Are you hurt?" She took his face in her hands and tenderly ran her fingers over his head.

Staring into his eyes, she noticed the edges taking on a red glow. His arms finally wrapped around her, but instead of a comforting embrace, they tightened as though he wanted to squeeze the air and life out of her.

"Himiin, I do not know why you want to hurt me. But if it is your wish, it is my wish as well." She pressed her lips to his, putting all her love and passion for him into the kiss. His lips remained straight and stiff. She ran her tongue along the seam, willing him to open to her.

When he opened, his arms dropped to his side, and hot air whooshed out of his mouth.

She stepped back, keeping hold of one hand as his eyes went blank. The hand became too warm to hold and his body sagged. Moving quickly, she dropped to the ground and caught his head in her lap when the large body slumped to the floor.

A hiss much louder than a snake, ricocheted through the cave sending the hair on her arms to spike.

She shielded her eyes as a streak of light shot out of Himiin's body and balled into a beautiful glowing orb before fading and shrieking into a streak of light once more. The beam zipped to the right, again rolling into a twinkling orb and fading before the shaft of light hissed skyward. The orb glowed, exploded, and a shrill whistle pierced the air, echoing through the cave.

The acrid scent of an extinguished fire lingered in the air as ashes, cold to the touch, fell around her. Fear for Himiin and her people throbbed in her heart.

She sat on the floor in darkness, cradling Himiin's head.

"What just happened? I do not understand." She ran a hand over his head and felt a bump above his ear. "Oh, Himiin, you have been hurt. No wonder you acted strangely." How was she to get Himiin out of the tunnel if he did not wake?

"What do I do?" she beseeched the Creator. Her words echoed through the hollow earth before silence pressed around her like falling head first in a snow drift. Quiet, cold, and suffocating.

She stared into the blackness with no notion of which way led them out of the cave.

The weight of Himiin's body on her lap and his strong face under her hand were welcome reminders she was not alone.

Staring into the darkness, she called to Himiin with her heart. He had to wake. Otherwise they would both perish in this tunnel and the Lake Nimiipuu would not be warned of the attacking Blacklegs.

Le'éptit wax lepít

(22)

Himiin's head hurt, and his body ached. A gentle hand soothed his brow while a melodic voice whispered his name.

"Himiin, come back to me. I need you. Our people need you."

Gradually, his head cleared.

He opened his eyes to darkness. Focusing on the voice, he gazed into Wren's worried face. The hard cold ground didn't bother him due to the soft warm lap cradling his head.

"You scared me." She trailed a caressing hand over his open eyes and down the side of his face, tracing his lips with her finger. "You have a bump on the head. Did you defeat whatever you charged after?"

His head swirled with thoughts. Who was he after? He closed his eyes and concentrated. He was inside Hawk and witnessed the Blackleg's cruelty to Wren. The memories made him flinch. He administered to Wren's injuries in the pool under the waterfall—these thoughts warmed him. Then he followed a buck to the Blackleg raiding party...

He'd spotted the dark spirit in this tunnel.

Fear for Wren pushed his body into motion. He tried to sit up, but his stomach convulsed. The sensation didn't make sense. He was a spirit. Physical ailments like this did not affect him.

"Did you see them?" he asked, ignoring the unsettling in his body.

"See what?" Wren held his hand.

"The red eyes." Her intake of breath told him she had. "Where did he go?"

"Who?" She stared at him, watching his every move.

"The Blackleg spirit. He has red glowing eyes. He was here. I tripped chasing him toward you." It was inconceivable the spirit had left without harming Wren.

"I-he-" She wiped her hand across her mouth. "You came up to me. I was happy to see you and flew into your arms. Only you stood so still, not returning my embrace." She searched his eyes.

He did not remember her embracing him, and he would not have stood still. He would have gathered her into his arms.

"Then your arms tightened around me. It hurt, as though you wished me harm." The confusion in her eyes, made his heart ache. He never wanted her to think he would harm her.

"I would—"

She placed her hand upon his lips, stilling his words. "I love you. I told you this and if you wished me to leave this earth I would." She gulped and raised a shaking hand to his face. "Your eyes were red on the edges. And I-I kissed you. Giving you all my heart. You became hot like an ember in the fire and fell to the ground."

She held his head in her hands. "Something hissed and white light flew through the cave, shrieking. The light burned out, dropping ash to the ground."

She took a deep breath as the knowledge which froze his heart, came to her.

"The Blackleg spirit was inside you."

"Yes." Himiin shook with anger. The spirit had invaded his vessel. Used Wren's love for him to get near her.

But the Blackleg's plan had not worked. The spirit was so full of evil and hatred, when Wren bestowed love upon him, he could not survive.

Himiin sat up, embracing her. He nuzzled her neck and clung to her scent. "He will never touch you again." He drew back, holding her by the shoulders. "Your love for me saved you. We will forever be as one." In the darkness, he kissed her, filling himself with her love. When she sagged against him and sighed, her hands moving over his bare back, his groin ached for her.

"We must hurry to the village." He regretted dragging her into more turmoil, but they had to warn Proud and Tall.

"Yes." She hugged him tight before leaning back.

He stood, drawing her up beside him.

"It is not far now. Come, we will be at your village at the early light." He took her hand, squeezed reassuringly, and continued down the tunnel.

They walked all night. Wren's steps lagged as a slight breeze brought warm fresh air. He stopped long enough to scoop her into his arms. The glow of a new day dimly lit the last length of the tunnel.

He stepped out of the cave. The morning sun peeked over the hill across the lake. He turned and glanced up the side of the mountain. The sunlight illuminated the snow-covered peaks and dusted a golden hue over the tops of the tall pines. The view and woman sleeping in his arms were all he would ever need to be content.

Below, at the edge of the village, the sun herald readied his horse to race through the village awakening the inhabitants to the new day. He shook his head. This day would not be as peaceful as those that had come before.

They were ahead of the raiding party, but by how far? He must hurry to warn Proud and Tall. They would need everyone to defeat the revenge seeking Blacklegs headed their way. He hoped the warriors of the Lake Nimiipuu were not on a hunt.

Carrying Wren's sleeping body, he ran down the side of the mountain weaving his way through brush, trees, and around boulders. The warmth of her body as she snuggled against his chest and the security of her arms wrapped around his neck, strengthened his conviction to keep her with him always.

First they had to tell her family and the band he was a spirit. Living among them would not work. It was inconceivable for him to travel as they did. He had to stay on the mountain and protect the harmony. Could Wren survive on the mountain through the cold weather?

His heart constricted. Without a way to keep her warm and fed in the cold time, she would have to travel with the band. To keep from becoming a burden upon her elderly father, Proud and Tall may make her marry. The thought of watching her with another turned his stomach. They had to find a way to be together.

His torturous thoughts obscured his vision as he raced down the mountain and into the middle of the village. The women carried baskets of food out to the fire while young girls stirred the coals and fed the flames. The boys filled pouches with food in readiness to head out to the meadows to watch over the horses.

He stopped and surveyed the village. The Nimiipuu watched him with suspicious eyes. They stared at his flaxen hair and then the limp body in his arms. He walked over to an old woman.

"Where is Chief Proud and Tall?" he asked, casting his gaze about, daring anyone to come closer. No one moved or offered any information. They stared at the woman in his arms. Her long, loose hair covered her face and upper body as she slept cradled in his arms.

"I am here," said a deep voice to his right.

Himiin carried Wren to her father. "Your daughter has much to tell." He nodded toward the lodge behind Proud and Tall.

The Chief's face became like stone, but he motioned to the lodge.

Himiin sensed the man did not trust him. Proud and Tall entered the dwelling first, keeping himself between Himiin and the women filling baskets near the fire.

Wren's mother and grandmother halted their morning preparations. The worry etched on their faces had to be from the disappearance of Tattle-Tale. The grandmother shook her head as Himiin stepped to the middle of the lodge, cradling Wren in his arms.

"You say this is my daughter. It is my son who is missing. My daughter is married to a Blackleg." Proud and Tall crossed his arms and glared.

Himiin sat down, cross-legged, holding Wren in his lap. He took her arms from his neck and tried waking her with a gentle shake and a kiss on the top of her head.

"Wake my little bird, we are here. Within the home of your people." He tenderly tucked her hair back behind her ear, revealing her face.

"My daughter? But she is to wed—"

He cut off Wren's mother with a scowl.

"She has much to tell. We have traveled all night. She is weak from her ordeal." Again, he gently shook the woman sleeping in his lap. "Wren, you must wake. There is much to prepare for."

Proud and Tall stood over him. "You have brought my daughter back. What of the peace with the Blackleg?" The wrinkles on the chief's forehead told of the trouble he saw ahead.

"I would rather you hear what your daughter has to say. It should come from someone you know and trust."

Respect flashed in Proud and Tall's eyes.

"Himiin? Why have you stopped running, we have—" Wren's eyes fluttered open. She saw Himiin's strong face and the love in his eyes. A movement caught her attention. They were in the lodge of her family. She had to warn them.

She pushed away from Himiin to stand. He smiled and helped her scurry to her feet.

"Father we must prepare for an attack. The Blackleg are coming to take the horses." She grasped her father's hands. He stood still, studying their clasped hands.

"What is this?" He held her hand up to inspect the red marks around her wrists.

"Hawk tied my hands—" She gulped back the shame as her eyes filled with tears. She wiped at the tears and glanced at her father. The recrimination in his eyes stung like a slap across her face. He thought she had wronged their people. Again.

"Did you do something to anger him?" Proud and Tall's incensed gaze rested on Himiin.

She stepped back, pulling her hands from his grasp. "This is one time I have done nothing to disgrace my people." Her father blamed her. Like all the times before. Never did he listen to the reasons for her disobedience. But this time… She glared at him. She would not allow him to pass the blame to her. The problem started when Hawk used her to get to the prized Nimiipuu horses.

"Then why are the Blackleg coming to take back the horses? You should be with your man, not this man." He stared pointedly at Himiin.

"They are not coming to take back Hawk's horses, they want all the horses." She grasped Himiin's warm comforting hand. "This man saved me." On the way to the village she knew her father would wonder at her return, but to challenge her and think she brought this upon them… Her heart ached with disappointment.

"Where is Hawk?" Her mother stepped into the discussion. "Did you become his wife?"

Wren's stomach twisted in disgust. She would never be a wife to such a vile man, even if he were still alive.

She grasped the bottom of her dress and peeled it from her body.

223

Her grandmother and mother stared at the green, blue, and purple bruises. Her father's gaze rested on the torn nipple.

"Does this look like the body of someone who has become a wife?" She walked to her father, pointing at the offending nipple. He turned his head. "This is the kind of man you gave me to. He looked after me well. He bit me, pinched me, and took me over and over again until I wished I were dead." Tears of fury replaced the shame.

Himiin walked up beside her and took her hand giving her more strength. "All he wanted was to use me to get back to the valley and take your fast horses. There was never going to be peace between the tribes. This was not my gift." She choked back a sob. "It was torture."

She stared at her mother. "No, I am not a wife, for his own people killed him, he was so vile." Glaring at her father, she added, "That is the one thing the Blackleg will forever have my gratitude. He was evil, and I would not have lived long with him, for it would be better to be dead than his wife."

Himiin picked up her dress and slid it over her head. Her body shook with fury. The people standing before her were hard to focus on through her haze of anger.

Himiin's strong firm voice, said, "Your son is safe." He faced her father. "Tattle-Tale is hiding. I told him to wait three suns before he came back to the village. I did not want him captured again by the Blacklegs."

"Again?" Proud and Tall's voice held accusations.

"The Blackleg raiding party coming after your horses took him hostage." Himiin glanced at Wren, then back at her father. His calculating eyes, revealed his decision of how much to tell. "I rescued him."

He took her cold hand into his warm strong one. "Do not worry that your daughter will disgrace you." He turned his passion-filled gaze on her, making her body tingle as he said, "She is my woman. We became one before she left the mountain."

Her mother's intake of breath and grandmother's disappointed head shaking did nothing to spoil the elation his words brought to her heart. She belonged to him. There was no other she wished to have. Wren held onto his strong hand as her heart pounded with happiness. His strength and love gave her the courage to tell her father everything.

"Hawk was never interested in peace. He planned to meet a group of his followers and come take all our horses. Before they showed up, he—" A lump of disgust made it hard for her to talk. Himiin's strong arm pulled her close. His closeness gave her the fortitude to face the man's wickedness.

"He violated me. When he left to meet his friends, he threatened worse treatment if I tried to get away. He never came back." She smiled at Himiin. He returned the smile and nodded his head to continue. "Himiin came to me and told me of Hawk's death and Tattle-Tale's capture." She grasped her father's hand. "We have to prepare for the attack. Himiin saw a Blackleg raiding party headed this way."

Her father's assessing gaze scanned the man standing beside her. "How do you know this? How did you know where to find my daughter?"

Her heart raced, fear clawed at her throat. What should they tell her father? Would he accept Himiin as a spirit?

"I witnessed the riders heading this direction. I saved your daughter because she called me." Himiin offered no more. He gazed into her eyes as he squeezed her hand. Their bond did not escape her parents. She watched them exchange glances.

"We will talk of you two later." Her father motioned to the flap of the lodge. "Come, we must warn the village of the attack."

Proud and Tall sent a messenger around to gather the band in front of his lodge. As the crowd grew, Wren watched the faces of her people. Most wore blank expressions, as though they waited to make a decision on her reappearance.

As usual, one voiced his opinion.

Eyes of Snake jeered. "I told you it was not wise to make peace with the Blackleg." He stared at her. "They used you to see our village and learn where our herd is kept."

Wren backed away from his vicious words and found the solid chest of Himiin behind her. She glanced over her shoulder. He glared at the warrior.

"They did use Wren." Himiin stepped around Wren, blocking her from any more ugly remarks. He leveled his gaze at those gathered, especially the warriors. "They used the whole band. Giving you hopes of peace, something they know the Nimiipuu desire. They are, after all, schemers."

The crowd shuffled their feet, and a low undercurrent rumbled through the group. Wren watched her father. He seemed older and more vulnerable than when she'd left.

"You must move the horses to a safe place." Himiin said to the group. No one moved. He glanced at her father.

"This man is right." Proud and Tall called to a cousin, Tattle-Tale's age. "You and the other boys move the horses to the valley beyond the lake."

Silly One nudged her brother with her elbow when he continued to stare at Himiin.

"Now?" he squeaked.

"Yes, now. Have you not heard a word that has been spoken?" Silly One chided her brother.

"How do we know this man who has entered our village with Wren is not sending our horses into the hands of the Blackleg?" Eyes of Snake stepped forward confronting Himiin.

Wren watched with trepidation as the two eyed one another. She knew Himiin would not fight, but Eyes of Snake was noted for his temper.

Chief Proud and Tall gave his attention to Eyes of Snake. "This warrior brought back our beloved daughter, and she speaks highly of him." In a low, even tone he added, "That is all I need."

Eyes of Snake dropped his arrogant gaze, but did not back away. The warriors around him muttered and retreated from his alliance.

Wren smiled at her father. Maybe, he finally saw her as someone worthy of his trust. In time, she would tell him the truth about Himiin. Until then it warmed her heart to know he trusted the man on her word.

"The women must go to the cave above the village," Himiin said, avoiding eye contact with her. "Wren knows the one I speak of."

"I will not leave the village. It is because of Hawk's greed the Blackleg are attacking. I will help." She shoved her hands on her hips and stared at the man she loved. How dare he expect her to abandon everything to stand on the mountainside and watch her village, her family, and the man she loved under attack?

"What he says is wise. Take the women and small children to this cave." Her father narrowed his eyes. "It is your duty to keep them safe."

She glanced from Himiin to her father. She loved them both in different ways and was not about to let them fight alone. Nodding her head in acceptance, she refused to look at either of the men. She would get the others to safety first, then come back and help.

"Come, all women and children. Bring a blanket and food. We know not how long this will take." She helped her mother and grandmother wrap food in their blankets.

The two women kept their eyes averted and did not say a word, an unusual trait for both. She did not know if they were appalled by what had happened to her or her return.

Wanting to know, she asked, "Why do you not show happiness at my return?"

Her grandmother directed a watery gaze at her. "You were with another before your betrothed arrived. It is no wonder this peace is being ripped apart. You failed us before you even left."

She stared at her mother and then her grandmother. They would forever believe she brought this upon the band. Even knowing the marriage to the Blackleg had never been her gift to the people.

"Himiin is the man of my heart. He makes me strong." She wrapped her blanket into a tight bundle and chose her words. "I believe my gift is yet to come to me." The women shook their heads, gathering their belongings in their arms.

Wren exited the lodge secure in her knowledge Himiin would always love her, no matter what. Her task at the moment was to get the women and children to the cave safely.

She led the group of forty-three women and children up the side of the mountain. Memories of the dark spirit gave her second thoughts about entering the cave. Even though she knew the spirit was dead, her encounter with him reminded her of the evil that could take over the Nimiipuu if they did not remain vigilant.

Silly One walked beside her. She gently touched the welt around Wren's neck. "How did this happen?"

Wren stopped and studied her trusted friend. "It is too ugly to tell."

Her friend's eyes became large with fear. "Hawk did not treat you well?"

"He did evil things to me. Things I do not wish upon any other woman." She grasped Silly One's hand. "When you are asked for, I

227

hope it is someone who you feel strong affection for, and he feels the same for you."

"How did Himiin find you?" Silly One whispered.

"I used this," she lifted the wolf fang and showed her friend, "to call to him. He heard my plea for help and asked the Creator to allow him off the mountain." She smiled, remembering the concern in his eyes when he found her huddled in the cave.

"He has spoken for you?" Silly One asked.

She was still unsure of why he spoke for her when they could never live as husband and wife.

"It cannot be. He has his mountain to care for, and I am a mortal. He will continue long after I have gone to this earth."

"But you can be together for that time," Silly One stopped her. "You have been through a lot. You deserve happiness with the man you love. And who loves you."

Wren continued to walk when the others caught up to them. She ducked her head and whispered, "I am going back when you are all safe in the cave."

Silly One shook her head in protest.

She continued, "I have yet to use my gift. It may be now, during this attack, that I will find my vision."

Her cousin stared at her, but uttered not a word.

She had made her decision. She would return to the village to save her people and the spirit she loved.

Le'éptit wax mita't

(23)

Himiin helped the Nimiipuu warriors ready their bows, arrows, knives, and clubs for the attack. The sun hovered directly overhead, leaving plenty of daylight for the raiding party to strike. Several warriors scouted the area on the side of the mountain he had last seen the Blackleg.

Boys, Tattle-Tale's age, watched the herd in the low valley far from the high meadows where the Blackleg believed the horses grazed. All other men of the village sat around their fires waiting.

Himiin peered across the dying embers of Chief Proud and Tall's fire. Wren's father appeared to have aged since the news of the raid.

"We will defeat the Blackleg," Himiin said, watching the tired warrior.

"Yes, we will defeat them, but what will we lose in return?" The chief's dark eyes dulled with sorrow.

The defeat etched on the chief's face bothered him. The chief should be as enraged as the younger warriors, ready for battle to save the people and village. Instead, he appeared worn out, ready to go into the earth.

Himiin's gaze traveled up the mountain side. He stared at the mouth of the cave. "If we are lucky, we will lose very little. The women and children are safe. The men of this village are strong and care about the survival of all."

"Have you fought the Blackleg before?" The chief stared at him.

"Not the people, but the essence." In truth, he had never fought a mortal. The one he killed had been by accident. He lived with the guilt every single moment. The spirits he dealt with never seemed to vanish completely. Except the Blackleg spirit that perished from Wren's love.

This unsettled him. Why had he not also perished if her love was so strong to take away a spirit?

"Why do you frown?" Chief Proud and Tall asked.

"You daughter has strong powers. Ones, which I do not understand." He wanted to tell this man the strength of his daughter, but to do so he would have to explain things he wasn't ready to reveal. Proud and Tall had too much on his mind right now to learn a spirit loved his daughter, and she returned his love.

"Yes, our Wren has always held this mountain and all who live here in reverence." He glanced at the mountain. "At times her love has caused this band undue hardships. Yet, when it was thought her weyekin asked her to leave, she did with honor." He shook his head. "She has earned my respect and the respect that this mound of earth means something special to her. It broke my heart to send her away, knowing her desire to never leave."

His gaze rested on Himiin. The sadness in his eyes reflected his soul. "Had I known of the Blackleg's actions and intentions for my daughter, I would not have sent her." He sighed. "It has been a long time since a man has fooled me so completely." He wiped a hand across his wrinkled face. "I believed he was a good man and wanted peace."

Himiin placed a hand on Proud and Tall's shoulder. "He fooled many. Even his own people. That is why they killed him. He deceived them as he deceived the Nimiipuu."

The chief nodded his head. "Then he met his fate."

Proud and Tall stared up the side of the mountain. "I have hurt Wren with my decision to send her away and my quick anger at her return." He shook his head. "I wanted peace with the Blackleg and did not think everything through as wisely as I should."

He knew the chief would not make the same mistake again.

Tears glistened in Proud and Tall's eyes. "Because of my actions, I have dishonored my daughter. She feels deep."

"I have learned this."

Before the chief could question him further a scout raced into the village.

"Aieee! They come! They come!" He zigzagged around the fire pits and lodges, pulling his horse to a stop in front of Chief Proud and Tall.

Everyone jumped to their feet and closed in around the rider to hear what news the warrior brought.

He slid from his sweating, snorting horse. "They are not far behind me. Their number is twenty. They and their horses are painted for battle."

Chief Proud and Tall raised his arms. "Take to the trees around the village. We will surprise them."

The men scattered, leaving Himiin and Wren's father standing in the middle of the deserted village.

"Come, we will wait in the lodge." Proud and Tall gathered his weapons and walked toward his dwelling.

"Should you not take to the trees as well?" He stared into the forest. There wasn't a flash of anything other than the rippling of leaves in the breeze.

"We will wait in the lodge." His statement was final.

Why did the old chief choose to wait for the enemy in the first place they would attack? The lodge of the woman who started the whole treachery—at least in the eyes of the Blackleg—would be the object of their rage.

Knowing the Blackleg could only kill his vessel, but not his spirit, he feared for the mortal—Wren's father. She would be distraught should anything happen to the chief. He would stay close to her father and try to spare him from the battle.

Entering the lodge, the flap fell behind them as the thunder of horse's hooves shook the ground and hammered in his ears. The arrival of the Blackleg wasn't the reason panic dried his mouth and shook his body.

Wren stepped away from the far side of the lodge.

"You were to stay at the cave!" He shouted and crossed the lodge, taking her by the arms. His fear for her safety shriveled his gut. She winced and he loosened his grip.

"I had to help. It is because of me this happens." She stood firmly, her face etched with determination.

"This has nothing to do with you. It is the Blacklegs' greed which caused the attack." He drew her to him. Her heart beat rapidly. "It was foolish of you to come back down here. We must hide you." He scanned the interior of the lodge.

"You will hide under the buffalo robes. They want blood and horses." He dragged her across to the pile of buffalo hides Hawk had given for her.

"I refuse to hide." She crossed her arms stubbornly.

He threw his hands in the air as screeching and whoops of revenge rang through the deserted village.

Chief Proud and Tall crossed to them. "Daughter, you will do as this man says. I do not wish the tortures you have endured to happen again." He touched her cheek and said, "I do not want you to fall into their hands. You are precious to me." He motioned for Wren to get in the pile of hides.

Himiin lifted several hides. She glanced from one man to the other, before crawling into the dark hairy pile.

"I will see you when this is through." Himiin bent, kissing the hard line of her lips. He dropped the hides on the woman who stole his heart and hoped she would not be foolish and emerge once he and Proud and Tall were engaged in battle.

From the sounds outside the lodge, much blood was being shed. He raised his face to the fire hole in the top of the lodge. Closing his eyes, he asked the Creator for forgiveness. There was little he could do to get through this day without blood on his hands.

With a heavy heart, he gripped a club and threw open the flap. Warriors from both sides wrestled with knives, while Blacklegs still on horseback rode through the chaos swinging clubs, knocking anything in their path to the ground. Dodging the bodies entwined in battle, he moved away from the dwelling and Wren. It would be impossible to watch all the Blackleg and hope none snuck into the lodge of Proud and Tall. He would find the best vantage point to watch the opening, without drawing attention to the structure.

He knocked the first Blackleg warrior to confront him to the ground with one blow. The hollow crack of the club as it met the man's head made him nauseous. He knew of no other way to stop the onslaught.

The fighting continued. Cries of anger, anguish, and agony rang out through the village. A lodge went up in flames. The acrid smoke swirled upward; the orange, angry blaze licked at the sky and reduced the dwelling to black ashes. The warriors continued to battle, ignoring the fire. The Nimiipuu outnumbered the Blacklegs, but the bitter warriors from afar fought until only a few managed to flee.

Himiin stood in the middle of the village. Stench of blood and death assaulted his senses. The carnage of the battle made his heart heavy with grief for the dead and the living who lost a family member.

Bloody, limp, Blackleg bodies were strewn across the ground. Several Nimiipuu also lay among the fallen. This should not have happened. Why must the Blackleg always use force to acquire things they could get in trade?

He raised his hands and face to the Creator asking absolution for his involvement. His name rang out above the moans and chaos. Jerking his head toward the sound, Wren threw open the flap on the lodge.

She scanned the crumpled bodies, her brow creased with worry. Her gaze came to rest upon him. She rushed forward. The joy in her eyes told him she believed he would no longer be standing.

Happiness swept through him at the sight of her. He opened his arms, eager for her to run into his embrace.

A flash in the trees behind her drew his attention.

He saw the arrow the same instant he heard the whoosh of air carry it toward Wren.

"No!" he shouted and ran toward her.

His warning came too late; his steps too short.

The 'thunk' of the lethal arrow pierced her back and echoed in his head like a clap of thunder.

Her eyes widened. The smile she held for him, convulsed into a perfect circle before she fell into his open arms.

"NO!" he bellowed, glaring at the sky. He had killed another innocent.

His knees buckled, taking them both to the ground. Rage clenched his stomach, his heart squeezed with fear.

"Wren!" he cried and kissed her soft cheek. His heart flickered with hope when her eyes fluttered open.

"Our love is forever." The words floated away on her last breath.

"No!" Rage, emptiness, and remorse shook his body as he searched the faces of the Nimiipuu warriors gathering around him. "She cannot go. It is I who should be taken. She has a pure heart." The men around him avoided his pleading gaze.

He had gone against the Creator. He fell in love with a mortal and let that love alter his devotion to his mountain. His selfish acts led to her death. He should be the one pierced by an arrow and his life taken, not the innocent woman in his arms.

He cradled Wren to his broken heart and stood. Lifting his face to the sky, he held her limp body above his head and chanted to the Creator.

"I have done wrong, not this little bird.
Take from me and give to her. She has yet to accomplish her gift.
I have learned of love from her and have nothing more to accomplish.
Take my spirit, giving it to her so she may live."

He opened his eyes and stared at the offending arrow protruding from her back. Gently, he lowered the body of the woman he loved. He crossed his legs and sat on the ground, draping Wren's body across his lap. The heels of his hands pushed the tears from his face. He kissed her cheek again and thought of her sparkling eyes, lilting laugh, and mesmerizing songs. How could she be taken away before she accomplished her weyekin?

He turned her face down on his lap and stared at the deadly arrow sticking out of her back. The ugliness of it made his chest constrict and his head pound.

He grasped the lethal shaft.

Warriors, at his side, lunged forward and grabbed his arm.

"She may be saved," one warrior said, trying to pry his hand from the wooden shaft.

Himiin glared at the men and waved his arms to get them all to back away.

"Only the Creator can save her now." He grasped the arrow and gave a swift yank, drawing the weapon from her body. Her warm blood mixed with his tears upon his hands.

Raising his blood stained hands skyward, he called to the Creator, "Give her back life and take mine."

Clouds converged overhead, sending a cold wind whisking across the lake and stirring up whitecaps.

Spirit of the Mountain

Wren's life meant more to the Nimiipuu than his own existence. She had a great gift to bestow upon her people.

Standing once again, he held his beloved over his head. Her arms, legs, and head dangled lifeless as he placed his hand over the vile bloody hole in her back and offered her to the Creator.

"Give this woman life. She is the heart and soul of these people.
I am merely your servant.
She is worthy of all you bestow upon her.
Give her my life."

The tension among the warriors as he continued to chant and spin in a circle was as palpable as the threatening storm. The scent of their fear flared his nostrils, but did little to deter him from his quest to give life back to the woman he loved.

Thunder rumbled and lightning split the sky. Himiin's muscles bunched in anticipation. He would hold her body thus, until the Creator granted him this one wish.

He chanted again.

"Give this woman life. She is the heart and soul of these people.
I am merely your servant.
She is worthy of all you bestow upon her.
Give her my life."

Darkness surrounded him and he collapsed.

Bright light warmed Wren's body. She opened her eyes and shook her head. Why was she face down across a body? She rose up on her forearms and stared at Himiin. The sight of him tipped her lips into a smile. He survived the attack.

His beautiful eyes were open, but they stared at her, lifeless. Why did he not smile back?

"Himiin?" She touched his warm face and still he did not respond. Panic squeezed her chest. Why did he not say something or look at her? She could feel the beat of his heart under her hand. He still lived.

The shuffle of feet and murmur of voices caught her attention. Glancing to her side, she noticed the warriors staring up into the sky. She shielded her eyes against the glare of the sun popping out from behind a huge dark cloud which moved swiftly through the endless blue.

"What happened?" she asked. The men jumped and stared at her as if she had appeared out of nowhere.

"Wren? But how?" Her father dropped to his knee, embracing her to his chest.

"Yes, how did I come to be face down on Himiin?" She peered down at her lover. Again, she did not understand the emptiness of his eyes. He did not smile nor reach out to her. "And what has happened to him?"

Proud and Tall picked up a bloody arrow. "This was in your back."

She stared at him and reached behind, feeling her back. She would know if an arrow had pierced her. Would she not?

He nodded toward Himiin. "He pulled it from you and called to the Creator." Her father raised his face, gazing at the blue vastness above them. "The sky became angry. He chanted until darkness came." Proud and Tall returned his gaze to Himiin.

"He dropped to the ground, and you are alive." Proud and Tall took her hand. "He gave up his life to give you yours."

She stared at the shell of the man she loved.

Flashes of their time together ran through her mind.

Her head throbbed. Her heart pounded.

How dare he leave the mountain! What made him think she would want to live without him?

Anger tore through her, vibrating her body and clenching her muscles. She glared at the glistening snow-covered mountain. The seriousness of his actions penetrated her fury.

He gave up the mountain for her.

Tears streamed down her face. She touched his cheek.

His eyes stared straight ahead, not seeing her.

"No!" She screamed and grasped Himiin by the shoulders, shaking him. "We need you!"

"I need you," she choked and flung her body across his.

Le'éptit wax pí-lept

(24)

"Daughter, you must eat." Morning Fawn waved a bowl of fish soup under Wren's nose. She gagged at the offending smell, and her already churning stomach lurched. She shoved the bowl away and clung tighter to Himiin.

She had refused to leave him even after the women and children returned and the bodies of the fallen were taken away. When her father tried to remove Himiin, she threw her body across her lover, refusing to move. His heart beat beneath her hand, and his body remained warm to the touch. He may be a living shell of a man, but she refused to believe he would never again walk upon the mountain.

The women wailing for their fallen warriors made a fitting backdrop for her inner turmoil. The warning she and Himiin brought to the Lake Nimiipuu had saved all but four warriors. Had Himiin stood beside her, this knowledge would have validated all she had gone through.

Listening to the keening of the other women, she refused to wail. Himiin was not dead. She saw the pulse in his neck and felt the puffs of breath when she leaned close to talk to him. His body lived; it was his spirit that had left him.

The sun settled behind the mountain, bringing the crisp evening air. The cold chilled her body to match her icy heart. The mountain and her people needed Himiin. How could he have given her life when his essence formed the heart of them all?

237

Silly One patted her shoulder.

"He loves you. You will never find another to give that much of himself so you may live."

Nodding her head, she wiped at the endless tears. She glanced at her cousin. "He is all I ever want. And everything our people need."

Silly One nodded to the mountain. "Take him up there, to where you met. Show him he is needed." She shrugged. "It cannot hurt."

Holding his limp hand in hers, Wren gazed at the mountain they both loved, and thought of the clearing where she first saw him as a man. Her heart raced when memories flooded her head.

"Come," she ordered and stood, tugging on Himiin's hand. His head turned to her, but the eyes remained blank. "Come," she said again. Silly One slid her hands under his arms and helped raise him to his feet.

"Daughter, are you well enough to leave?" Her mother hurried to her side. She grasped Himiin's other hand, stopping their progress. "What if the Blackleg have not left the area?"

"I must take Himiin to where we met. I will talk with the Creator. I must show him Himiin is needed." She tugged on Himiin to make him walk.

"But the Blackleg?" Her mother clung tight to Himiin, keeping them captive.

"The village is safe. Father has sentries watching the mountain." She studied her mother, then the man who captured her heart. "My life means little without Himiin." She reached over, taking Himiin's hand from her mother. The shock on Morning Fawn's face made her only slightly guilty.

"You cannot think such things. You have a gift to bring to your people. No man is more powerful than your duty." Her mother raked a cold stare up and down Himiin.

"He holds my heart and the heart of the people. I will never be able to fulfill my gift if he is not the spirit guiding me." Wren jammed her hands on her hips, determined to make her mother see the bond between she and Himiin involved more than making babies.

"If you leave with this man, you will turn your back on your people."

She glanced at her father. Did he believe this as well? His posture showed he listened. Why did he not side with her? Did he also believe she betrayed her people by clinging to one man?

Few Nimiipuu married for love. It was the way of life.

She knew her parents had become fond of one another, but they had never been touched by the love she and Himiin shared. She had always believed to have marriages without feelings hindered the happiness of the entire village. For how could the Nimiipuu prosper in spirit, when made to live and have children with someone they held little respect for, or worse yet, found it hard to rest their gaze upon?

"Bringing Himiin's spirit back is good for the people. If I fail—I have failed my people." She turned to leave.

"You are not doing this for the people. You are doing this for yourself." Her mother's accusation darkened her heart. She did want Himiin back for her and for the people. Her weyekin had finally shown himself. She knew her gift to her people would only come through the love she and Himiin shared.

"Believe what you believe."

Ignoring the glare of her grandmother and the sorrow in her father's eyes, she led Himiin into the forest. Climbing the mountain was slow. Himiin followed like a blind man. His feet shuffled along, skittering the rocks and sending forth the scent of decayed plants and damp earth. Low limbs stopped his forward motion when she forgot to guide him around the trees.

Even though his eyes remained unseeing, she pointed out some of the special places they had shared on their outings.

"Remember resting on this boulder and watching the clouds?" She watched him. His eyes remained blank, his lips slack. They climbed higher. She heard the splash of water rushing down the mountain side.

"When you caught the fish for me to eat, you showed great skill." She had watched his agile body that day as he slipped about the stream in his attempt to provide her with food.

Today, his body appeared strong, barely taking in air as they climbed higher and higher. Her heart ached, watching his expressionless face. She wished he would do anything, even look upon her harshly rather than with the unseeing eyes.

The Creator had to hear her plea. The Lake Nimiipuu needed the Spirit of the Mountain to sustain them all. She needed Himiin to carry out her gift to her people.

As she hid in the lodge, listening to the battle between her people and the Blackleg, fear for Himiin and the others nearly crushed her heart. During the battle, she realized her gift had nothing to do with actually saving the Nimiipuu from a threat. Her gift was to teach her people, and her children, and their children, the wonders of the mountain and the surrounding valleys. To bind the hearts of the people closer to Mother Earth, so they may prosper and build a strong band— one with leadership which surpassed all others.

She glanced at the man walking alongside of her, and her heart ached. His duty to the mountain and the people was more impressive than anything she had to give. But together they could do great things for the Nimiipuu. This was the man to help her fulfill her gift. She had to make both Himiin and the Creator see this.

At the clearing, she led Himiin to the center. His distant stare as he stood among the fragrant colorful flowers and tall grass sent shivers of apprehension down her back. Could she bring him back? Was her love for him and her conviction to fulfill her gift strong enough to make the Creator see Himiin must return?

A sliver of the moon shone overhead, casting a faint light over the meadow. Taking Himiin's face between her hands, she stroked her thumbs back and forth across his angular cheeks. She pulled his head down, rose onto her toes, and kissed his lips, savoring the softness of them. When he did not return the kiss, her resolution wavered.

Tears burned her eyes. She swiped at the wetness and set her jaw. To give up now would not only give up on Himiin and their love, but her people as well. Pushing his loose flaxen hair behind his shoulder, she slid her hands down his strong neck. Her thumbs rested on the gentle pulse. His blood still moved.

Life stirred in him.

Wren tipped Himiin's head down. His lifeless eyes stared back. Where was the dark blue color they turned when his emotions raged? If only some spark of recognition would light his eyes.

"When others would have shamed me for what the Blackleg Hawk did to me, you gave me the strength to continue and prosper. When I would have rather stayed in the cave, never to have another set their gaze upon me, your gaze warmed me and coaxed me out." She swallowed the memories of the Blackleg's assault and brought forth the warmth and love Himiin had bestowed on her.

Pressing her body against his solid form, she wrapped her arms around his middle and snuggled her head against his chest, continuing to speak to his heart. "When I thought I never wanted a man to touch me again, you showed me gentleness and love. For these reasons I have brought you into my heart and do not want to let you go." She shook her head. "These reasons are selfish.

"However, I believe you are the only one who can help me fulfill my gift to my people. Together we will teach the Lake Nimiipuu to open their hearts to each other and explore life with new meaning. In this way we will help them prosper and become strong in number and in heart."

Standing on tiptoes, she kissed his lips, his neck, and down to his shoulder. She gazed into his eyes. Nothing changed his expression, but his pulse beat stronger in his neck. Placing their hands palm to palm, she raised them in the air and chanted to the Creator.

"Oh Great One, this man gave you his spirit so I may live, but I am not living if he is not beside me in every way.
He is goodness and strength. He has given his very essence for me and I for him.
Give us the gift of one another. It is our gift to bring the Nimiipuu people back to Mother Earth.
To teach them this land is part of our being.
Without it we shall perish, just as sure as I will perish without the guidance and security of Himiin."

With their hands still linked and her face tilted to the moon, she continued chanting. A tremor shook his hands. Her heart skittered. She glanced at his face. A faint glimmer of hope sliced through her. His eyes grew darker.

"Himiin, I am yours forever. Show me you are mine." Squeezing his hands, she lowered them, and placed their clasped palms between her breasts. "My heart yearns for your strength and guidance. Help me take our people on the path of knowledge."

A shrill whistle pierced the air and grew louder. Her ears ached, but she refused to let loose of him or take her eyes from his. She must instill in him her love, trust, and acceptance.

A flash of light blinded her. Heat ripped through her body where their hands rested between her breasts. She gasped for air waiting for her sight to return.

She blinked rapidly to clear away the shards of light and wished desperately to see Himiin. She growled with frustration. When the light faded and she could see, her breath caught as Himiin looked down, first to their clasped hands, and then into her eyes.

Tears tickled her cheeks.

He was back.

Tipping his head, he brought his lips to hers. A flash of light and bolt of energy jarred her to her toes. She wrapped her arms around his neck.

"You're back," she whispered, dropping kisses across his chin and throat.

"I'll only leave you in death," he said, embracing her.

"Yours or mine?"

"Both."

"You're no longer a spirit?" She bit her lip. Would he one day feel cheated he had lost his immortality because of her?

"The Creator has granted me life as a mortal for my selfless act of giving you life." The smile lighting his face chased her fear away. "I will spend the rest of my days loving you and helping the people."

"No more nightly howling?" she asked, a bit disappointed she would not hear his call and experience the tingle of excitement.

"I may not be a wolf, but I can still show you I care." He swept her off her feet and into his arms.

"Forever, you will hold my heart," she whispered just before he kissed her and gently placed her on the soft sweet grass of their mountain. His tender kisses and caressing hands revealed his love and filled her heart. In her dizziness, she thought she heard someone call her name.

Himiin sat up, drawing Wren with him. He knew the voice which called Wren's name and the cadence of the light footsteps that approached.

"Tattle-Tale. I wondered when you would make it to this side of the mountain." He stood, pulling Wren to her feet beside him.

The boy watched them warily before stepping forward. "Who are you?"

"I am Himiin."

Tattle-Tale pointed to Wren. "How do you come to know me and have my sister?"

Wren stepped away from Himiin to stand next to her brother. She placed an arm around his shoulders, hugging him. "It is a long story little brother. As I believe you have a tale for us as well."

The boy glanced back and forth between them, his brow creased in puzzlement.

Himiin smiled. If only the boy knew they had met before. This was one time when the tattle-tale did not know everything.

"You need food. We should return to the village." He slid an arm around Wren's waist and gestured to the boy to start down the mountain.

"Why are you giving orders?" The boy took a stubborn stance. One Himiin had seen before.

"Because, he is right. Come." Wren grasped her brother's hand and pulled him along.

After some cajoling by Wren, Tattle-Tale could not keep his angry silence. He began with finding a wolf, an eagle, and an elk seemingly in conversation. Himiin's step faltered at this news. The boy had been within sighting while he and his siblings worried and talked about him.

"One night I was so sleepy, I could not keep my eyes open. Heat surged through my body, and I awoke in the middle of the Blackleg raiding party." His eyes held confusion.

Unease clenched Himiin's insides. The boy had been invaded by the Blackleg spirit. He hoped with the dark spirit in ashes, the boy would no longer experience the Blackleg's presence. Or his evil.

Tattle-Tale continued to tell how Hawk saved him. "Where is Hawk? He said he would find you." The boy studied Wren. "But you are with this warrior." Tattle-Tale narrowed his eyes on Himiin. "What have you done with Hawk?"

Himiin shook his head. "Hawk was not a good man. He has gone to a place where he can no longer hurt others."

Tattle-Tale opened his mouth to say more, but the sentry announced their arrival.

Wren led her brother and Himiin out of the trees and into the village. Proud and Tall was the first to approach, followed by Morning Fawn, who ran forward, hugging her son to her bosom.

Tattle-Tale squirmed from his mother's embrace.

Wren smiled. Her brother's escapade had finally given him a

reason to grow up.

Silly One hurried over to her. "See, your love for your man is strong." She leaned forward and whispered, "Everyone is talking of this man who gave you life. Will you tell them he is a spirit?"

"He is no longer."

Silly One's eyes widened.

Wren grasped Himiin's hand. Everyone from the village appeared to be present. Now would be a good time to explain.

"Please listen!" she called. Her father raised his hands and all the people quieted, gathering close.

"Himiin is—was—The Spirit of the Mountain." She squeezed his hand as tears burned the back of her eyes. His sacrifice for her was greater than anything she could ever do for him.

"He rescued me when I was hurt and lost, bringing me back to my people." A tear slid down her cheek. He caught it with his finger.

"When an arrow took my life," the group all murmured and she smiled, "he gave me his." Gazing into Himiin's eyes, she knew he would not regret his sacrifice. The love shining in the depths of his blue eyes warmed her and showed her they would enjoy many years of togetherness.

"On the mountain of both our hearts, I asked the Creator to give Himiin life so we can fulfill my gift to you, our people, together."

Himiin raised her hand. "Wren is strong and with her guidance, we will all prosper." He kissed her hand and motioned for her to continue.

"The Creator gave Himiin a mortal body. We will be together until we are given to Mother Earth."

She faced Proud and Tall. "Father, Himiin told you earlier I was his." She glanced at Himiin over her shoulder. "And I wish to be of his lodge."

"He has no lodge," Tattle-Tale stated, stepping up to Himiin and looking him up and down.

Himiin stared back at her brother, his face still as stone. She did not fear his anger, for she trusted this man with her every breath.

He broke into a smile, his eyes sparkling mischievously as he said, "I will before morning if you help me—brother."

She held her breath, waiting for Tattle-Tale's response. The gleam in her brother's eyes made her breath catch. Would he accept Himiin?

Tattle-Tale placed his hand on Himiin's shoulder and smiled. "Brother."

Paty Jager

Epilogue

Himiin sat by the lake in the full moon waiting for his sister and brother. He smiled, thinking of the years of love he and Wren shared. The dozens of children and grandchildren they raised to love the mountain and the people.

His heart yearned to see her smile, but Wren passed during the cold time when they wintered away from the mountain. He fought with the elders and won, bringing her body to the mountain, giving her to Mother Earth when the snow had melted.

He knew his time was upon him, he felt it in his tired bones. The memories of the days before he became mortal were vague. But he remembered his spirit brother and sister with clarity, and the times on the mountain he and Wren shared when he roamed the mountain as a white wolf.

The lake came alive with splashing and whitecaps as Wewukiye stepped from the water. He shook, flinging droplets over Himiin.

Himiin pushed the water from his skin and glared at his brother. "You would think after all these years I would get use to you making me wet."

"There is no need to growl at me. I tried to tell you, you would one day tire of being a mortal." Wewukiye tossed his massive head and stared into his eyes. "You miss her."

His heart squeezed. "Yes." He stared at his regal brother. "But I will be with her shortly."

Wewukiye stepped closer. "You are leaving this earth?"

"If the way I am feeling is true, yes."

246

A shadow fell across Himiin. He knew from where it came. The swoosh of air and scratch of bark told him, Sa-qan had arrived.

"I'm glad you could be here," he said, stroking the white feathers upon her head.

"Why have you called us together?" She watched him closely and blinked.

"He is leaving us," Wewukiye said hoarsely.

"Do not worry for me. I'll be with my Wren. But I want to make sure you will watch over the Lake Nimiipuu. We have grown in number and prosper, but we have seen the people whose skin is the color of antelope. They are coming our way." He stared across the lake. "We must not give up this land. We will perish and all Wren has worked for will be lost."

He stood. "Promise you will keep the land for Mother Earth."

"We will do our best to keep the Nimiipuu on this land," Wewukiye said, nodding his head and watching him closely.

Sa-qan glanced at the moonlit village. "You should return to your lodge. You do not look well."

He smiled. His mortal body was tired and ready to rest, yet his heart sung like the first time he'd shared his heart with his beloved. He smiled at his brother and sister and nodded. "Take care, my brother and sister. I will be with my Wren tonight. Forever."

About the Author

Award-winning author Paty Jager ranches with her husband of thirty-five years raising hay, cattle, kids, and grandkids. Her first book was published in 2006 and since then she has published seventeen books, five novellas, and two anthologies. She enjoys riding horses, playing with her grandkids, judging 4-H contests and fairs, and outdoor activities. To learn more about her books and her life you can visit her website.
http://www.patyjager.net

Other books in the Spirit Trilogy
Spirit of the Lake
Book Two - Wewukiye's story
Spirit of the Sky
Book Three - Sa-qan's story

Halsey Brother Series
Marshal in Petticoats – Gil's story
Outlaw in Petticoats – Zeke's story
Miner in Petticoats – Ethan's story
Doctor in Petticoats – Clay's story
Logger in Petticoats – Hank's story
Halsey Brothers Series – Box Set
Halsey Homecoming trilogy
Laying Claim – Jeremy's story
Staking Claim – Colin's story
Claiming a Heart – Donny's story (coming soon)

Other Historical Western Romance
Gambling on an Angel
Improper Pinkerton
For a Sister's Love
Christmas Redemption
Western Duets: Volume One
Western Duets: Volume Two
Western Duets: Volume Three

Western Anthologies
Sweetwater Springs Christmas: A Montana Sky Short Story Anthology
Rawhide "N Romance: A Western Romance Anthology

Contemporary Western Romance
Perfectly Good Nanny
Bridled Heart

Historical Paranormal Romance
(Native American)
Spirit of the Mountain
Spirit of the Lake
Spirit of the Sky

Contemporary Action Adventure Romance
(Isabella Mumphrey Adventures)
Secrets of a Mayan Moon
Secrets of an Aztec Temple
Secrets of a Hopi Blue Star

Thank you for purchasing this Windtree Press publication. For other books of the heart, please visit our website at www.windtreepress.com.

For questions or more information contact us at
info@windtreepress.com.

Windtree Press
www.windtreepress.com

Made in United States
North Haven, CT
09 October 2024

58566342R10157